THE KINGDOM'S PROTECTOR (SETH'S POV)

LAUREN MOON

Book #2 in The Moonlit Prophecy Series

To my dog, Bosco, I miss you beyond words. This way you can live on forever in my stories... I will never stop telling our story. Thank you for everything.

To my cat, Saint, I love and miss you so much. Thank you for the countless smiles and the amazing memories. You were taken from me too soon. Thank you for being the best kitty.

TRIGGER WARNINGS

The Trigger warnings for this story are listed below. They are not limited to this list, your mental health matters to me.

Death
    Pregnancy / Pregnancy involving multiples
    Nightmares
    Murder
    Possessiveness
    Obsessiveness
    Violence / Thoughts and threats of violence
    Mentions of Sexism
    Mentions of Misogyny
    Stress
    Anxiety
    Mention of Panic attacks

AUTHOR'S NOTE

Before you dig into The Kingdom's Protector I just wanted to give you a little helpful information.

This book is written from the main male's point of view, if you would like to read from his mate's point of view, please look for the other version of the story Ruthless Kingdom!

When you see italics, it's the characters speaking in the other's mind.

If you find any errors or have any questions! My email is Authorlaurenmoon@gmail.com or you can message me on Instagram @Heartofanalpha! I'm always open to talking!

PROLOGUE

Scarlett laid there unconscious and naked as I gently picked her up in my arms. This can't be happening... She can't be dead. Not like this. Not for me. The shadows faded away, the brightness of the full moon shined down on us. Tears streamed down my face as I held her to my strong body.

Please... I closed my eyes as I bit my bottom lip. If you're listening to me Goddess... Take me. Don't take her. Don't take my babies. I can't live without her. I want to die with her.

Reign was speechless and that just caused my body to ache more.

I felt like I was slowly dying with her. My power drained into her, I was giving her all of my strength. Allowing my power to seep through the land before I give it right back to her. I thought it would do something. Anything. To give me back my life.

"Please baby... Please open those pretty brown eyes for me my love... I need you to wake up." I said, my body was shaking as I looked down at her.

I placed my hand gently on her face, my hand glowing red.

I felt the power role through the land, going through my legs. Up my body and through my hand on her face.

She needs to live... She has to wake up. She can't leave me. I won't let her leave me. I stared down at her, willing and praying that she would open those beautiful brown eyes and look at me. Or say anything. I just need something.

"Baby... Wake up!" I ordered, my power rolling through my command.

She gasped, her eyes opening, shining a powerful purple.

Oh my Goddess. She's alive.

"She's ALIVE!" Reign shouted, staring with me.

"Oh thank the Goddess!" I said, holding her tightly to me.

Scarlett held me back weakly as I stood up with her in my arms. "We're heading to the hospital."

She has to be okay, so the doctor needs to look at her to make sure she is okay.

"N-no..." Scarlett said, shivering slightly as she cuddled into me.

I disappeared, before appearing with her in my arms. We were standing in an empty hospital room in Scotland. I'm assuming her private room at the hospital.

"You are not giving me no for an answer. You heard your mother, why did you continue to fight? You could've untied me and then I could've done it." I told her, gently laying her down on the bed.

I reached behind the bed and pushed a button to send a notice to the desk that someone in the room and waiting.

Someone. More like the most important person in the whole world. But yeah, someone is another word for her.

"I thought she was trying to mess with me. I heard your concerns but I couldn't snap out of it. Xena was in control, and she wanted blood. Pete's blood. We need to go to Ireland and make sure that the land is starting to heal." Scarlett started, groaning as she tried to sit up.

I growled, gently pushing her to lay back down.

"When does this woman never stop?" Reign stared in complete shock.

My answer is never.

"I will handle that. Ireland is not the top priority. Scotland is not the top priority. You are the top priority. I should've figured out that you could be pregnant... Alpha's are more fertile than omegas... And are even more fertile during heat. So I should've put it together, but you weren't acting differently. Nothing changed..." I said, staring intently at her.

My eyes haven't gone back to brown yet, I felt Reign standing at attention. And I don't think he's going to calm down for a while. Scarlett leaned back against the pillow on the bed.

"Can you at least give me a shirt?" Scarlett asked, shivering slightly from the cold air.

I frowned, digging into the cabinets to find something for her. I guess we both needed clothes.

"It's so much more fun when we're naked." Reign whined.

And I knew that, but until I knew she's okay... Nothing is going to happen.

"I'm sure the doctor will be here soon... I thought that your clothes would be here..." I started to mumble, before grinning as I found shorts and hoodies.

I sniffed the air and I growled, not liking the scent of different males on it. Scarlett couldn't help but laugh, knowing exactly what I was upset about.

Forgive me for not wanting my mate to smell like another male.

"I'm sure they just come in here and wash them every once and a while. I haven't been to the hospital in a while... I typically care for my wounds at home. It has been that way for a long while. I didn't feel safe enough to come to the hospital. Everyone would talk about their Alpha who got hurt and back then my reputation was weak and I couldn't risk it." Scarlett told me as I walked back over to her.

My muscles were tense, my veins bulging with my stress.

Even though I knew she was okay... She was alive right here. She was okay. I just couldn't shake the feel of her dead weight in my arms... She was dead. She died. And I'm... I'm not okay.

"Tell her... It's okay..." Reign assured me.

But it's not okay.

I absentmindedly started to rub the clothes against my skin, marking them with my powerful scent.

"I understand my love... I hope it is different now." I said, helping her get dressed.

I was gentle with my touches, not wanting to cause her any pain. Scarlett was shaking slightly, trying to help me. I felt her body was still weak, and I wish that I could help with that. I continue to let my power drift through our bond, to try and give her my strength.

At least when people smelled her, they would smell two alphas instead of just one. I gently slipped the shorts up her legs, lifting her enough to move the shorts to her hips. The next was her hoodie, I closed my eyes and allowed my power to put a hoodie on her. I was too scared to push moving her anymore.

"I'm here now... We have a bond... We may have kids on the way. You will be the first Alpha in the entire world to have three packs under her control." I assured her, gently laying her back down on the bed.

I quickly slid on a pair of gray sweatpants. I felt my power drift back through my body and I went rigid. "I would fight and kill anyone for you. Why are you not drawing on my power?"

She's giving me my power back. I don't like it. She needs it more than I do.

"Bite her. Send the power straight through her mark. She can't send it back that way." Reign explained.

And I honestly might do that. Maybe it will give me some comfort in feeling our bond strength.

Scarlett closed her eyes, her skin was slowly coming back to its normal color. "I am okay... I'm just tired is all. Going home to our bed sounds really nice. But someone is insisting that I get checked out."

She smirked slightly, peeking her eyes open to tease me. I smirked, sitting beside her legs and gently massaging them to relax her.

Sleep will help. Sleep will let me also freak out and get my witts together before she wakes up.

"You can tease me all you want. But until I make sure you're okay. We're not going home. Yes there is a possibility that your mother was lying. But I think there is a possibility of your mother being right. So yes, you're staying here. And if the doctor doesn't get here soon, I'm going to go out find him and drag him here myself." I told her, licking my lips slowly as I eyed her body.

Scarlett's cheeks heated up as I looked at her, she bit her bottom lip.

And I would do it too.

"YEAH!" Reign shouted. *"I like that plan!"*

"I'm sure he's just getting his daughter settled with Alex... Everything will be fine." Scarlett promised, reaching down to hold my hand.

I intertwined our fingers, rubbing my thumb over her hand gently. I felt her warm skin... I heard her heartbeat.

She was alive... And okay. Why can't I calm down? I feel like my body is still in my fight response.

There was a soft knock on the door, before the doctor peeked his head in. "Alphas?" The doctor called out, before walking in.

Doctor Hunter closed the door behind him, striding into the room. Well finally.

"It took you long enough." I huffed out, causing Scarlett to giggle.

He took his sweet ol' time getting here.

"Seth!!" She laughed, smiling as she tried to stop laughing.

Doctor Hunter chuckled, shaking his head slightly as he brought an ultrasound machine closer to the bed. I flinched slightly, not wanting anyone near her. But at the same time, I knew she needed to be checked out. To really show she was pregnant.

It could've been a joke by her mother to throw us off. I need to know if she is pregnant.

"I do know that I took a hot minute to get here... I didn't know that I was supposed to come here. Didn't quite think that I was going to be the Alphas personal doctor." He smirked slightly, turning his focus to me.

I don't like him.

"Me either." Reign growled, he was standing on edge.

I was on edge. We were both losing it. It was taking too long to find out if my mate was pregnant.

I growled, baring my fangs at the doctor. My eyes dark red, as I didn't take them off of him. One wrong move. I'm gonna kill him. The doctor shifted uncomfortably.

"Can you lift her shirt up please?" The doctor asked, keeping his gaze down.

Scarlett smiled, squeezing my hand gently.

"Baby... He's not going to do anything to me... He just

wants to make sure I'm okay..." Scarlett spoke to me soothingly.

I calmed down a little... But not much. "So let's just lift my shirt up and then after he checks to make sure I'm okay. We can go home and cuddle and watch a movie okay?" She told me, knowing I was stressed and anxious.

She felt my worry and pain like it was her own. I nodded slowly, helping lift Scarlett's hoodie up to expose her flat stomach to the doctor.

If she was pregnant... Why is she so skinny?

"He's just anxious... Everything is just a bit overwhelming for the both of us." Scarlett explained, keeping her eyes on me to keep me calm.

I growled softly, watching the doctor's slow movements. Slow precise movements. I don't like him at all.

"I understand... So Alpha Knight... I'm going to apply this gel to your stomach. It's going to be cold. And then I'm going to use this doppler and place it on your stomach. Nothing is going to hurt. All the doppler does is show me what's going on inside of your stomach." The doctor informed, telling me his actions before he did them.

I tensed, watching the doctor apply the gel.

"I still say we should kill him. Then no one will be touching Scarlett." Reign offered again.

And I agree with him. It's looking good.

"If you hurt her, I'm gonna kill you." I snapped.

Scarlett smiled at me, gently rubbing her leg against me to keep me calm. It's more so adding fuel to my ever present need to claim her in front of everyone. But that's not happening till I know she really is okay.

"I'm okay baby..." Scarlett assured, peeking over at the Doctor. "I appreciate you coming here so late."

Like I wouldn't have gone to his house and drug him out of bed by his legs. But he doesn't need to know that.

The doctor smiled, bringing the doppler to her stomach before turning his focus to the screen. "I'm just going to move the doppler around a little bit to see what's going on..." He told us, gently moving the wand around.

I inhaled sharply at the movements, rubbing my stomach absentmindedly. It tingles and feels so weird and cold.

"I feel that like it's on my stomach." I told her, smiling as I was slowly calming down.

Doctor Hunter chuckled, smiling as he turned his focus to us instead of the screen. "Congratulations Scarlett. You're pregnant."

CHAPTER
ONE

I stared at the doctor, before flicking my eyes over to the monitor that showed two little figures on the screen the size of an orange. We're having twins... We're having babies! My bottom lip trembled as I finally looked down at Scarlett.

"Wow! We're going to have BABIES!" Reign howled with excitement.

We're going to have a baby! Babies! Twins. Just like her and Gray. I'm so beyond excited.

Scarlett sniffled, her eyes watering. "We're going to have a baby..." She smiled.

I couldn't say anything, I just cupped her face gently and kissed her. My power seeped through her body, giving it a faint red glow. Hmm... That's a little different. Kind of cool. I like it.

"You... Gave me everything.." I sat down on the bed, running my hands all along her body.

I needed to make sure she was okay... Touching her body... Feeling her skin warming underneath my touch. I needed to touch her, to feel that she's alive. She could've died... She could've left me. I can't handle it if she dies.

I brought my hand to his lips and kissed it. "I'm sorry for fighting... I had no idea I was pregnant..." She frowned. "I wouldn't have if I knew."

"Tell her to shut her pretty mouth. She's alive. That's all that matters." Reign growled, baring his fangs.

I might just bite her. She likes it. I'll feel better.

I shook my head. "Stop. It's okay... None of that matters. The only thing that matters to me is that you're here. You're alive. You didn't leave me. And that you and our babies are okay." I explained, kissing her hand again.

I turned my focus to the doctor that was still in the room. Why is he still here? Is everything fine? Or is he trying to wait until we're focusing on him to talk? He needs to talk and tell me what is happening with my mate and my children. Reign growled in agreement.

"And they are okay, right? Her and the twins? Nothing is wrong with them, right?" I asked, my eyes slowly turning red as my anxiety rose.

I might kill him if he doesnt start talking.

"Oh yeah. Do that. Definitely do that. I second!" Reign nodded in agreement.

I knew I could always count on him to agree with me.

"Two peas in a pod. I got you." Reign laid down in the back of my mind.

After not agreeing with him for the longest time... It feels good to be able to count on him for stuff. The doctor smiled, before shaking his head slowly.

"No. As far as I can tell. Everything is okay with all three of them. There's a lot of things we should discuss about her pregnancy..." The doctor trailed off, as Scarlett glared at him.

What are a lot of things? What's going to happen to Scarlett? Why is she glaring at him? I have too many questions and not enough answers.

12

"But. We can schedule an appointment to come back to discuss everything we need to. So we can go home, snuggle, and watch a movie. Whatever you want, my love." Scarlett smiled, squeezing my hand gently to bring his attention back to me.

I feel like the room is spinning... My vision starts to darken. I don't know what I'm going to do.

Scarlett kept her eyes on me. "Breathe with me." She told me, breathing in deeply and holding her breath.

I nodded, following her breathing. Scarlett released her breath, having me follow right after her. I need to tell myself she's okay... But I feel like I'm going to kill the doctor if he looks at her one more time.

"Yes... I'll have my assistant schedule something with Grayson." The doctor nodded. "Sooner rather than later."

"Thanks Doc..." She smiled at me. I growled, not liking him. "He is just helping us. Shush."

I don't like that he wants to see my mate so much.

I growled again, earning a laugh from her. "I'm going to take you home. And you're not going to leave my sight ever again." I told her, before getting up and picking her up in my arms.

No one is going to take her away from me. I won't let another person touch her... I can't. I shook my head. I can't let anyone take my life away from me. My body was tense, nearly vibrating as I held her tightly to my chest. Feeling her weight in my arms, gives me a sense of peace and comfort. She's alive... She's okay.

She's not dead.

"What happens if I gotta pee?" I asked, smiling up at him as she looped her arms around the back of my neck.

I've gone to the bathroom with her before. I can always just do it.

"I can come with you. I just want to be able to protect you... I just..." I trailed off, not wanting to continue this conversation until we were alone.

Scarlett nodded, knowing exactly what I was thinking. I took a deep breath in... I can't survive without her. She's the air inside my lungs... She is the reason I get up in the morning. I'm in love with her. I refuse to live without her.

Suddenly we appeared in our bedroom back home. I laid her gently down on the bed. "I... I don't want to leave you. I can't."

I know I'm being ridiculous. But... It's just that she was dead. She looked dead... She was dead. She left me and then she just wasn't. I shook my head. No. I need to stop thinking about that.

Scarlett frowned, whimpering softly. "I'm sorry baby... I'm okay. We can lay down together... I'm sure nothing is going to happen... Probably until tomorrow morning." She tried to reassure me.

I growled, taking off my shirt before climbing into the bed beside her. She needs to relax... To calm down. To take things easy. I won't let her overwork herself. Not anymore.

"Yeah. Because you're the big Alpha and everyone needs you. Yeah well guess what. I'm going to be right there with you. No one is going to push you. You have to be careful now." I laid down, before reaching over and pulling her so she was laying on my chest.

This is where she belongs. On my chest. Touching me so I can feel her warmth... So I can know that she's alive.

"I would've moved if you didn't grab me." She teased gently, wanting to calm me down.

I smirked. Too slow. I needed her against me immediately. I missed her touch as soon as I put her down.

"You took too long for my liking." I shrugged, trying to relax. S

carlett frowned again, feeling my body still tense. I feel like my body is in this... Fight mode. Like if I close my eyes, I'm going to wake up and she's going to be dead.

"I can't help it... I can't help it at all. We could've lost her." Reign whimpered at the thought.

"Do you think letting Reign out would be a good idea?" She offered. "The bed is big enough for him to lay in?"

I shook my head no. "No. No. He just is tense... And needs to hold you so that he knows you're okay."

We both need to know that she's okay.

Scarlett nodded quietly, before laying her head back on my bare chest. I wrapped my arms tighter around her, looking at the outside to make sure we were safe.

They took me from that door... They took me like I was nothing to her... Then he tried to take everything from me.

A bang on the door caused me to move quickly so that I was covering Scarlett's body.

Nothing ever stops to let us relax do they?

CHAPTER
TWO

Scarlett placed her hand on my chest, her power slowly seeped through my body. It took everything in me not to groan at the feeling her power gave me... It's like the most addicting drug.

"I think it's just Stormy." She whispered.

I growled, baring my fangs at her.

"Only Scarlett would say "Oh I think it's just Stormy." After you know. Almost DYING!" Reign growled, baring his fangs in annoyance.

Agreed. She needs to be smarter about these things.

"I know you're going to stay here until I know who is out there." I narrowed my eyes on her. "I don't trust anyone."

So help me. If she tries to sass me about this.

Scarlett smiled, nodding her answer. "That's my good girl." I praised, causing her cheeks to turn pink at the praise.

I bit back a smirk. I could smell just how much she loved it when I praised her.

"I told you we should've waited until tomorrow or something." Stormy's voice could be heard from our bedroom.

I kind of maybe just a little bit. Hate the both of them.

"And I told you I'm not waiting!" Kingston snapped.

I growled, climbing off of the bed. I definitely hate Kingston more though. He could've stayed back at their home.

"I'll go kick them out?" I offered with a smile.

Maybeeeee she'll just let me do it? Or maybe I should just do it without asking. Scarlett rolled her eyes, smiling as she shook her head.

"You don't have to kick them out. I'm sure it's a misunderstanding..." Scarlett got off the bed with me.

I frowned, holding my hand out to her. A misunderstanding or Kingston is just trying to start a fight like usual.

"Yeah, but I can't stand her mate." I huffed, when she took my hand.

We walked out to the living room together. I'll happily throw Kingston out of my house.

"*Stormy can stay! Just not Kingston.*" Reign nodded in agreement.

Smart man.

"I know baby..." Scarlett squeezed my hand gently, as I pulled her into my side so I could support more of her weight.

I don't like that she's up and walking around. But I knew she wouldn't want me to kick them out. And I one hundred percent guarantee that I could not stand Kingston's smell in my bedroom. No. I can barely tolerate his smell in my house.

"They don't just get to keep us here!" Kingston snapped. "She wanted you here. But hasn't spoken to you, hasn't done anything to spend any time with you. We can't even go into town because of her pack."

"I'm going to cut you off right there." Scarlett growled, causing both Kingston and Stormy to shoot their attention to her. "My pack is her pack. And no one said you guys couldn't go into town."

I held Scarlett against me, one wrong step by Kingston and I'll be able to easily put her beside me. I don't trust him.

"Don't even try that with me Scarlett. I may not be a wolf. But I'm not stupid. We went into town once, and all we got were dirty looks and everyone whispering about us. I also had someone come up to me and say Elves are not allowed in their territory. So look me in the face and say we're welcome here. Tell me our child, who's going to be half elf. Is going to be welcome among the mutts of your pack." Kingston's eyes were starting to glow blue as he stood up to Scarlett.

Stormy immediately grabbed his hand to try and calm him down. I refuse to let him talk to my mate like this.

"Yeah! You get him!" Reign cheered. *"You've got this!"*

Before Scarlett could even say anything, I stepped in. I growled, my eyes turning a darker red. "First off why don't you look who you're talking to before I throw you out of my house."

"I'd love to see you try. If I'm kicked out. Stormy is coming with me. And I promise you we'll never step foot in Scotland again." Kingston was fuming angry.

Stormy tried to step in front of Kingston, but he wouldn't let her. Their relationship is weird. Reign snickered in the back of my mind. He can't tell me I'm lying!

"Okay... Okay... Why don't we calm down here?" Stormy laughed nervously.

Scarlett looked at her sister. Finally Stormy is talking. Kingston has some nerve walking in my house and talking to my mate this way.

"What is this all about Stormy? You know you're always welcome in my house? And same with Gray too. Where is this all coming from? Or is it just coming from Kingston?" Scarlett asked, looking between the two now.

Kingston's right hand started to glow, but before anything could happen Stormy grabbed his hand. Hm... That's something. I narrowed my eyes at his hand. Is that how he uses his power?

"No. It's not just Kingston. Honestly, I don't like that you would think I would let something like that happen." Stormy glared. "I don't feel like I have a place in this pack. Not before I left, and especially not now when my mate is an Elf. And he has a point. Our children are going to be outcasted. Just like we were because our powers are different than theirs. I don't want that for my kids." She tried to explain, Scarlett nodded as she listened to her sister.

He really doesn't have a point. What the Alpha says goes. If the Alpha says not to outcast her nieces or nephews. It just simply won't happen. No one has a choice but the Alpha.

"*Duh. It's not like it hasn't been bred into our DNA.*" Reign rolled his eyes. "*We would be having so much more fun if we were naked and in bed.*"

I couldn't help but groan at the thought. I'm hoping no one could hear me.

"I can't stop you from leaving. And I can't promise you that things aren't going to be harder for you guys here because of what Kingston is. But I can promise you that your children will be included if that's what they want. They'll be the Alpha's nieces or nephews. They won't be messed with. I'll have guards around them if that's what you want. I don't want you to leave, we've been dealing with a lot lately. I haven't been able to see much of anyone." Scarlett said, a shiver racked her body.

I growled unhappily as I picked her up in my arms. I don't know if she's cold. Or just tired from everything she's gone through. But I'm hoping that either way this will help her.

Kingston rolled his eyes, obviously not believing her. "We'll stay, okay?" Stormy said, obviously just wanting to leave. "We're fine here. We prefer being out in the woods anyway.

But if one more person says anything to my mate, about how he shouldn't even be allowed in this territory. I'm going to break their necks."

Scarlett nodded. "I'll put out an announcement, before we announce anything else. I'll say Kingston is a part of this pack, and if anyone messes with him. They'll be messing with the Alpha's family. I'll try to be better about spending more time with you as well. Just please give me some time for everything to calm down?"

Stormy looked up to Kingston. "Is that better King?" She asked with a kind smile. Kingston, who hasn't smiled since he got in my house, looked down at Stormy and gave her a small smile.

"Is that better King?" See. I knew he was the cause of all of this. He likes to start problems just to be able to start an issue.

"If that's good enough for you. Then it will be good enough for me." Kingston said, brushing a piece of hair behind her ear.

Stormy leaned into his touch. They're so gross. I want them out of my house.

"I second that." Reign agreed.

"If that's all. You guys may leave now." I said, turning around to head back to our bedroom.

Time for Scarlett to go back to resting. I don't care if it hurts their feelings or not.

"Wait!" Stormy called out, causing me to stop and turn around.

Scarlett had her head against my chest, as she was growing more tired. I feel her body relaxing... Her bond is opening up more. I feel her energy is low and I don't like it.

"Kingston had something he wanted to say. Right King?" She looked up at him again.

He glared slightly at her, before shaking his head no. She

growled, before stepping on his foot. Kingston grabbed her quickly, forcing her back to his front.

"*Ew. I'm going to throw up.*" Reign gagged.

"You're getting it when we get home for that one little one." He growled in her ear, causing Stormy to squirm. Kingston looked up to me and Scarlett.

They just wanted to be disgusting in my house? I didn't need to see that.

"I've been around for a long time. Which means I hear things, and know more about other people. Your pack can't mindlink with each other right?" Kingston asked, bringing his eyes to Scarlett causing me to growl to show my unhappiness.

King smirked, before looking back at me. He didn't need to look at my mate. He can just keep looking at me.

"Yeah. That's right. But it's been that way for as long as I can remember. Why?" Scarlett asked, not understanding where this was going.

"One of your Elders doesn't like that you're a female running three packs. Says it's unnatural or whatever, but they're closing off their side of the bond. Stormy says that that could lead to malfunctions in the pack bond. Just thought I would tell you." King offered nonchalantly.

Scarlett stared at him, before she growled. So obviously she knows who he's talking about?

"Is his name Scott by any chance? Scott Armstrong?" Scarlett asked.

I looked confused, but didn't want to interrupt her. She can have her conversation and then just inform me later on the details.

"Yes." Was Kingston's short reply. "We're going to be going now."

But before Scarlett or I could reply, they were gone. I

sighed, finally heading back to our bedroom. Hopefully he took his stink along with him.

"I can't stand that guy." I growled, gently placing her on the bed.

Scarlett tilted her head, obviously interested in the story behind this. I don't really think it's an interesting story. She might get upset about it.

"Come on now. You can't just leave me on that." Scarlett whined, wanting to know more.

I chuckled, climbing into bed beside her. She should know by now, maybe I can talk her into me telling her tomorrow.

"You've seen every memory from my life. You already know." I teased, before bringing the blanket up and over the both of us.

"It's not like I remember all of them! We get to see it once, and then never again. Which I honestly think is messed up if you ask me." Scarlett groaned. "I want to know, please. Pretty please."

I smirked at her. "It's not as interesting as you might think that it is."

Well... Since she asked so nicely.

"Don't act tough. You can't tell her no." Reign teased.

He is completely right. I can't tell her no.

THREE

"No matter if it's interesting or not. It's about you and I want to know everything." Scarlett smiled. "So go on! Tell me!"

"She's adorable when she wants to know information so badly." Reign laid down to watch.

Well she's adorable all the time. But I agree... I don't know how she didn't have Alphas bending to her will.

I laughed, shaking my head. "I don't know if it's necessarily all about me. My father was the one who was Alpha at the time... He was the one who was dealing with Kingston."

Obviously... Considering I was in a prison cell. But that's not the point of this story.

"But obviously you were a part of the story?" She offered, wanting me to go on.

I tried my best not to fidget... I hate having to say this. I was such a puppet to my father. I hate it.

"I guess so... Obviously everything before the whole imprisonment thing is kind of hazy. Um, but I remember when

I was about six or so. My father had a meeting with Kingston."
I started, rubbing the back of my neck uncomfortably.

I swallowed thickly... Kingston wanted peace. My father
didn't like that.

"What was the meeting about?" Scarlett pressed on slowly,
not wanting to push it.

*"At least she respects you enough to drop it if it's too hard to talk
about."* Reign whimpered softly.

This is my past... It doesn't define who I am. I'm okay to
continue.

"Kingston wanted a small piece of land to stay on. He said
he wouldn't bother us, and in return we wouldn't bother him.
But my father denied him. Said something about how he won't
look weak to his pack, especially not to a weaker species like an
elf." I looked away from her, unable to look at her reaction.
"Kingston went on to start a small battle. We lost many that
day... It was one of the first interactions I was involved in..."

I have to admit Kingston is strong. Powerful. He's good in
battle. But I will never tell him that. I don't want him to think
that I like him.

Scarlett's mouth fell open. "You fought him... At six?"

My father needed my help... I was the only one who could
do it. My mother hated that I was involved so soon.

I nodded. "I was the only one who was able to wound him.
I was small enough to run in while he was fighting... And be
able to stab him in the leg with a blade covered in my blood. It
ended up making him run away. I guess my powers didn't mix
well with his."

Thinking back on it... I wonder if part of it had to do with
my future involvement with Scarlett. An Ember wolf's power
and a Shadow wolf's power would do great harm to Kingston's
kind.

Scarlett frowned, moving so that she could climb into my

lap. "I'm so sorry baby... You shouldn't have had to deal with that."

I wrapped my arms around her gently... The weight of her sitting in my lap calmed my racing heart. She is the only peace I feel right now.

I was quiet, just holding her to me. I was staring outside, a blank look on my face. I kind of want to redo this wall... Make it not glass so no one can just walk right into our bedroom and take her from me.

"Is that why he has a hatred towards you? Or just the whole wolf versus elf thing?" She asked, gently dragging her fingers down my bicep to draw him back to the present.

Her fingers against my skin made me snap back into focus. I don't want to go back to that day. It's one of my worst memories.

"How are you so calm around him?" I asked, looking back at her finally. "It makes no sense." She shrugged.

That's my question. How is she so calm? Elves are the most hated enemy to wolves. And to her? It's like nothing is different about him being here.

"It's cause she's special. She's powerful. She's secure in herself. I don't know. She's unique and not much can bother her." Reign shrugged, trying to give me an answer.

I appreciate him trying to help me. But... I want to know her answer.

"I've been around a lot of different creatures... And control has never really been a major issue with me. After everything with my father and sister. I'm... One with Xena and she doesn't really care about the fact he's an elf. I mean sure it's annoying because he calls us mutts and talks down about us. But his species doesn't annoy me. His attitude does." Scarlett tried to explain, but she was just confusing herself.

She might be confusing herself, but I know what she's trying to say.

I breathed out, before rubbing the side of my face. Doesn't mean I have to like it.

"I guess that makes sense. But I just don't know. Maybe it's because he's an inferno elf? And they are the only other creature besides your breed of course. That can kill an Ember wolf. I don't know. But I just don't like that guy."

"I understand it." She kissed my cheek. "I don't really like him so far... But he makes Stormy happy, and he seems to be able to stand her teasing and playfulness. So he seems pretty perfect for her. As long as she's safe and happy... That's all that matters to me honestly."

She's a lot nicer than me, that's for sure.

"Eh. It can be like good cop bad cop! We can be the mean one, she can be the nice one." Reign flashed his fangs at me.

I actually like that plan.

"What a good big sister." I teased, causing her to laugh and shake her head.

"Stormy was so young when I took control of the pack. She didn't understand it, and I never expected her to. I did everything I did to make sure she was safe. I don't regret it. The only thing I do regret is that I wasn't able to spend more time with her and Gray." She frowned, but she shook her head. "Nope! No more sadness. We've had enough sadness and stress. So let's change the subject!"

I laughed. I can change the subject. That's fine.

"You are something else, my love. Something else." I laid her back down on the bed so I could lay beside her. "Are you hungry?"

"I just want to lay with you." She told me, before laying her head on my chest. "I just want to rest. I'm so tired."

I started to gently run my fingers up and down her back to help her relax. "You went through a lot... Go to sleep. I'll be right here when you wake up. I promise."

No one is going to take me away from her... I plan to stay up for a little while longer... I want to make sure she's okay.

CHAPTER
FOUR

I laid there against the grass with my eyes closed. Scarlett was
*tattooing my chest, it was Xena's paw mark. She said something
about wanting to mark me... Reign rumbled his approval. She'll
have his mark next.*

*The sound of the machine made me zone out... I don't think I've
ever been more peaceful.*

"Seth!" *Her voice shouted.*

I woke up with a start. I immediately looked down at Scarlett who was sweating as she laid beside me. What happened?
I don't even remember falling asleep!? I don't know what I did!

I sat up, gently squeezing her shoulder. My heart started to
race, my eyes shifting colors. Not now Reign! I need to stay in
control! "Scarlett." I said, shaking her gently.

When that didn't wake her up, I started to panic. "Scarlett!" I shouted, shaking her a little harder this time.

"*Let me wake her up! I can do it!*" Reign howled, fighting
against my control.

Her skin started to heat up, but before it could go any
further I growled. My growl was low, a rumble across her skin

made her sit up with a start. Ah ha. There we go. Her eyes were glowing purple as she looked around before she made eye contact with me.

What was her nightmare?

I gently cupped her face to give her a form of skin to skin contact. "Shhh precious... Shhh... I'm right here. I'm right here. You're okay. I'm okay. We're both safe." I soothed, gently rubbing my thumbs across her smooth skin.

She looks panicked... She looks like she sees a ghost. What happened while I fell asleep?

Scarlett inhaled shakily, her eyes slowly fading back to their deep brown. "You're okay..." She repeated. Placing her hand against my chest to feel my heartbeat. "You're safe."

My heart has started to calm down... Seeing her awake helps... She can see that whatever she saw is not real.

I smiled, leaning forward to press a kiss to her forehead. "We both are okay... We're both safe... Do you want to tell me about your nightmare?"

I want to know... I should've stayed awake. How long was she having this nightmare? I could've lulled her back to sleep.

Scarlett's bottom lip trembled. "It was... Y-you against the tree again. I couldn't do anything... I..." She swallowed thickly. "I couldn't save you."

Oh my sweet amazing mate...

"*So this is going to torment the both of us for a while...*" Reign frowned.

It is... But we can work through it together.

I wrapped his arms around her before pulling her into my lap. "You did save me my love. You saved me like you always save me."

I breathed in her powerful scent... Her amazing scent... She's alive and healthy.

We both are.

Scarlett was trying her best to not cry. "I'm sorry..." She whimpered, shoving her nose into my neck.

My frown deepened as I tightened my hold on her. Did I do something that upset her? She has no reason to apologize.

"Why are you sorry babygirl?" I asked, gently rubbing her back to help sooth her.

I want her here with me, not in her mind and panicking about something.

"I... I'm not normally like this." She told him, before leaning away from my neck. "I normally can keep my emotions in check."

It took everything in me not to chuckle. I should've expected a response like this. She's so used to not being able to let her emotions free. I want her to be safe with me. I want to know all of her emotions.

I playfully rolled my eyes at her. "You are my mate. My other half. You are the air to my lungs... You are my alpha. I want to hear every single little tiny detail about you. But I know how hard it can be to talk about the nightmares... So I'm not going to make you. But you don't have to be scared to talk to me about things. Okay?"

We're a safe place... For each other. She doesn't have to be the all powerful alpha with me.

Tears slowly trickled down her cheeks as she listened to me talk. "T-thank you... I just... It's going to be hard now. I won't be able to protect you like I usually do. I feel like everything is changing all at once." She was going to go wipe at her cheeks but I beat her to it.

I gently wiped away her tears while I paid attention to her. Caring for her is my duty... Easing her worries is something I'll always do.

"I'm nervous that something bad is going to happen... Whether that be an attack... Or you're going to get tired of me not being able to protect you like I once did... I'm worried you're going to leave me..." Her voice broke as she sniffled.

I whimpered, hating seeing her so upset. I hugged her tightly to my chest again. I wish I could talk all of her worries. She is mine until the end of time. Not even death will take her away from me.

"I promise you Scarlett. That no one is going to take me away from you. There is nothing in this entire world that I would let take me away from you. I'm never going to leave you, because you're mine." I told her, gently gripping her chin so she locked eyes with me.

I need her to know that this is the truth and for that to happen. She needs to look at me.

"You. Are. Mine." I repeated, needing her to know that I was telling the truth. "Nothing in this world will ever change you being mine, okay? Nothing. I want you to repeat it for me."

Nothing will take her from me. Nothing will stop me from loving her. I would fight to the ends of the Earth to keep her mine.

Scarlett nodded, the tears finally stopping as she felt better with my promise. "I want you to repeat it to me." I repeated, giving her a low growl causing her to squirm in my lap.

Scarlett's cheeks turned red as she bit her bottom lip. Ms. Dominant Alpha likes to be told what to do. I could make this work.

"Oh yeah we can." Reign licked his lips at the thought.

"Nothing in this world will ever change you being mine." She repeated, I grinned.

Such a perfect response.

"Good girl." I praised. "You're mine. Forever until time ends. You're mine. Now... Do you want to get something to eat? I don't want you to be hungry."

I don't want for her to be hungry, or the twins. She needs to eat more for the twins.

"I guess food would be great. Before we have to go to the pack house." Scarlett told me, moving to get up.

But I gripped her hips and kept her in my lap. She doesn't have to walk. She has me for that.

"You don't have to walk." I told her, getting up and still holding her. "And you don't have to remind me." I rolled my eyes, showing that I didn't want to do that.

I want for us to be alone... To have some time before we have to go and deal with people.

Is that too much to ask for?

"I know..." Scarlett sighed. "But... You know. We have to do things we don't want to do sometimes. I would prefer for us to just go back to the cabin and be alone for a while. But with us taking control of your territory again. Everything will need to go back to before, where The Bloody Rose wolves go back to their homes."

"We have Betas and Deltas for a reason. Hello what is Max for?" Reign rolled his eyes.

That's my point.

"Can't we just make Max and Alex and that other guy? Your previous Delta do it?" I asked, causing Scarlett to laugh.

I wonder what happened to that guy. Max and Alex do a better job anyway.

"Madoc... Now runs the pack orphanage. He and his mate do it together. I think I pushed him into being my Delta when he didn't want to." Scarlett shrugged. "He always loved the orphanage, getting to help all the kids. So when Alex came into our little mix of things, they talked about it. I got a text and okayed it."

I nodded. "We'll have to stop by there eventually to see

how things are going." I gently placed Scarlett down on a chair by the island.

Scarlett couldn't help but laugh.

"And here I thought you didn't like him." She teased.

Oh. I hate the guy. I hate any guy that thinks they can just talk to my mate. Which means a lot of people.

"I don't, but now that he has a mate? And doesn't work under you. I like him a little more now." I teased right back.

Scarlett laughed harder, shaking her head.

"You my sir are a possessive mate. Good thing I like it." She winked, smiling as she watched me move around the kitchen to make us breakfast.

CHAPTER
FIVE

After we ate breakfast, we were on our way to the packhouse. I took a deep breath in. Just because we aren't alone... Doesn't mean that anything is going to happen. Everything is going to be fine.

But I found my body tensing more and more the closer we got to the building. Scarlett frowned, sensing my anxiety through our bond.

Realistically? Anything could happen. Would I be prepared for it?

"We have to be prepared. Anything could happen. Anyone could try and take the Alpha position right now." Reign reminded me.

He was on edge... I was on edge. I can't lose control right now.

"Everything will be okay. Nothing is going to happen to me." She assured, squeezing my thigh gently. "You'll be right there with me. You don't have to even leave my side!"

I gave her a small smile as I pulled into a parking spot. I brought her hand from my thigh up to her lips. "Right there with you... Every step of the way." I repeated before kissing her hand gently. "Don't leave my side."

I might lose it if she does.

"Not even if I have to go to the bathroom." Scarlett teased with a playful grin.

"Your private bathroom in your office is big enough for us both to shift in and we'd still have plenty of room." I smirked, causing her to lean forward and kiss the tip of my nose.

I tried my best not to scrunch my nose. It's one of the most delicate things she does to show me her affection. It's adorable.

"Uh duh. That's why I mentioned it. Don't need to leave my side EVER. Even if it wasn't big enough we would've made it work." She nodded once. "Are you ready to get this over with?"

I snorted, climbing out of the car to get her door. "Might not want to say that too loud. We wouldn't want anyone else to hear?"

Could you imagine the rumors that would start if they heard this?

Scarlett laughed, taking my hand before getting out of the car. "They all know I prefer doing my work from home. Less noise. Less distractions. It's calm and peaceful."

Less people. She's in her own personal comfort zone. I completely understand it.

I put my arm around her shoulders, pulling her into my body. "Well, I'm here now so I'll tell everyone to shut up and leave you alone. After all, you're pregnant... You need to keep calm. Speaking of that... When are we supposed to tell people?"

"So help me if she says I don't know." Reign growled slightly.

She's so going to say I don't know.

Scarlett shrugged, following me into the building. I didn't say anything as I kept her against me tightly. Scarlett gently placed her hand on my chest. I looked around the hallways, no one even really paid attention to us walking in here. Which is probably a good thing.

"Right there with you... Every step of the way." She repeated to me.

I couldn't bring myself to say anything as I led us to her office. I don't need to talk to anyone. It's completely fine. She has to, I don't.

It didn't take us long to weave our way through the halls, I opened the door to her office for her. She frowned, looking up at me.

"Are you sure you're wanting to be here? We can go back home. Have Max and Alex meet us there?" She asked, obviously worried about me.

Of course she's more worried about me. When she is the one who almost died. I shook my head before shutting the door behind me. As long as she's with me. I can handle anything.

"I'll be fine. As long as I feel that you're here with me." I explained, grabbing her and pulling her against my chest. "No one will take you away from me."

Scarlett giggled. "I never want to be without you."

"That's what I like to hear." Reign growled with approval.

"You'll never be without me ever again. What are we going to do first here?" I asked. "Because the quicker we get things done, the faster we can go home."

"Talk with Grayson and Alex about how we need to start having the people who live in Ireland move back to their homes if they want to. Change our guards to stop guarding the border between Scotland and Ireland since we're one now. Ask about getting everything back in Ireland started again." She named off a few things.

I picked her up, making her wrap her legs around my waist.

41

She's the hottest woman I've ever laid eyes on. Who knew I'd be with such a dominant Alpha? I freaking love it.

"Why is it just so hot when you talk about your duties as Alpha?" I questioned, my voice was holding a hint of a growl to it.

I placed her on her desk before leaning down and kissing and nipping at her neck. She's my drug of choice. Her smell. Her taste. Her everything. I can't get enough.

Scarlett couldn't help but moan as she moved her head to the side to give me more access. "I don't know." She gasped when my teeth grazed against her mark. "Maybe you like me being in charge." She taunted.

I growled, leaning back to look her in the eyes. I lifted one of my hands to her throat, causing her to grin as she was excited. "If you weren't already pregnant." I growled, my eyes turning a dark red. "You would've been now. I would've bent you over the desk and not stopped until you were telling the whole world my name."

"Oh she likes this." Reign grinned.

I know she does.

Scarlett giggled, leaning into my hold on her neck. "I just want you to know... I really really really like this new side to you."

I smiled, leaning down and kissing her gently. "Well thank you baby. Thank you for letting me be like this and not getting mad at me."

"I would've told you if I was uncomfortable with something. But I'm pretty open for anything with you." Scarlett winked, dipping her hands into the waistband of my pants.

I bit her bottom lip, letting my fangs dig in enough to draw blood, which I greedily licked it up. I'm so obsessed with her taste.

"Everything about you is delicious. My absolute favorite

treat." I growled, she laughed as I was leaning down to nip her lip again.

"Are we interrupting something?" Alex asked, a disgusted look on his face as he watched us interact.

"They always interrupt us. Freaking brothers." Reign complained.

"I don't know if I'm supposed to be happy for them? Or grossed out that they're all over each other and smell like... Like they just want to rip each others clothes off? But also mixed with a different scent I can't really put my paw on." Max added in, sniffing the air in the office.

"She's mine. I'm allowed to be all over her. Plus she likes it, so it's not like I'm doing anything wrong." I bared my teeth at them.

Scarlett laughed, before rolling her eyes.

"We have a very consenting relationship so as long as we're being safe and we're having fun with it. Then just be happy with us. But don't worry, we have safe words." Scarlett teased them, causing Alex to gag dramatically.

I laughed. I love how she wants to tease them. It's freaking hot.

"That's just disgusting, I don't want to know about that!" Alex whined.

Max smirked, crossing his arms.

"Eh, I'm with Scarlett. As long as they're having fun and being safe, I don't care. Are we going to talk about the pack stuff now?" Max asked, before sitting in a chair in front of Scarlett's desk.

Scarlett nodded before both her and me moved to the back of her desk. I sat down first, before pulling her right into my lap. We can sit like this because it's just them... They won't tease her. And if they tried, I'd put a stop to it.

"This is so comfortable." She grinned, cuddling into me.

I wrapped my arms around her tightly. Alex sat down in the last free chair. Let's get this over with so we can go home.

CHAPTER
SIX

"So tell us what happened!" Max said, bouncing slightly in his seat.

"I mean nothing important..." Scarlett trailed off, causing me to growl unhappily.

"Oh nothing important. Nothing at all." Reign rolled his eyes.

Yeah. That's my girl for ya. Always downplaying what happens to her.

"Scarlett nearly died. I killed Pete. We took control of The Bloody Rose Pack." I shrugged, obviously not wanting to discuss it into great detail.

I don't want someone to accidentally over here something they shouldn't. That could make things really bad.

"Scarlett nearly died!?" Both Max and Alex said at the same time.

"Keep your voices down! Everyone has super hearing here!" Scarlett said, rubbing her ear slightly. "I don't think I almost died. But obviously I wouldn't know. The important thing is that everything is fine now. We need to focus on

47

moving everyone to where they want to be. Whether that means they go to Ireland or stay here in Scotland."

I huffed. "We'll make an announcement. Preferably today, saying that it's clear to go back to Ireland now. Nothing is dying anymore, and it's safe to go back to their homes."

It will also show our people that Scarlett and I are fine. That we're powerful because we're taking over Ireland without a second thought.

Alex nodded, typing out a list on his phone. "Okay, so after this we'll have an emergency meeting outside? Or do you want to do this online like livestream it?"

"Livestream probably isn't the safest idea because then anyone could watch it." Max offered, leaning back into the chair. "But then again everyone is going to find out about this shift of power anyway. So we'll have to call a meeting of Alphas."

I'm pretty sure Scarlett is going to hate his suggestion of the meeting of the Alphas. I don't like it myself.

"We will not have to call a meeting of Alphas." Scarlett rolled her eyes. "They're nothing but a group of sexist male Alphas who don't like to listen to me. Last time there was a meeting of Alphas I killed one of them, and I can't keep doing that."

"Well you could. You would just be the alpha of four packs and not three." I added in causing Scarlett to smirk.

I'm completely right. That would be hate. Being the Mate of the first Alpha in history to run four packs.

"But didn't you say that you killed Pete?" Alex asked, looking up from his phone. "That would mean you're the Alpha not her."

"I have no interest in being the Alpha of that pack." I snapped, flashing my red eyes at him. "They've done nothing for me my entire life. Why would I waste my time in trying to be the Alpha of them? No one would respect me."

Our previous pack did nothing for us. Did nothing to help us. Heck Alex even ran to Scarlett's pack instead of staying in the other one. Why would I want to be the Alpha? Why would I want to lead people who didn't help me out of the worst time of my life?

"I mean I agree." Max leaned forward, placing his elbows on his knees. "They didn't do anything to get rid of dad, and they didn't do anything to save us from being tortured."

"At least we know Max is on our side along with Scarlett." Reign shrugged slightly.

"We'll still have to have a formal ceremony, marking The Bloody Rose Pack as ours." Scarlett explained, talking over the rest of us. "I'm sure they'd appreciate it if we stuck to tradition."

"You know the ceremony is just a big show of you submitting to Seth right?" Alex asked, wanting to make sure she knew. "Like, get on your knees in front of him. Hang your head. Bare your neck. Shift when he tells you to. The whole thing is you submitting in front of everyone to your "alpha"."

Over my dead body will she do that. I don't need her to submit to me. I know my place. I'm secure in our relationship. I don't need her to lower herself for me.

"Yeah! Look at you being all confident!" Reign cheered.

"Yeah well she can't do that." I didn't think about it before I said it.

"Why not?" Max asked, shifting his eyes to Scarlett.

Oops.

Scarlett smiled. "I trust that you won't go telling everyone this but. At the fight... There were some things said. I thought it was just a way to try and throw me off my game. But after I almost died or whatever. Seth took me to the hospital, and we found out that I am pregnant with twins. And one of the main things I can't do is shift. Which is going to be difficult." She sighed. "I love letting Xena out to play."

"I'm gonna be an Uncle!!" Max was so excited, he jumped out of his seat and rushed over to give us both a big hug.

I wonder how long it's going to take him.

Alex froze for a second, before it dawned on him.

"Hey! Wait, I'm gonna be an Uncle too!! I always forget that we're like half brothers." Alex jumped out of his seat to go and get in on the group hug.

Scarlett laughed as we hugged them back. After a minute, Alex and Max went back to sit in their seats. "Yes. You're going to be uncles. But you have to keep it quiet. No telling anyone, your mate is okay. But tell her she's sworn to secrecy."

We'll keep this between the families until we have a better game plan. We don't need it getting out before we're ready.

Alex nodded. "I'll tell her later. Let's figure out some things today. Mainly the announcement to have people move back to their homes if needed. Then we can just take it slow. Do one thing at a time. Today's task... Telling everyone to move back home if they want. Tomorrow's task is heading to Ireland to make sure everything is going okay."

"And we'll keep going like that. We'll make sure the secret stays a secret until you're ready to announce it. Will you be doing a formal naming ceremony too? Or well... Two? I don't know if we could do just one? Twins aren't the most common in Ireland." Max said, rubbing his jaw as he was deep in thought.

I like the plan of doing one thing at a time. That way she doesn't get overwhelmed.

Scarlett's heart started to race at the thought. I was immediately able to hear it. Okay. Time to get this moving along.

"We'll think of that when it comes closer." I told. "We don't

have to think about it now or any time soon. Naming ceremonies aren't a thing in Scotland. So we'll just think about it
and table it for a different day."

Max made sure to type it into his phone. "Perfect!"

"So we decided that it's not going to livestream the
announcement. We'll just go out, schedule the announcement
for what? An hour? Maybe two?" Alex asked, looking at Scarlett
and I now.

Two so she can eat, maybe it'll calm her down a bit.

"Two maybe? That way it gives everyone enough time to
get here to hear it from the Alphas themselves?" Max said,
looking at us as well.

"Two hours." I nodded. "That way I can get her a snack
beforehand."

Scarlett laughed. "So I'm just going to get fat sooner rather
than later huh?"

"The faster people know you're pregnant with my kids. The
better." I grinned happily.

I want everyone to know that she's mine. I don't care how
fast. The sooner the better.

CHAPTER

SEVEN

Two hours passed, Scarlett was sitting at her desk eating a sandwich that I made her. I liked being able to provide for her... Cook for her... She cared for me all the time when she first brought me home. It's my turn to return the favor.

I leaned against the large wooden desk, just watching as she stuffed her face. I couldn't help but watch... Staring as she shoved the sandwich into her mouth. I could smell my own lust. I don't need to say anything.

"Oh but I will! I like watching this." Reign told me.

My cheeks heated. I'm so not telling her you said that.

Scarlett looked up at me, a slight tilt to her head. "What?" She mumbled around a mouth full of food.

I smiled, leaning down to press a kiss to her head. "Nothing. I just... I love you so much."

More than any word in the entire world could express.

Scarlett beamed happily up at me. "I love you so much." She repeated to me after swallowing her mouth full of food.

I laughed, brushing a few crumbs off her lips.

"Are you ready to talk about what you want to say to everyone?" I asked, shifting my weight uncomfortably.

I know she'll know exactly what to say... But it still makes me anxious... There's going to be so many people. Scarlett moved her chair to be right in front of me. She dipped her fingers in the waistband of my jeans.

Mmm... I love that she's so confident with putting her hands in my pants.

"I typically just... Well I typically just wing it because that's what I'm best at for speeches." She laughed slightly. "I've never been one to really talk in front of big crowds. I always thought people didn't like me."

I frowned, getting on my knees in front of her. "Even if they don't like you. I do. That's all that matters."

We will make the world respect her.

Scarlett smiled, leaning forward to kiss me on the lips. "All I need is you."

"All I need is you." I repeated with a sharp nod.

Then there was a knock at the door. I couldn't help but growl. Scarlett laughed, shaking her head. It's like they have some sixth sense. It's annoying.

"It's okay baby... Really. Remember what Alex said. We're going to take it one thing at a time. The announcement is today. We'll handle tomorrow's thing tomorrow. That way we can take it slow... Take it easy. Not push either one of us into losing it. Because if you lose it I'm gonna lose it." She explained with a slight smirk as she reluctantly stood up.

"*Well when she puts it like that. I'm not allowed to lose it.*" Reign groaned.

Nope. Because if you do it. Xena will and that will put the kids at risk.

"I'm not going to lose it." I sighed. "Even though I'm sure people would be terrified of me and think I'd be perfect for you."

Two crazy peas in one pod.

Scarlett laughed as she walked to the door. "Yeah, everyone already knows that I'm a wildcard. Who knows, maybe you'll just be the tamer of this wildcard who let's me have my fun when it's needed." She teased.

I smirked, walking up behind her before spanking her butt. "I think I like being a brat tamer. It can be quite fun." I whispered into her ear before following her out into the hallway.

It's one of my favorite pastimes.

"How many people are out there?" Scarlett asked Alex.

Alex smirked slightly.

"Everyone." He responded simply.

Everyone!? My chest began to ache at the thought of so many people around Scarlett. She sensed my worry, before leaning her weight back into me for a moment.

How did everyone get here in less than two hours?

"You're going to be right there with me... Every step of the way. I won't leave your side. And you won't leave mine." Scarlett assured, repeating herself to me again.

I couldn't bring myself to speak, I just nodded my reply.

Before we walked outside, we could hear the noise from the crowd through the front door. And when we opened the door, everyone immediately quieted down staring at Scarlett and me. One by one they slowly started to drop to their knees. Showing their respect and submission to their Alphas.

Wow.

"Double wow..." Reign whispered in agreement.

Scarlett grabbed my hand, pulling me to stand right beside her. "Every you may rise." She commanded, causing everyone to slowly get to their feet. "I know times have been crazy... Things moved... Well they moved rather quickly these last few weeks. Things died off in Ireland, causing you to move here. Your past Alpha threatened and attacked me several times.

Which ended him in challenging me for my Alpha position in which he lost."

A few gasps left the crowd as they took in what she said. Scarlett squeezed my hand, a silent way of telling me that I could talk if I wanted to. I swallowed thickly, moving my arm around her shoulder to pull her into me.

I need to talk. I have to or they are going to think I'm weak.

"Can't have that. I don't want anyone getting any ideas into trying to take her away from us." Reign growled.

"Pete thought he could take down the only female Alpha in the entire world. He thought just because she is a woman that it would make her weak. What you're thinking is true. Alpha Scarlett Knight is the first Alpha in history to have three packs under her control. Ireland is safe to return too. I know many of you love it here. As do I.

But if you want to. You can return to your homes, if you would like to stay in Scotland. After this, please meet with Alex or Max and we will figure out something to permanently move you to Scotland." I told the crowd, smiling down at Scarlett. "We want this to be as easy on you all as possible. So we're leaving the decision up to you where you would like to stay."

I feel myself calming... Maybe it's her power. Maybe it's Reign wanting to show the world that we're powerful and we can handle being with the World's Strongest wolf. Maybe it's who I was always meant to be. Who knows.

"Things will not change." Scarlett stepped in. "Just because we have another pack to be in charge of doesn't mean that we're going to drop the ball on anything else. Ireland is just as important to me as Scotland and Spain. You all are my pack. There's no more The Winterfalls against The Bloody Rose Pack. We are one. We are no longer enemies."

"Long Live Alpha Scarlett and Alpha Seth!" Someone shouted from the crowd.

"Thank you for saving us!" Another shouted.

More shouts echoed throughout the crowd. I smiled, my heart warming at the praise from the crowd. It's like they're accepting us as a couple. Or I'm going to take it like that at least.

Scarlett looked up at me. "This is not just for me... But you as well." She told me placing a hand on my chest. "This is because of the both of us."

I leaned down, pressing a gentle kiss to her lips. "Thank you..."

"For what?" Scarlett asked, not understanding what I was thanking her for.

For everything? For keeping me? For saving me? For letting me be her mate? I have so many things to be thankful for.

"For letting me be your mate." I smiled, pressing another kiss to her forehead.

Before she was able to respond, I raised a hand to quiet down the crowd in front of us.

It's time to show the world that I'm an Alpha by birth... Even though I don't know if I want to be one.

"Thank you all for meeting us in such a short time... For now this is all the information we have. But we're not going to stop here. A lot of things are coming and we won't hesitate to keep you all informed. Remember if you want to stay in Scotland, meet with Alex and Max and they will make sure to get you settled." I called out to them, causing them to nod.

Scarlett smiled as I led her down the steps to the pack house and to where our car was parked. It's finally time to go home.

"And get naked. Just kidding. Maybe. Probably not. Being naked is more fun." Reign sing songed to me.

I couldn't hide the laugh that left me.

CHAPTER
EIGHT

The next day, I was the first one awake. I couldn't sleep... I feel on edge, like something bad might happen. Scarlett was laid against me, resting her head on my chest and her leg over my waist. Her weight should calm me down shouldn't it? Even when I was asleep... I felt her weight and I knew she was with me.

I smiled as I looked down at her peaceful face, I put every single detail of her face to memory. Her soft cheeks, her perfect skin, her full lips, everything about her called to me. My peaceful angel... My saving grace.

I didn't want to get up, not wanting to disturb my peaceful angel. She practically whimpered in her sleep, her body shifting slightly. I frowned, gently running my fingers down her face.

"What could she be dreaming about?" Reign asked me.

I don't know... Part of me wants to look.

"You're safe..." I whispered, allowing my power to slowly flow into her body. "I won't let anything bad happen to you..."

Scarlett's eyes slowly opened, her eyes a dull purple as she looked at me. "Seth?" She yawned, before snuggling deeper into my chest.

Wait... Why were her eyes that dull? I need to look again.

"My love..." I said, worry laced my voice as I didn't like how dull her eyes were. "Can you look at my eyes please?"

I don't think that's a good thing.

Scarlett nodded, before shifting so that she could look at me better. I let my eyes start to glow red, wanting to see if I could get her eyes to brighten up.

"Xena should want to show me her power when she sees mine..." Reign told me and I agreed with him.

When it didn't work, my heart skipped a beat. "Are you feeling okay? You slept okay didn't you? No nightmares or anything?" I quickly asked, shifting so she was laying on her back and I could look over her entire body to make sure she was okay.

Nothing happened while I was asleep did it? Why did I go to bed in the first place! I shouldn't have taken my eyes off of her.

"I'm really tired... I don't know why. I didn't have any bad dreams. I don't even remember what I dreamed of." She leaned back into the fluffy pillow that her head was on.

I squeezed her arm. I don't want her to go back to sleep. I want her awake so I can watch her and make sure she's okay.

"Don't go back to sleep. I think we should go to the doctor." I said, climbing off of the bed. "I don't like how dull your eyes are."

Definitely should go to the doctor.

"But let's make it sound like she has a choice." Reign snorted.

"But the bed is so warm... And comfortable." Scarlett complained, bringing the comforter up over her body.

I frowned further, gently taking the blanket back off of her. As soon as I know she's okay. I will happily bring her back to this bed.

"I know the bed is so warm and comfortable. But I don't know if something is wrong. And if something is wrong, I would rather have the doctor check you out with all the right machines and stuff to know what is happening." I told her, before I quickly grabbed a pair of shorts and one of my hoodies to put on her.

My scent should help keep her calm and comfortable. At least I was hoping. Scarlett frowned, reluctantly sitting up.

"Who said that something was wrong?" She asked, helping me as I put the clothes on her.

I shook my head, after I was done helping her get dressed. I quickly changed myself. One thing at a time Seth... One thing at a time.

"I never said that something was wrong. I just said I want you to be checked out if something is wrong. Your eyes are an extremely dull purple, when they should be brown. I don't like it, and I just want to make sure everything is okay." I explained, when I was fully dressed.

I went back over to her and picked her up in my arms. Reign growled his approval, showing that he loved her being in our clothes. I loved it too... Especially since we're going to the hospital with other men.

Instead of driving, I closed my eyes and transported us to the hospital in Scotland. I'm getting better at this. I immediately put Scarlett down on the bed, before rushing to the door and opening it.

"Get me the doctor. Now!" I commanded, my power rolled through the hallway causing the nurses to rush off to find the doctor.

Scarlett was still sitting in the same spot I had set her down. I took a deep breath in. Everything is okay... She's alive.

"She's alive." Reign repeated.

"I feel okay, I don't think anything is wrong." She tried to soothe me.

I shook my head, heading back to sit with her. I really hate that even when she's not feeling well. She's still focusing on me instead of herself.

"It's better safe than sorry. Let me see your eyes." I said, gently lifting her chin to look into her eyes.

Scarlett opened them completely, letting me see into her dull purple eyes. They're still so dull... I don't know what to do.

"They're still really dull. I don't like it." I shook my head again, before sitting right beside her on the bed.

I don't want to do anything that could hurt her or the twins. Scarlett smiled.

"Gimme some of your power then." She said, like it was no big deal.

"What?" I asked, scrunching my nose.

"Maybe that could work?" Reign offered.

"You heard me. Gimme some of your power. It'll brighten my eyes up." She explained. "Really. I think it'll work!"

"Or it could have a bad effect." I didn't like her idea.

But she pouted, giving me puppy dog eyes. I also hate it when she does that. I can't say no to her! It's not fair.

"Ah stop looking at me like that. If the doctor says that it's a good idea. We'll try it out okay? But not a minute before that."

Scarlett grinned, leaning over to kiss me on the lips. "You won't refuse me anything." She teased.

"Simp." Reign snorted.

I laughed. "You are the Moon to my stars baby. You mean

the world to me. You are the air inside of my lungs. I will never tell you no or refuse you anything." I promised.

The doctor knocked on the door before peeking his head in. "How are we doing in here my alphas?"

Ew. It's him again.

CHAPTER
NINE

"To be honest?" I said, looking at Scarlett and then the doctor. "Really worried."

It's better to be honest with him than lie. I might not like him. But he's still her doctor. Unless maybe Carter can do it?

"You don't like her either." Reign reminded.

Yeah... I don't like anyone besides Scarlett. It's fine.

Scarlett leaned into me, knowing her body weight would help me relax. "I slept all night, and I've been listening to what you said. But I woke up today, and I'm really exhausted. Seth said that my eyes are a dull purple. Obviously I can't tell, but it's worrying him."

I probably should've taken a picture but it's a little too late for that.

The doctor nodded as he listened to her, he placed his tablet down on the bedside table. "Well... It's a good thing that he brought you in."

"See!" I said, causing Scarlett to playfully shush me.

I'm not crazy.

"We touched base about it a little bit, but you know things

are going to be different than a regular pregnancy." He explained, bending down slightly before using a flashlight to look in her eyes.

After about thirty seconds, Scarlett growled, showing her unease to the light being shined in her eyes. I wouldn't like a light being shined in my eyeballs either.

The doctor laughed, immediately putting the light away. "Sorry about that... But that's a good sign that Xena is obviously okay. How are you feeling other than the exhaustion?"

"Um... I think pretty normal. I mean I just woke up and Seth immediately brought me here. So I'm still not really awake awake yet. But I'm not feeling any pain or soreness. Just extremely exhausted. I can tell Xena is super exhausted because she's more irritated and hasn't been talkative." She tried to explain, thinking about anything that might be out of the ordinary.

"She had a bad nightmare the other day. Could that have caused something?" I asked, looking at the doctor for an answer.

I'm going to be a little snitch about everything. I want everything to be okay. With her... With the twins... Nothing bad can happen to them. I won't make it out alive. The doctor smiled.

"No... You both went through something extremely traumatic so nightmares are normal. It's to be expected for some people. In others, they black out the entire memory, refusing to let themselves even relive the memory in any way." He explained, holding his fingers against Scarlett's wrist to check her pulse. "If the nightmares were forcing her to sleep walk? Sleep shift? Then I think there would be an issue. But if it was just a nightmare in bed, I don't think there's anything to worry about. But if she tries to hurt herself in her sleep. Bring her back in here and we'll see what we can do about it."

"I'm not going to try and hurt myself in my sleep." Scarlett interrupted. "I would never do that!"

"How would you know that you're doing it, if you're asleep?" I asked her with a slight smirk on my lips.

Oh I hope she bites me. That would be so hot. Scarlett bared her fangs at me causing me to chuckle.

"Someone's feisty when she's tired." I couldn't help but tease her.

Scarlett shook her head at me before turning her focus back to the doctor.

"So what do you want us to try to help with my dull eyes?" She asked, before placing her hand on my thigh and squeezing it.

I let my eyes drift down to her hand and I wanted to move it... But I have self control. I do.

"Well, something you can try. I'm not sure how well it'll work. But you can try and have Alpha Knight let his power run through you. Like have you draw his power, to energize you again. You could be really tired because you're growing two babies that are half ember wolf. So they're not getting the usual power they get from ember wolf mothers." He tried to explain, putting his hands in his pockets. "It's honestly a guessing game. No one has anything written down about half ember half shadow wolf heirs."

"I'm just saying you should listen to me more often." Scarlett smirked at me.

I rolled my eyes playfully at her. She's such a brat.

"You should just nibble on her ear. It'll make her squirm. A silent little reminder of who is in control here." Reign told me, getting excited about the thought.

I bit back a groan. I love it when she squirms.

"I still think getting checked out was the best idea." I shot back, causing her to smile.

67

Again... I really wasn't giving her an option.

"Don't be afraid to come back, even if you don't think it's something that needs to be addressed. It's better safe than sorry, and that way we can have notes for when you have more kids." The doctor explained, grabbing his tablet. "I'm assuming that you would want privacy?"

"Well, we're not going to stay here. I'm going to take her home." I said, picking up Scarlett in my arms. "There's no point in staying here."

We both hate hospitals, we'd be more comfortable at home.

"We both don't like hospitals." Scarlett explained.

But before the doctor could even reply, we were gone and back in our bedroom at home.

"He really is going to think you hate him." She teased me.

Well. I do. I don't think it takes a rocket scientist to figure that out.

"Well, he's only good enough to make sure you're okay." I shrugged, walking us to our bed.

I gently laid her down first, wanting to make sure she was comfortable.

"I know and I appreciate that so much." Scarlett smiled at me. "I'm sorry that this is going to be a kinda rough pregnancy at first."

"I'm not. I wouldn't change anything about us." I huffed, sitting down beside her on the bed. "So you want to do that right now? Like the whole give you my power?"

I wouldn't change a thing for the world... This is how our lives played out to get to each other. This is what the Moon Goddess had in plan for us.

Scarlett nodded, turning so she could hold my hands. "I think that would probably be best. You've given me your power before. It's nothing bad or difficult."

I nodded, biting my bottom lip. "Okay... Well. If I'm giving you too much power. Just let me know and I'll stop. I don't want anything to happen to you."

"I think it'll be okay. I'm not worried." She assured me. "I trust you more than anything."

"I trust you more than I trust myself." I told her, wanting her to know.

There is no one in this entire world that I trust more than her... She has my life. She is my life.

CHAPTER
TEN

Oh I really don't want to do this. I don't want anything bad to happen to her or the kids. Scarlett closed her eyes, preparing herself for my power. I couldn't close my eyes, I needed to watch her.

I needed to make sure she was okay... I slowly allowed my power to go through our connected hands.

"Tell me if it's too much." I repeated, causing her to squeeze my hands gently.

My heart started to ache at how fast it was beating... I need to calm down before Reign takes control.

"I can feel your panic." She teased. "We're all going to be okay. All four of us."

"I know... I know." I answered her, before forcing myself to close my eyes.

But before she could even respond to me, we were both dragged under.

When we opened our eyes, we weren't in our bedroom. We were in the woods, no one was around.

71

If this is the Moon Goddess. I might have some choice words with her.

"Where are we?" Scarlett asked, still holding my hand. "Don't let my hand go." She demanded.

I brought my arm up and around her shoulders to pull her against me. Just in case this isn't the Moon Goddess... I'd rather be prepared to protect my mate.

"I will never let you go. You're stuck with me." I promised as we walked through the dark woods around us. "Do you think this is the Moon Goddess' doing?"

"Wouldn't she be here by now if it was from her?" Scarlett asked, tilting her head slightly. "Does this place feel... Familiar to you?"

I don't know? But kind of I guess?

I looked around us, looking at the tall trees, letting myself listen to the animals around us. "It feels familiar to me... But I don't remember this place. It doesn't look like I've been here before."

I don't know where we are though... But it does feel like I've been here before. Maybe it's somewhere I saw in Scarlett's head?

"I don't think I've been here before either?" Scarlett continued deeper into the woods. "But maybe I came here when I was a kid and I don't remember?"

Maybe when we marked... That's how I saw this. I don't really know how else I would be able to know what this place is?

'Memories are a funny thing. Sometimes we remember them... Other times we do not. Our lives are long. We experience so much.' A strong feminine voice called out.

Scarlett and I stopped dead in our tracks, looking around for where the woman might be.

I totally called it. It's the Moon Goddess.

'Things are different now my sweet children. So many things are different than before. Back when you were children.' The voice continued, but the Moon Goddess never appeared. 'These trees hide *a power that hasn't been awoken in centuries. They haven't needed to show their faces.'*

"What are you talking about?" Scarlett asked as she didn't understand what she was explaining. "Yes, times have changed. But we only listened because you told us what we were supposed to do."

I didn't understand what she was saying either. Why can't she just come right out and say it?

I nodded. "I agree with Scarlett. She went through so much to get to where she's at now." I called out to the woods around me. "Why did you take us here?"

What's so important about these woods? It's not the fields where Scarlett killed her father?

'Everything will make sense my children. I would never move you in the wrong direction.' The woman called out. *'I would never let anything bad happen to those who are most faithful to me. Think about these woods... Let yourself feel the power... Let yourself remember what happened here.'*

Scarlett shook her head at me, silently telling me that she wasn't following the conversation. I wasn't following this conversation either. At least I'm not alone.

"I don't remember anything about this place?" I called out.

"It only feels familiar to me... I don't think I've ever been here before?" Scarlett answered her.

'You have... Both of you have... At the same time... Think back... Think about what has happened here... Then and only then will you be able to find out why you have to find this place. Find the power that's hidden here.' The woman called out.

I've been here before? In the middle of a tree, a purple and red glowing light appeared.

We looked at the tree, before heading closer to it to check it out. When we got close enough, the tree stopped glowing, showing the necklace in the middle of the tree. The necklace was gold, with a talisman of a wolf with a crescent moon behind it.

It's really delicate and beautiful.

'Your destiny awaits... Your power awaits...' The voice called out. 'Trust me... Think about what you've witnessed...'

And with that, the world around us melted away.

When we opened our eyes, we were back in our bedroom.

"What was that all about?" I asked, tilting my head slightly.

Scarlett didn't answer, she just stood up and headed out of our bedroom. And where does she think she's going?

"She says we've been there before... She says we should know." Scarlett mumbled, her brain working a million miles a minute as she tried to figure it out.

I was quick to follow after her. I think I want to go through her thoughts so I can really understand what she's thinking... Or maybe I should just ask.

"Are you willing to tell me what's going through your mind babygirl?" I asked, following her out to the garage.

"Is she okay?" Reign asked.

I'm not completely sure.

"I have drawings... Of things I used to dream about when I was a kid. Different things, not all of them were good. But I think I've drawn this place before. It seems too familiar to not have seen it before." Scarlett told me, opening up the garage door and immediately heading to where she kept her old sketch pads.

I actually really like that she used to draw. I wish she would actually get back into it.

I stood beside her, letting her dig through the container on the floor. "I think I would feel better if you sat down."

That way she doesn't accidentally hurt herself.

Scarlett rolled her eyes playfully before sitting on the concrete floor. "Happy?" She teased.

"Of course I am. Thank you. Are you finding what you're

looking for?" I asked as she was just tossing random books out of the container.

How many does she have?

"*A lot.*" Reign shrugged.

"I'm trying..." She mumbled before her eyes lit up. "Here we go!!"

CHAPTER
ELEVEN

Scarlett raised her hand to me to help her up. I laughed before taking her hand and pulling her to her feet.

"Oh but she said she didn't want to sit down." Reign rolled his eyes playfully.

She's stubborn. It's in her DNA.

"Okay. What are we looking at in here?" I asked, tapping my finger against the cover of the sketch book.

There could be many different answers to that question. But obviously it has to be important. I wish I could just know what she was looking for. I could help her. Scarlett opened the book, flipping through the many different drawings she had.

"She's insanely talented." Reign complimented.

"If I drew those woods, it would be in this sketch book. I know this one has all of my different drawings of woods and stuff similar to it." She explained, before she stopped on the drawing she had of the woods that we just saw.

Okay... That's weird.

"Don't call my mate weird." Reign growled at me.

I wasn't calling her weird. I was saying it's weird that she has the same exact woods drawn that we just saw from the Moon Goddess. Don't try to get me in trouble, Reign.

"Oh... But think about all the fun we could have if we did get in trouble." Reign groaned at the thought.

I don't need to be thinking about this right now. I need to focus.

"Doesn't this look like the woods we were just at?" She asked, letting me take the book in my hands.

I took a minute to look over the entire page, memorizing every single detail that Scarlett captured perfectly. It was the same woods that we just saw too... Why is this piece of land so important?

"Yes... Actually. It does. Do you remember anything about this dream? Or any hints on where this is?" I asked, looking down at Scarlett now.

Before she said anything, she moved the page to let me see the back of it.

'New woods? No one was there but me. But the power there is... Unique. Powerful. Nothing I've ever felt before. I might have to find where it is if I need to see anything else. Maybe the Moon Goddess wants this to be an addition to my territory? I smelled rouge.' Was scribbled onto the back of the page.

I couldn't help but laugh at the messy writing. She scribbles on like everything. It's probably one of the cutest things she does.

"Alpha Scarlett Knight. Only alpha female in the entire world can't sit still long enough to write a paragraph?" I teased, causing her to blush in embarrassment.

"I just wanted the basic details down, so I didn't forget anything. I honestly never thought I was ever going to see those woods again. Yes I originally thought that it might be an addition to my territory. But as time went past... I figured it was just one of those weird vivid dreams that I had from time to time." Scarlett shrugged like it was no big deal.

I nodded, listening to her speak. It's definitely something to look into. But I don't know how. This literally could be anywhere in the entire world. Maybe it's where Stormy met Kingston?

"Leave the puzzle pieces connecting to Scarlett. She's way better at it than you are." Reign teased me causing me to smirk.

You're so mean to me. But it's okay. I love you anyway.

"Well apparently it's something we need to look into. Why do you think she showed us a necklace?" I asked, gently taking her hand to pull her into the house with me.

I love seeing how her mind puts things together, so I ask as many questions as I can think of.

"I don't know. I've never seen anything like it before. But it felt like I needed it. I felt like it was calling out to me." She tried to explain, before bending back down and picking up an empty sketch pad.

Oh? She's going to start drawing again? She started to walk back into the house, causing me to follow quickly after her. For being shorter than me... She sure can walk super fast.

"She's like barely shorter than you." Reign told me.

I know that. I can walk just as fast as her with no problem. I just wanted to make an observation.

"What's that for?" I asked, easily keeping up with her as she went into the livingroom to sit down.

I really want for her answer to be for her to start drawing again. She seemed to really enjoy it.

"I want to draw the necklace... I want to remember it. Especially if we're going to have to go and find this necklace?" I growled unhappily at her words. "Or have someone go and find this necklace for us? They're going to need to know what it looks like so they know if they're getting the right thing."

I will chain her to the bed if I have to.

"Oh! Do that anyway! She would be so into it." Reign panted at the thought.

Nope. Gotta focus. But I know she would totally be into it.

"You're not going." I told. "You're not going, I'm not listening to you argue about it. You're pregnant and it's simply not happening."

She doesn't have a choice in this.

Scarlett smiled at me, before she sat down on the couch she kissed me on the lips. "Even if I did go, you'd be stuck with going with me. And I don't think it's a good idea... Not just because of me being pregnant. But things are finally starting to... Well they're starting to go back to normal. I just don't think the pack would like it if we had to leave again."

I wouldn't like it if she left again either. Not being pregnant with my kids.

I smirked, grabbing a pencil from the junk drawer in the kitchen. I walked back to the living room, before sitting down beside her. She took the pencil before propping the book up on her lap.

"To be fair, the last time we went away. It was a lot of fun for me." I kissed the top of her head. "We should do that more often."

That would actually be super relaxing to me. I'd actually really enjoy myself.

Scarlett laughed. "What, have a vacation to have sex for two weeks straight?"

"YES!" Reign answered, but I wasn't going to let him tell that to her.

"Well not just sex. But just... Have time for us to be us without anyone else around. I like private time with you. Because you are the best thing to ever happen to me." I smiled as I watched her focus on her drawing.

I love when it's just me and her... It makes me feel whole. Comforted. Safe. I don't have to worry about someone hurting her.

"You are the best thing to ever happen to me. I wish I didn't have to be the Alpha sometimes... I'd much rather be spending time with you instead of them. Yes, I love my pack. But I wish I had the time to well... Be a kid." Scarlett told me, her brown curly hair falling past her shoulders.

I nodded, gently moving her hair to her back and braiding it to be out of the way. Reign growled softly, showing his approval of me taking care of her. I would do anything to make her life even slightly easier.

"You deserved so much better than the start up you got... I wish I was able to do something." I frowned. "I wish we both had a different start, but where we're still able to get to where we are now. Together."

If I could be promised that we would come back together and have a better start? I would want us to have a better childhood.

Scarlett looked back at me. "I might have had a bad child-hood. But I wouldn't change it... Because it brought me to you. You made every bad thing that's ever happened to me or that's been done to me worth it. You are worth it." She told me, bringing her forehead to my forehead.

She is the best part of my times... No matter how dark my life was... As soon as I met her. She was my light. She had been my light for as long as I can remember.

"You are my everything." I whispered, locking my eyes with hers.

"You are my everything." She repeated with a smile. "Now... Let's finish this. And then call Alex and Max to see if they want to head to Ireland with us."

CHAPTER
TWELVE

I had brought out my phone, sending a quick group text to Max and Alex asking for them to come to the house. Scarlett had moved to lean back against the couch. I wonder how much time I have until they come to the house.

"You thinking what I'm thinking?" Reign asked me.

More than likely. Yes.

"Maybe..." She mumbled, before she wrote out a few words about the wolf sitting in the crescent moon.

I looked at her, I had been sitting silently beside her while she drew. I looked down at the writing she was doing. At least this time she took her time to write so it wasn't a scribble.

"I dare you to tell her that." Reign snorted.

Yeah, absolutely not.

"What?" I asked, wanting to be included.

"Well... I was thinking. What do you think of The Rose Fell pack? To combine our pack names... This wouldn't include Spain's pack... Although maybe it should since I run that pack. But I figured that since Ireland and Scotland are side by side. That it would be easier for everyone if we had one pack name.

And this." She tapped her pencil against the wolf howling in front of the crescent moon. "This could be a logo type thing for the pack."

I smiled at her excitement about it. "I like it, and I think the logo type thing would be perfect for it." I teased with a smirk. "We'll figure out what to deal with Spain later. Octavia and Lincoln have things under control so we shouldn't worry."

Spain. Scotland. Ireland. I wonder what other territories she'll take? One things for sure is that I know she's the hottest woman I've ever laid eyes on.

Scarlett nodded. "I wanted to visit with him eventually just to check on things. But I think it's more important to have things settled here before checking on our other pack. Especially since we're going to have to think about ceremonies and different things."

And here I thought I was going to be able to get away with not talking about it.

I groaned, dramatically leaning against the back of the couch. "I knew this topic would be brought up eventually."

"How your pack has a ceremony for the Alpha's mate to submit in front of everyone?" Scarlett teased gently, turning to watch me as I sat there.

My pack. I hate how she says that. I haven't felt a part of that pack in a very long time. I don't claim them as mine.

"How my "pack" is going to expect the only female Alpha in the entire world to submit to me? And in turn that would make other Alphas think less of her? You already have to deal with so much. Adding on my old pack's old ceremonies? That's not something you have to do. Especially not for me." I shook my head. "I don't want anything to happen to your standing in the world."

Which could happen. They could use this as an excuse to respect me more than her.

"We have an Alpha for a mate and we LIKE it! I don't want that to change." Reign pouted.

Scarlett smiled, moving so that she was straddling my lap. "You my beautiful handsome mate... Are truly one of a kind. Yes... I guess the Alphas would think less of me. But hey, think of it this way. I can always kill one of them again and have them all terrified of me again."

She says that like they aren't already scared of her.

I laughed. "Again? Like they still aren't scared of you?"

Scarlett smirked. "Well I guess you have a point. But my point of that whole thing was... I'd do anything for you my love. I would let anyone think less of me. Because what they think doesn't matter to me... What you think of me does matter. That's the only thing that actually matters to me."

Her being respected by the world matters to me, and her being seen as the Alpha matters to me.

I wrapped my arms around her, pulling her closer to my body. "You are the only thing that matters to me. Can we just talk about this a different day? Let's just focus on today's task. Heading to Ireland to make sure everything is going okay. Then our next thing is... I don't know making sure people are okay in Scotland?"

"Yeah what happened to one task at a time?" Reign asked.

Scarlett rolled her eyes playfully. "The next thing to think about is the ceremonies. Either starting with Scotland or Ireland. Or we could do it all in one. Make new traditions. Make our traditions... And tell the old ones to go away."

I definitely would want the old ones to go away.

I nodded, listening intently to what she was saying. "We'll talk about it... I don't think we should talk about it with Max and Alex. Because one of them will say that we should follow traditions to make The Bloody Rose Pack feel heard... Important."

I bet it's Alex.

Scarlett shrugged. "We'll make the decision... Because we're the Alphas. We will know what's best for our pack... And us." She leaned forward, kissing me gently on the lips.

I do love it when she says we. Showing that we're one.

"Mmmm..." A rumble of approval vibrated in my chest. "You wanna know what I want right now?"

Scarlett's eyes were glowing purple causing me to smirk. There's the power behind the purple.

"There's those beautiful eyes I love to look into so much. Back to their powerful purple."

"What do you want?" Scarlett asked, her hands trailed down my torso slowly to pull at my shirt.

"I want you." My voice was deeper than usual, holding a hint of Reign's growl to it.

"I always want you." She answered as one of her claws ripped off my shirt.

I couldn't help but laugh before flipping us so her back was on the couch and I was hovering over top of her. I'll always be ready for her. No matter what.

"Well good thing I'm always ready for you." I said, I looked down at her smaller form.

My eyes slowly taking everything in until they landed on her stomach. Her almost completely flat stomach that holds my kids in there...

"I wonder if it's some special power that Xena has... The ability to hide her pregnancy? Like she can change her scent?" Reign wondered.

Scarlett shook her head, before bringing my face down to hers.

"Are you seriously thinking about how I'm pregnant right now?" She teased me, before booping my nose.

"Read my mind. You'll know exactly how hot I find it that

you're knocked up with my kids." I winked, tearing off her shirt to expose her skin to me.

She wrapped her legs around my waist before pulling me down to her. There will never not be a day I don't love having her pregnant.

"Well, I think you should reward me then." She whispered against my lips. "For being such a good girl and getting pregnant."

I groaned, my eyes rolling into the back of my head. "That's probably the hottest thing I've ever heard you say. But you're right. You are such a good girl, and I'll make sure to praise you everyday for getting pregnant."

I leaned down, kissing her deeply. She immediately opened her mouth, wanting to feel my tongue against hers. I brought my hand up to the back of her neck, pulling her closer to me. She moaned into my mouth. And I ate it up.

But before we could go any further, the front door burst open.

"And the BROTHERS are here!" Alex's loud voice echoed throughout the house.

I hate him.

THIRTEEN

I growled, lifting myself up only enough to see above the back of the couch. I will kill them if they try to see my mate in the state she's in.

"Yeah! Threaten them!" Reign cheered.

"I'd stay there if I were you. If you see my mate without a shirt, I will personally gauge your eyes out." I threatened, my eyes glowing red as my two brothers stopped before they entered the living room.

Scarlett laughed, before my eyes cut down to hers. What is she laughing at? She's not going anywhere without a shirt on.

"If you think about moving, I will spank you. I don't care if they hear." I threatened, causing her to smirk.

Oh she thinks I'm joking?

"Oh. This is going to be fun." Reign grinned.

"Don't threaten me with a good time baby." She winked, before pointing at the blanket at the end of the couch by our feet. "That's what I was going to reach for. So no one gets to see me but you." She booped my nose causing me to nip at her finger.

I want to be biting something else.

"Yeah, cover up the goods. I don't want to see anything." Alex hollered.

I growled, before reluctantly sitting up and grabbing the blanket. I should've just told them to meet us in Ireland.

"I wish I would've waited to text you guys to come over." I huffed, annoyed with my brothers.

"I told you we should've gave them more time!" Max said, causing Alex to shrug.

I gently wrapped the blanket around Scarlett to cover her exposed torso up. Max is smarter than anyone I know.

"I guess you guys can come in now." I sighed causing Scarlett to smile at me.

Not like I have any choice.

"We will have plenty of time later to be alone." Scarlett reassured me. "So did you guys already go to Ireland?"

"Carter didn't like it, but yes. I got up early and went on a run through Ireland. Everything seems to be doing pretty okay. A lot of people have already gone back to their homes, and they're starting to fix things up from how Pete left it." Alex informed. "I... Well I was in my wolf form or else I would've taken a picture of everything. I think it would be nice for the pack to see you guys checking in on everyone."

I think the pack can suck it.

"I thought he would say that so whenever you're ready I have your guards ready. The caravan style like you like. An SUV in front and behind you. Are you wanting one for yourself? Cause it'll take one call." Max asked, he was always jumping at the chance to help us.

Scarlett looked at me, before looking back at Max. "Yeah. We'll take an SUV. It'll be much more comfortable in the back, so we'll want someone to drive us as well. Is that alright my love?"

People. People I don't know and don't trust. Absolutely the freaking heck not.

I breathed in deeply before nodding. "Yeah... I'd like that better than the sports car. You'll be able to be more comfortable. So I want that."

Her comfort is the most important thing to me.

Scarlett kissed my cheek. "You are the cutest."

"Okay, I'll make the call. Do you want me to give you like twenty minutes to get ready and maybe get some food for the trip? I'm assuming I'm going with you?" Max asked, pulling out his phone as he was about to call them.

"If you want to come with us you can. You can either ride with us or whatever you want." Scarlett offered. "But yes, twenty minutes should be good. Right babe?"

I looked down at her. "Yeah. That'll be just fine. It won't take you but a minute to put a different shirt on. Then we can get snacks ready for you."

"Perfect! I'll get the cars ready and then over here in twenty minutes." Max said with a smile, before pressing his phone to his ear.

Alex groaned. "He's so on top of things. I don't know how." He followed Max outside.

It's because Max knows what we need before we even know it.

FOURTEEN

A couple of hours passed, Scarlett and U were in the car heading to Ireland. The closer I got to Ireland... The more stress I felt. I don't want to be here. But I don't want my mate going here without me. Scarlett fidgeted causing me to tilt my head as I looked at her.

"Is she okay?" Reign asked.

I don't know...

"Are you okay?" I asked, turning my body more towards her.

"Yes. I'm just uncomfortable." She huffed, before deciding to lay her legs across mine. She smiled at me. "You should rub my feet."

Has she wanted me to rub her feet all this time? I wish she would've told me.

I laughed, pulling off her shoes before gently starting to rub her feet. "Why are you uncomfortable?"

"I... I don't know how to explain this. But with Grayson... I have this extra sense. He's my twin, so of course I feel it. But he's... I don't know. He's uncomfortable about something, like he wants to talk to me but he's not letting himself." Scarlett tried to explain before she rubbed her chest. "It's making me anxious."

Makes complete sense to me. Twins are unique.

I frowned. "Well... Maybe that can be tomorrow's thing? You send him a text and say you wanna see him at the house. Could tell him something about you wanting to catch up? That way you aren't lying to him and you'll be able to tell what is going on with him." I offered with a slight shrug.

Also if he's here in front of her. She'll be able to smell the lie.

"That's actually a really good idea, I'm going to do that." Scarlett smiled, taking her phone and quickly sending a text to her brother.

I smirked as I looked over her body. I love how close she is with her brother.

"I'm just saying, if he wasn't your twin. I would rip his throat out." I flashed my fangs at her, causing her to giggle.

She may be laughing. But I'm telling the complete truth. I didn't stop rubbing at her feet.

"I find that so hot." She laughed, before groaning as I moved my hands up to her calves. "Ugh, that feels almost better than sex."

"Did she just say what I think she just said?" Reign asked, growling with his unhappiness.

I stopped, before glaring slightly at her. "Better than sex?" I repeated.

Scarlett smirked. Oh I so want to spank her.

"I said almost. Nothing is better than sex with you, okay? You are the best thing to ever happen to me. In more ways than one. Better?" She smiled innocently at me, causing me to nod and go back to rubbing her legs.

A lot better.

"Better. We're almost there, so you'll be able to stretch your legs. And see everything... As it should've been before Pete was the Alpha." I closed my eyes, taking a deep breath in.

I don't need to think about him. I don't want to think about him. He's dead. No one can hurt my mate nor my unborn children. Scarlett moved, grabbing my bicep.

"Look at me..." She purred gently, wanting to bring me out of my thoughts.

When I opened my eyes and looked at her, they were red and showed my stress of being back in Ireland. I hate this place. Scotland is my home. Scotland is where I belong.

"Pete is dead. No one is going to take you away from me. You say the word and we'll leave okay? You don't have to stay here, you can take a car home and I'll be home in a few hours." She offered.

I growled, my eyes flashed a darker red at her as my power soaked the car around us. That would never happen. Over my dead body.

"No. I'm not leaving you in this country without me. No." I shook my head, my hands tightened on her leg. "No."

"*Bite her!*" Reign told me.

Scarlett frowned. "Look at me." She said, but I had my eyes closed, refusing to open them. "I said look at me." She commanded, her power rolled through our bond quickly, wrapping around me and forcing me to open my eyes and look at her.

"*I like it when she commands us.*" Reign flashed his fangs.

Scarlett smiled. "Isn't that my good boy?" She taunted, knowing she wanted to bring me out of my thoughts.

"*Ew. Put a stop to that immediately.*" Reign almost gagged.

I growled, moving quickly so that I was positioned over top of her. My hand moved to wrap around her neck, just resting there and not applying any pressure. I don't want to hurt her. I want to prove a point though.

"You are my Alpha baby..." I whispered into her ear. "But never forget who's in charge." I nipped her earlobe causing her to moan. "You are in charge in front of everyone, but I know you love giving me the control. Letting your body calm down, relax, and give into me and my demands. You're my good girl, don't make me have to show you why you love to be my good girl so much. Because I will... And I'll love it."

I will submit to her no problem... But in the bedroom. When it's just us? I'm in charge and she knows it.

Scarlett giggled, squirming slightly underneath me. "Do it, show everyone why you're mine." She grinned.

I shook my head with a smirk. And this could be her punishment. Being teased. Left wanting more and I won't give it to her until later.

"If only I had the right amount of time to properly pleasure you baby..." My voice was a whisper against her neck. "But I can't..." I whispered, kissing her mark gently. "So I won't tease you. I don't want to have to kill people for smelling your arousal."

Scarlett whimpered, shifting her hips up to try and feel me. "Please?" She begged.

I shook my head, reluctantly pulling away from her. She'll learn her lesson.

"Nope. I guess you'll learn your lesson not to taunt me." I smirked, moving her legs so I could sit down again.

Scarlett groaned, dramatically laying back against the bench seat.

"I think you're incredible, your confidence is so hot. But gosh dang it, I wish we were back home." She told me, causing me to chuckle.

"This is incredible." Reign laid down.

"We're here anyway babygirl." I told, the laugh that was once in my voice was gone now. "Welcome to my childhood home..."

Welcome to my own personal Hell.

CHAPTER
FIFTEEN

"Do you want to see your childhood home?" Scarlett asked softly, waiting for the car to park.

I shook my head. I would rather die than have to go and look at my childhood home. That was absolutely terrible.

"No. I don't want to have to relieve it again. Let's just check and see how everyone is doing and head back home." I said, my eyes drifting away from hers.

I don't want to have to think about everything that's happened in that house to me. She frowned, gently taking my chin in her hand and moving my face to look back at her. I took a deep breath, inhaling her scent. It's like her scent brings calmness to my body. It brings a sense of peace.

"If this is going to set you back... You need to go home." She explained. "I'll be fine, I'll be safe here with Alex, Max and the guards."

I shook my head no. "Absolutely not. I'm not leaving you alone in this country. Ever." I said, swallowing thickly. "No. I can't do it. Last time..."

Last time she almost left me. The time before that she got

seriously injured. No. I'm not letting her stay in this country without me. I need to protect her.

Scarlett quickly brought my face closer so she could kiss me. "That's our past. This is our future." She whispered against my lips. "I'm yours. I'm alive. No one is going to take me away from you."

Reign shivered in the back of my mind. I nodded quietly, but I couldn't bring myself to say anything. There was a gentle knock on the door. "Alphas. Are you ready?" A guard called, but he waited for the command to open the door for us.

"*At least we know that he doesn't want to die.*" Reign said, laughing at his own joke.

I knew this was him trying his best to calm me down. But I don't think I'll be calm until we're back at home. Or at the very least in Scotland.

"Are you ready?" Scarlett asked, wanting to make sure before she said anything.

Nope. But we're going to deal with it anyway.

"*Yeah! We're fine. Everything will be fine. They better not even think about touching Scarlett.*" Reign growled, showing his unease in the situation.

"I'm ready... Just don't leave my side please..." I almost begged, causing her to give me a soft smile.

If I have her by my side. I can handle anything.

"Not even to use the bathroom." She winked, earning a small smile from me. "You can open the door. We're ready."

I moved to get out first once the door was open. When my feet hit the ground, it was like my heart started beating faster at the location I was in. I thought my stress in the car was bad. This was awful. I forced myself to turn around, holding out my hand to Scarlett to help her out of the SUV.

Scarlett took my hand and climbed out of the SUV. She

looked around, people stopped and were staring at us. My hand tightened in hers, before she gently squeezed my hand.

Everything is fine. I feel her power dancing into my body and I knew that everything was going to be fine. I just need to stop freaking out.

"How about you show us around Alex?" Scarlett said, looking to Alex now.

She stepped into me, letting me put my arm around her shoulders to keep a better hold on her. I need to be prepared for whatever comes next... I need to be prepared in case someone comes after her.

Alex looked at me, my body language showing how tense I was. I'm tense. I don't know how to hide it. I don't exactly want to hide it either. It's exhausting trying to be okay when I'm not.

"Alright! My mate is currently working in the hospital so she's taking control of getting that all back up and running. But right now, we're focusing on everyone getting back into their homes. Then back to their jobs and regular everyday lives." He started to explain, leading us down the street from where the fleet of cars were parked.

Scarlett and I's guards circled around us, making sure no one got too close to the group. "Are the guards helping you calm down? If not I can have them move to in front of us and behind us, instead of all around us." She offered, sensing my stress through our bond.

No it's better to have them around me. They'll be able to get Scarlett away from me if I lose control of Reign.

"*Hey! I'm not going to lose it. As long as you don't lose it. I won't lose it.*" Reign huffed.

"No... It's fine. They're fine. I like that they're keeping everyone away from us." I explained, constantly looking around us to make sure no one is going to take Scarlett away from me.

I don't want anyone close to me.

"Okay... Just remember. When you want to leave. We'll leave. No questions asked. We'll just leave." She repeated to me, causing me to nod.

Alex continued to talk, pointing out things to us. Why is he so excited about this? I would think he would hate Ireland just as much as me.

"Everyone should be settled back into their homes by tomorrow... Then what happens next would depend on what you guys want." Alex explained.

"We'll let them have a break. Let them get resettled into the calm here in Ireland. They can return back to work when they're ready. We'll still be living in Scotland, but we'll appoint someone to be in charge here like we did with Lincoln in Spain." She explained.

GOOD! I don't want to live here.

"Pretty sure you've made that abundantly clear." Reign laughed.

Alex looked at Max as he shrugged.

"She's the boss, don't ask questions." Max warned.

"Will this be a discussion for later?" Alex asked, looking to his Alpha.

I growled, my eyes flashing red at my brother. He doesn't know how to shut his mouth does he?

"No. It's not a discussion for later. We're living in Scotland. Case. Closed. Drop it." I ordered, my body was shaking with restraint.

"Punch him!" Reign growled.

Scarlett brought her hand up to my chest.

"Shh... It's okay..." She purred, her power going through his body to help calm him down. "I'm right here... We're going to

102

live in Scotland, we won't have to come here often at all. I promise. Do you want to keep going? Or do you want to go home?"

Nope. We're here so might as well get this done and over with.

"We can keep going." I breathed out, giving her a reassuring squeeze.

Scarlett smiled, nodding to Max. I hope Alex goes away to see Carter. That would help me a lot.

"How about you talk now? Let Alex go and see Carter. It'll give us one on one time." She smiled.

Alex's eyes shined with excitement at the mention of his mate.

"Yes!!" Alex said quickly before running off. Max rolled his eyes.

"Well, he talked a lot. But he pretty much said everything that needed to be said. Everyone will expect an Alpha ceremony but that doesn't have to happen anytime soon if you guys don't want. I spoke with a bunch of people, they said they would prefer to have everything settled here again before getting any formalities out of the way." Max explained, rubbing the back of his neck awkwardly. "I don't really remember too much about the ceremonies... So I'm sorry I won't be much help with that. But I can always ask around to get as much information as you guys will need. Even if you just want it to make a decision about what you're going to want to do."

He's the sweetest I swear. Always trying to take as much as he can off of our plates. I appreciate it more than he knows.

Scarlett smiled. "Thank you for your willingness to help out. Information would be nice, that way we can decide what we think is best. Right baby?"

I nodded, forcing a small smile so Max didn't think I was

mad at him. I might be in a bad mood. But I don't want to take it out on him.

"Yup. Information would be great since I don't remember much either."

Max nodded, turning back forward as we continued to walk down the street. Scarlett stumbled slightly, her vision growing blurry as she clutched onto me tightly. I immediately had her in my arms.

What's happening? I thought everything was fine!? She was fine.

"What's wrong?" I asked immediately, looking her over intently.

Scarlett shook her head.

"I... I don't know..." She shivered, her body moved so that she was curled into my embrace.

I looked at Max, but before anyone could tell me anything. I took off running towards the hospital.

CHAPTER
SIXTEEN

I made it to the hospital in record time. My heart feels like it's going to beat out of my chest. Is it the air here? Is it stress? Did I do this to my mate? I looked around, before finding the stairs. I took them two at a time until I reached the top level of the hospital. Scarlett groaned.

I'm not going to slow down until she is seen by a doctor.

"You're bouncing me around." She complained.

Crap. I should've gone slower. I frowned, trying to steady her more as I rushed onto the floor. I feel terrible.

"I'm sorry baby... I'm not trying to. I just need for you to be checked out." I explained, growling unhappily when I saw Carter standing at the nurses station. "I really wish we didn't come to Ireland today."

I guess today is the day where we see Carter's ability as a Doctor.

"I'm okay... Really. I'm just tired. I think I overdid it." She tried to calm me down.

Always trying to calm ME down.

"Well... Yeah. That's kinda her thing." Reign explained.

I huffed, walking over to Carter.

"Come check Alpha Knight out. Now." I ordered, leaving no room for discussion as I walked to the VIP room at the end of the hall.

Scarlett looped her arms around the back of my neck.

"I'll feel better if you would give me more of your power, just like the other day." She told me, but I just shook my head.

That didn't help for long... I don't want to keep throwing power at her problems if it doesn't help.

"Nope. Not until I get the okay from Carter." I said, trying to contain the roll of my eyes.

Scarlett saw it though, causing her to laugh. I don't know how I feel about Carter. If she can help my mate. I'll like her a lot more.

"You could've brought me home." She teased. "But okay... Maybe she'll know something else." She offered.

I smirked as I laid her down on the bed. Doubtful. No one knows anything about our breeds mixing.

"Doubtful." I kissed the tip of her nose.

Carter and Alex entered the room right after them, letting the door shut behind them.

"Alphasss!" Alex greeted with a smile. "What made you come here so quickly?"

His positive attitude is going to make me punch him.

I growled at him. "Stop messing around. You." I pointed at Carter. "Check out my mate right now. If you so much as hurt her." I threatened, immediately turning my focus back to Scarlett.

I gently brushed her hair behind her ear. I don't feel anything weird coming from her side of the bond. I don't think anything is happening? If so wouldn't I be able to feel it?

"Are you okay? Are you feeling better?" I questioned, closing my eyes to listen to the heartbeats.

The twins' heartbeats are strong... So is Scarlett's. Scarlett smiled at me.

"I'm feeling a little lightheaded, kinda hungry. But other than that I think I'm feeling okay." She thought, letting Carter take her blood pressure. "Maybe the traveling was too much?"

I should've just transported her. Would've saved so much time.

Carter was quiet as she closed her eyes, just letting her power go through Scarlett's body. I don't think I like this. I don't know how I'm supposed to feel right now. My eyes were glued to Carter not knowing what she was doing.

"Just... Let her do her thing. She has a unique gift... Especially for pregnant women. She can see if anything is wrong by letting her power go through their body. It might even give you an extra boost to get through the day." Alex offered, leaning against the wall so he was out of the way.

It was quiet for a moment longer, before Carter's pink eyes opened up and looked at Scarlett. "Everything is okay with the twins. Xena is a little tired, but that's to be expected. Have you been seeing my dad regularly to make sure everything is okay?"

Scarlett nodded. "I think we have appointments set up... Like every month to keep things checked on. But I can see him whenever I like pretty much, just in case anything happens like today. I got really exhausted all of a sudden, so Seth wanted me to get checked out." She explained, before grabbing my hand to intertwine our fingers.

I hate her father. So much. I nodded, holding her hand tightly.

"I apologize for the harshness... I get worried." I trailed off as I sat down beside Scarlett.

I shouldn't have been so rude... I feel a little bad.

"*Eh... That's alright.*" Reign shrugged.

She smiled as she curled into me, letting her legs go across my thighs.

"There's no need for apologies Alpha Knight. I completely understand. It's a really good idea for you to come and get checked when you're feeling exhausted like that. Other than having your mate give you his power, I'm not sure of what to tell you. I'm sorry." Carter explained, looking towards Alex.

Alex smiled as he stepped up to us. He better not be all peppy. I might slug him.

"They'll figure it out. They always do. I'm shocked they even let you check her out in the first place." Alex teased, causing Scarlett to laugh.

"Well. We didn't really have a choice," I teased right back.

Carter smiled awkwardly as she shifted closer to Alex, he wrapped his arms around her and held her.

"Really... Thank you." Scarlett said giving her a slight nod of approval. "Can we head home now?"

Carter nodded, giving them her answer. "Great." I said, before scooping her up in my arms and heading to the elevator.

No use in staying in here! I hate this place. But when the doors opened, Max was standing there. His eyes lit up when he saw us.

"Is everything okay? I figured you'd take care of Scar while I took notes for you on how everyone is settling in." He said, motioning to the tablet he had in his hands. "I have pictures and videos so that you can see it first hand."

I don't know what we would do without him.

Scarlett smiled. "You're such a blessing to me." She complimented. "Everything is okay, I was just doing too much and I got tired. We're going to head home, so if we have to come back we will. But it won't be anytime soon."

Max nodded. I breathed out a sigh of relief. "I feel like

Ireland is just bad karma for me and everything I hold close to me."

It's bad juju or whatever they call it nowadays.

"Nothing bad happened to me. I'm okay, I just have to take it easy." Scarlett pouted. "And I'll do that when we get home. Is the caravan ready?"

Max nodded. "They're waiting outside, I figured you'd want to go home so I had them move the cars here. And I also have food for you in the car." He beamed with happiness.

I grinned at my brother. I love him so much.

"You are incredible. Honestly incredible. You've thought of everything. Good job, I'm proud of you." I smiled.

When the elevator doors opened on the main floor, we all walked out.

Since the hospital just reopened there weren't many people. Thankfully. I quickly made it outside, causing a guard to scramble to get the back door open to the middle SUV.

"Thanks. Take us home now." I ordered as I climbed into the car and sat down on the back seat.

Max climbed into the front beside the driver so he could get on his tablet again. Scarlett smiled as she looked up at me. We're alone back here and I'm thankful.

"I don't know what I did to get so lucky... To get such an incredible mate that wants to take care of me and carry me." She smiled, laying her head on my chest.

I tightened my arms around her. My whole world is laying in my arms right now.

"I'm the lucky one." I explained. "I'll never understand what I did to get you. But I promise everyday to cherish you."

CHAPTER
SEVENTEEN

When We got home, neither of us were tired so we decided to head out to our favorite field together. I had my hand on the small of Scarlett's back. This field gives me... Peace... Comfort...

"This would be a perfect place for a house. Secluded. Safe." Reign told me.

And that gives the perfect idea.

"What are you thinking of this whole thing?" I asked, wanting to know her true feelings.

Scarlett tilted her head slightly, a fry halfway to her mouth. Was she paying attention to what I just said?

"Of what whole thing?" She asked, she wasn't paying attention.

I chuckled, helping her to sit down on the ground before I sat beside her. The stars were out, a beautiful crescent moon could be clearly seen in the sky. The moon was gorgeous tonight...

"Not more beautiful than Scarlett though." Reign smiled.

"Of us having kids... Twins. What are you thinking about

it?" I asked, holding her food in my hand so it didn't touch the ground.

I know how she feels when her food sits on the ground. She won't want to eat it. She leaned back against the grass, just looking up at the stars.

"I'm excited... I'm so happy." She smiled, propping her head on her hand so she could watch me.

I kept my eyes on her, loving how relaxed she looked right now. She must love it here on this field too.

"Have you thought about names yet?" I asked, curious about her answer.

I have a few ideas. But I'm not sure what she would like the most.

"I have... A little bit honestly. I figured we could kinda take it one kid at a time? Well one pregnancy at a time." She smiled. "I really like the name Kourtney, with a K. To match Knight."

That would be adorable.

"So Kourtney Rose Knight? So she has your middle name?" I offered, reaching over to brush a piece of her hair behind her ear. "I want her to have a part of you. She'll be just like you."

I want for our daughters to act just like her. Powerful. Know they're strong and they don't need a man to do anything for them.

"We raise powerful women." Reign snorted.

Powerful woman. Just like their powerful Mom.

Scarlett looked surprised. "I didn't know you knew my middle name..."

I grinned. "I have my ways babygirl. But what do you think?"

It's so much fun to make her surprised.

"I love it. So We have one name picked out... Should we have two girl names and two boy names picked out just in case?" She asked, laying back down to look up at the stars.

114

I placed her food back in the bag before laying down beside her. I guess that would be a good idea. Just so we have all our bases covered.

"Hm... What do you think about Zeva? And again Rose for the middle name?" I asked, reaching over to pull Scarlett closer to me so we were touching.

I won't let that one go. I want our daughters to have her middle name. She smiled.

"I love that name. But wait... You know my middle name. What's yours?" She asked, peaking a glance over at me. "I never really thought about it. It's been so long since someone has even mentioned my middle name."

I don't think I have one? I've never thought about it at least.

"I don't have one. Or if I did, I was never told about it." I shrugged. "You could give me a middle name if you wanted?"

Scarlett leaned up, moving so she was straddling my waist to look at my face.

"You would let me give you a middle name?" She asked. "Isn't that supposed to be important?"

Why wouldn't I? She's the smartest woman I've ever known. I trust her with my life.

"You're naming my children. So why not? I figured that if you give me a middle name then at least one of our sons will have that middle name too. So then it's like a two for one special." I grinned up at her, my hands went to grip her hands gently.

Scarlett laughed before shaking her head. A two for one special. Just like her pregnancy.

Scarlett looked over my face, before gently running a hand through my hair. Reign wanted to purr at the relaxing feeling.

"What do you think of the middle name Blaine?" She

asked, curling a piece of my hair around her finger. "Seth Blaine Knight."

I smiled. "I love it... And in return. What do you think of the name Sebastian? Nickname Bash?" Scarlett grinned, she squirmed slightly.

"I think that's adorable! Sebastian Blaine Knight! Okay. So we have two... Since you gave me two names... Do you want me to pick the next boy name? If you want to pick it that's completely fine too." She asked, before laying down beside me again.

I like how we're agreeing on everything. It makes everything super easy. I placed my palm on her belly again. This is my favorite place to keep my hand.

"Sure. I'm honestly happy with whatever you want to decide." I explained, turning on my side so I could watch her better.

I want to draw her under the stars... She's gorgeous.

"Hmm... A boy name that goes well with Blaine as the middle name." She thought out loud.

I laughed. At least we're on the same page.

"It doesn't have to go with Blaine. I'm sure we'll have other boys. So it doesn't have to be this one that follows after my middle name." I reminded.

Scarlett grinned at me.

"I think it would be nice to have the first borns have our middle names. So maybe... Liam? Or Asher? I really love both of their names. Gray was almost named Asher actually. Could you imagine that? Scarlett and Asher?" She snickered. "I think Scarlett and Grayson sound much better together."

I nodded in agreement. "I agree. But I like either one of them, and I think they'll both sound perfect with Blaine. So either Sebastian, Liam, or Asher. And then our girl names are Zeva and Kourtney with a K." I smiled. "I like this plan."

"Definitely Kourtney with a K." Reign told me.

It was beautiful.

Scarlett yawned, closing her eyes as she relaxed next to me. "I like Sebastian and Kourtney together, and then Liam and Zeva. What do you think?" She asked, not opening her eyes.

I smiled as I took out my phone and took a picture of her relaxing in the moonlight. If I can't draw her. I'll take a picture.

"I love anything you do." I told. "As long as I have you... And we have happy healthy children. That's all that matters to me. Is our happy family."

Scarlett moved closer to me, her leg went over my waist. I looked down at her, noticing that she was asleep. I couldn't help but chuckle softly. I knew that she was going to fall asleep. She might've not been tired. But this field always relaxes her enough to make her sleep.

"I love you more than anything My Ruthless Queen." I kissed the top of her head, before managing to get up with her in ny arms.

I sighed in relief when I noticed she was still asleep.

CHAPTER
EIGHTEEN

The next morning Scarlett was awake, laying her body against mine. Hmm.. I love waking up with her right next to me. I groaned, tightening my hold on her as I rolled us over so I could shove my nose into the crook of her neck.

Her scent is my favorite thing.

"What are you doing up so early?" His voice rumbled against my neck.

Scarlett smiled as she moved her head to the side so I could have better access to her neck.

"Just nibble... Nibble her. Bite her. Mark her more." Reign groaned at the thought.

"I'm having that same feeling as yesterday..." She started before I abruptly brought my body off of hers to look her in the face.

What did she just say? Is she okay?

"Not the whole lightheaded feeling. The feeling about Grayson. I just feel like he's hiding something from me... I don't know what it is. Or what I even did to make him feel like he couldn't come and talk to me immediately about it."

Oh. Okay. That makes me feel so much better honestly.

I nodded, before laying back on top of her. "Well... At least he's going to come over today and you'll finally be able to find out what he's trying to hide from you. Doesn't he have the whole sixth sense thing too? I guess my question is wouldn't he know that you'd be able to tell what he's feeling?" I asked as I started to draw random shapes on her bare arms.

He could've forgotten about it? Since he doesn't have as much power as her? I don't know. That's just a thought.

"I feel his emotions more often than he feels mine... I'm so used to closing my emotions off from everyone. He could've forgotten by now that we can tell each other's emotions. Especially with the whole elder problem we still have to deal with." Scarlett growled slightly, causing me to smirk.

I'm excited to be able to get to hear and see her scare someone.

"Ah, just go and scare him. It'll be fine. Him being the elder, not your brother. You might make him cry." I teased.

Scarlett laughed. That would be hysterical, watching a grown man cry.

"He won't cry, but I'm not going to scare him. He's seen enough scary parts of me in his lifetime. But we'll handle it. It's on our one thing a day list." Scarlett smiled, scrapping her nails gently down my bare back. "I like that you don't wear a shirt."

I nearly grunted at the feeling. It shoots pleasure all around my body. I leaned up, smirking down at her. "I like when you don't wear a shirt."

"Oh imagine my surprise. But I can't exactly wear no shirt all the time, huh? With your brothers coming over whenever they want?" She smirked as my eyes darkened.

Next house we get. I'm so making them call before they come over.

"They ever see you naked, it'll be the last thing they ever

see. I don't care that they're my brothers." I growled, my brown eyes turning a dark red.

I'll make them blind. I don't care.

Scarlett giggled. "I love my possessive alpha. What are you wanting for breakfast?"

I smiled, kissing her lips gently. "I want you to eat more than you did yesterday. I was thinking yesterday, that maybe upping your food intake would help you keep your energy up for longer?"

I'm going to try whatever I can to get her to feel better.

"It's worth a shot, I'll try it." Scarlett told me. "Does that mean you have to eat more than yesterday too?"

I rolled his eyes playfully. "If you want me to, I will." I said, climbing off of the bed to head to the kitchen.

Scarlett followed quickly after me. She could've stayed in the bedroom for breakfast in bed.

"Of course I do. I want you to take care of yourself like you take care of me." Scarlett told me, watching as my back muscles moved and rippled as I walked.

I feel her eyes on me. I love how obsessed she is with watching me. I walked in front of the kitchen island.

"You will forever be my top priority. Obviously with the kids too. But you are my mate. My number one." I promised. "I take care of myself too. But I just know you babygirl. You like to think of everyone but yourself. So yes I want to make sure you're taken care of."

I want her to know that she's my top priority. Even if she doesn't do the same for herself.

Scarlett blushed as she sat at the kitchen island. "I just..."

"I know... You've been so used to doing that for the longest time. But now I'm here. I'm here to put you first. I'm here to save you. I'm here to be able to do everything for you." I winked, causing her to laugh.

I'm here to serve her. To please her. To be her everything.

"You are my greatest blessing. Oh! We should totally have strawberry waffles! With bacon!" She nodded, her stomach rumbling at the thought.

I smirked. So I see her cravings have started quickly.

"Are you really that excited about it?" I asked, wanting to make sure as I got into the fridge.

"YES!" She said, a little too loudly. "Of course I am! It sounds so good. Are you going to eat it with me?"

I nodded. "Yeah of course, would you like me to make some for your brother too?"

I don't want to be rude. I don't think her brother thinks I like him.

"Well maybe, I don't know if he ate before coming over or not?" She said, rubbing her stomach slightly. "I'm going to be selfish and ask for you to make mine first."

I chuckled. "I was, I'm always going to make yours first. You should call your brother and see when he's going to come over." I told her, causing her to nod.

She comes first always.

"In more ways than one." Reign growled.

Scarlett was about to get up for her phone, before the door opened and Grayson walked in.

"Why call me when I'm right here?" He asked with a dazzling smile that matched Scarlett's.

"Why is it that both of our brothers walk in here like they own the place?" Scarlett asked, teasingly.

CHAPTER
NINETEEN

"Well someone told me that I was welcome here all the time." Grayson smirked. "Is she regretting it now that she has a mate?"

Yes. I am regretting it for the both of us.

Seth laughed. "Nope. Because his brothers act the same exact way, so it's not like I can walk around naked or anything." She teased.

Grayson gagged at the mention of his sister being naked. Mmm... I'll have to get us a new house. She'll be able to walk around naked then.

"Okay gross, I didn't need to know that. But at least I'm not the only brother that does it. It feels great finally being back in Scotland... And it not being so crowded everywhere I go." He said, sitting down beside Scarlett at the island. "How have you guys been?"

"Stressed." I answered with a shrug. Scarlett looked at me. "He asked."

"Does she want you to lie?" Reign asked with a slight chuckle.

Probably. She doesn't like to be honest when it comes to her own health.

Grayson laughed. "Yeah... Being with the only Alpha Female in the entire world isn't easy. Especially her being as stubborn and strong headed as Scarlett." He bumped against Scarlett's knees.

"We've just had a lot of stuff going on recently. How are you doing? I've been feeling... A weird feeling coming from you." Scarlett said, wanting to cut straight to the point.

Grayson's cheeks turned pink. "I always forget that you can sense my feelings. I never can sense yours. I guess it's that Alpha power huh?" He asked, fidgeting in his seat.

She can hide her emotions from anyone. She's strong enough to do that. I don't know anyone else who could do that.

"Either that, or Scarlett is extremely sensitive to other's feelings in general. It's probably just a part of her personality, her power. She has stronger power, so she's more hypersensitive." I explained, putting the fresh bacon on a plate in front of Scarlett.

There's no problem with her being hypersensitive. But she can feel more than a normal alpha.

"I mean that makes sense..." Grayson looked at Scarlett.

"And the fact we're twins. We're more connected in that way too." She told him. "So what's going on? What are you hiding from me? Is the pack saying crap to you again about me? Cause I'll handle it if so."

This has got to be good.

"No, they're pretty good right now actually. I think they're happy with you guys being Alphas together actually. It's actually about when I went to find Stormy..." He trailed off as he averted his gaze from Scarlett.

I looked at Scarlett before turning my focus back to cooking her food. I'm not going to burn her food... But I'm so guessing that he found his mate.

"Eh. Probably." Reign offered.

"And..." Scarlett urged, needing to know more information.

"Well... I found my mate. And I moved her here, that's why it took me so long to get back here. I was helping her pack and getting her brother to be okay with her leaving his territory." He said, his cheeks turning a shade darker.

Scarlett smiled. I don't think I like where this is going.

"Oh that's wonderful Gray! If you would've told me I would've came to greet you guys! That's so exciting!! Who is she? Why didn't you tell me before? Haven't you been home for a while? Why didn't you bring her today?" Scarlett asked, her excitement obvious.

"Well... About that... I didn't tell you because I know how you feel about her brother." He said, biting his bottom lip as he forced himself to look back at her.

Oh this is not going to be good at all.

"What?" Scarlett asked, tilting her head slightly. "What do you mean?"

"I mean... I found her in Hunta..." Grayson laughed awkwardly.

"So neither of my siblings like to tell me anything." Scarlett said with a roll of her eyes.

"I feel like I'm missing a big piece to this story." I said, looking between the siblings.

Scarlett kept her emotions the same, only showing her excitement for Gray. But I could tell she was mad at the outcome.

"Scarlett doesn't get along with Silver Huntington..." He said, before he was cut off by an unhappy growl.

"Yeah, don't say it like it's some stupid fight. He came here for an Alpha meeting, and disrespected me continuously. Lied to me continuously. Tried to tell my military to leave my pack and join his. And don't let me forget! By the time he left, he had stolen something from the pack house. An antique piece of jewelry from our ancestors. So don't say it like it's some stupid fight where I got my feelings hurt." Scarlett growled, flashing her purple eyes at Grayson. "Silver is not welcome on my land. Ever again. If he ever comes back, I will lay him out like I did the last time he was here. When he thought he could just tell my whole pack he could take me in a fight. And I showed him and his pack that I'm more of an Alpha than he could ever be. So little Alpha got his panties in a twist and left my land with his tail between his legs."

I chuckled at the way she told the story. "I don't blame you, I just wish I could've been there to see you lay him out. I bet it was hot." I winked, plating the waffles and placing them in front of Scarlett so she could eat. "Would you like something?" I asked Grayson, causing him to shake his head no.

I would pay good money to see her lay a grown man out like he was nothing.

"That is such a turn on." Reign groaned.

I know. Her confidence is so sexy.

"Vi isn't like her brother... I swear. She's honestly so amazing... I think you'd really like her if you got to know her. Please don't hate her just because you can't stand Silver." Grayson frowned, looking down at his legs.

Scarlett had to finish the food in her mouth before turning to look at her brother. She gently pulled his face up to look at her.

"I don't hate her because of who she's related to. If she makes you happy, that's all that matters to me. But don't expect me to make nice with Blackguard because you are mated to his sister. That's not something that I'm willing to do. Unless he gives me back the piece of jewelry he stole from us and apologizes for being a sexist idiot." She told him with a smile. "And to sweeten the pot, I won't even bring up the fight between me and her brother. I'll act like nothing is wrong. I'm pretty good at that."

It took everything in me not to snort at her comment. An Alpha is always super good at keeping control.

Grayson forced a smile. "She already knows about you guys not getting along... She didn't even want to move here. But she knew how important you are to me so she moved... She even said she would go visit her brother without me so she didn't upset you. She's looked up to you for so long. Please give her a chance. I'm sure she would be able to talk him into returning whatever he took from you."

"I will give her a chance. I promise. I'm not going to treat her differently because of who she's related to. You matter more to me than some fight with someone... You know that right?" She asked softly, reluctantly moving her hands back down to her thighs.

It would be just like her to put her differences aside to make her brother happy. I was eating my food, slowly just in case Scarlett had wanted some of mine.

"Of course I do... I guess I just worry. I also didn't know how Seth would react hearing about Silver." He shrugged.

I smirked, swallowing my mouth full before replying. "Well, the thing is. If he wants to try and disrespect my mate in front of me. He'll be six feet under." He said, keeping direct eye contact with Gray. "I don't care if he's your mate's brother. He speaks down on my mate. He's a dead man. And if he doesn't listen to my mate's orders and steps foot on our territory. Any of our territories. He's a dead man."

I'll happily do it. No one gets to talk down to my mate. I don't care who they are.

Scarlett grinned as she finished her plate, she reached

across, stealing a piece of bacon from me. Called it. "That's probably the hottest thing you've ever said."

Grayson made a face. "You two are disgusting. I'll make sure Silver remembers not to come here, but I'll see if Vi can get him to give you back what belongs to you. What is it anyway?"

Scarlett shrugged, covering her mouth so she could talk. "I don't remember, it happened so long ago... And so much has happened since then. But I did want to tell you something..." She said, turning to look at me to make sure I was okay with it.

As long as Grayson can keep his mouth shut, I'm fine with her telling him. Grayson looked between us, obviously not following. I gave her a single nod in confirmation.

"I'm pregnant..." Scarlett smiled at her brother.

Grayson's eyes lit up with excitement.

"Oh wow!! Congratulations guys!" He smiled, hugging Scarlett gently.

"Yeah... We actually have been having a few slight problems..." Scarlett trailed off, her mind running a million miles an hour. "No. No. No." She abruptly stood up, heading to the living room.

I followed after her quickly. What is it now?

"What are you doing? Are you feeling okay?" I asked, worry lacing my voice.

"It can't be. It can't be." Scarlett said, grabbing her sketchbook.

TWENTY

"What's going on?" Grayson asked, as he wanted to be included.

Scarlett was flipping through her sketchbook to bring up the talisman she drew. Or at least I'm assuming. That's the last thing she drew.

"This. This is what the Moon Goddess showed us." She said, giving it to me to hold.

I took it in my hands, keeping it open to the page that she had it on. I'm just going to follow her lead on this one. Because I have no idea what's going through that mind of hers.

"But that. That is why it's familiar. I can't believe I never remembered. We had that necklace in our collection. But that's what he stole! That's what he took! It's the necklace of the first female Alpha of this pack." She said, grabbing her phone and calling someone.

"Who is she calling?" Reign asked.

I don't know. I want to know though.

Scarlett put the phone on speaker, waiting for them to answer. When they finally did, she didn't give them time to talk. "Get me the book in my office about every antique that my packs ever had. It should say something like The Winterfall history on it. It's big, it's black. I don't remember anything else about the book. Get it over to me now." Then she hung up.

I looked at her, waiting for her to explain herself. Is she feeling okay? I'm assuming she called Max if she's asking where something was.

"What are you talking about?" Grayson asked, keeping his distance from her.

Scarlett glared at him slightly. I stayed close to her... I feel her energy start to rise. I can't let her shift. No matter what I have to do to stop her.

"Do you really think I'm going to shift right now? I actually can't. So I'm fine." She said, "It's not like before, I'm not going to lose control of myself."

"I know that." I said, before Grayson nodded in response as well.

I trust her... But I also know that sometimes you don't have an option. They take control so fast.

"I'm talking about this talisman." She tapped the page since I was standing right beside her. "This. This is what was taken from me by Blackguard. He took the talisman that belong to our ancestor Caitriona Winterfall. That was hers. No one was supposed to touch it besides me!" Her eyes were slowly turning purple, the ground underneath us was starting to vibrate.

I dropped the book immediately, before placing my hands on her cheeks. I need her to come back to me.

"Baby look at me. Look at me right now." I said calmly, letting my eyes glow a deep red to help her fixate on me. "I need you to calm down."

I know I have this... I know I can get her to calm down.

"Xena wants out. Let me out to calm her down!" Reign demanded.

NO! I have this under control. I have this handled.

"I need my talisman back!" She growled, her eyes changing to a deeper purple.

Xena was itching at the surface. I squatted down slightly so we were face to face.

"I said you're going to calm down." I growled, my order rolling over her skin in large waves. I pulled at every once of power I had. I needed it and then some more to get her to listen to me.

"You're going to sit on that couch and you're going to listen to me." I demanded.

Scarlett felt the need to fight it for a second before she moved to the couch. She sat down, before moving to the back of the couch to get comfortable. There's my girl.

"Good girl." I praised. "Now. You're going to lay down and relax. You're going to lay with me and we're going to relax. We're going to calm down. If you fall asleep, I'll handle everything. But you need to calm down."

Grayson was sitting in a chair, looking down at his legs to show his submission. I heard Reign snort in the back of my mind.

"Baby." Reign chuckled.

He just isn't an Alpha.

"He could've been." Reign shrugged.

Could've. But he's too submissive to be an Alpha.

Scarlett laid down on the couch, giving me enough room to crawl behind her so she could move up against me.

"I'm sorry..." Scarlett frowned, cuddling up against me.

I wrapped my arms around her to hold her. That's why I'm here... To keep her in control.

"It's okay baby girl." I kissed the top of her head. "You just need a break. We'll lay here until Alex finds what you're looking for. Everything will be okay, but I just need you to calm down so nothing happens to you or the twins."

Scarlett nodded, shifting back closer so there was no room in between our bodies. "I'm okay... I don't know what happened."

"Over stimulation probably. It's something that you've been upset about for a while. So all of the emotions came rushing to the surface, it's okay. Just know that we're going to handle everything together." I assured, rubbing her arms to help relax her.

A nap would do her good.

CHAPTER
TWENTY-ONE

An hour later, Alex was walking through the door with three large black books in his arms. *So help me. If he wakes her up. I'm gonna break his legs.*

"*YEAH! I wanna see that!*" Reign nodded with excitement.

"I found three books that I think might've been it. But if you wanted the right one sooner, you should've called Max. He knows your office like the back of his hand." Alex called out as he walked into the living room.

"What are you doing?" Alex asked, plopping the heavy books on the coffee table.

I was still holding Scarlett as she was resting against me. Grayson was still sitting in the chair. Holding my mate. What does it look like?

"*I think he was talking to Grayson.*" Reign offered.

"Things well... Things happened. And I didn't realize Seth could command me and I don't think I like it." Grayson said with a funky look on his face.

"In my defense, I didn't remember you were here." I teased

139

as I continued to rub Scarlett's back. "My mind focuses on this girl right here."

At least I know I could command him.

"Well okay then, at least Seth is getting his confidence back." Alex smiled. "Are you gonna wake her up?"

"Her is up." Scarlett spoke as she reluctantly sat up out of my hold. "I wasn't sleeping, just laying down waiting for you to get here. Since you took your sweet ol' time getting here."

I'm surprised she didn't just immediately call Max. Max would've taken less time than Alex.

"You asked me to find you something! I don't even know where most of my stuff is. Carter does, she has to find things for me all the time." Alex complained. "Max knows where all your stuff is."

Exactly my point.

"Max makes me so proud." I grinned, sitting up beside Scarlett. "He's been doing such a good job with all of this. I mean so have you."

I would lose my mind if it wasn't for Max.

"You can say that again." Reign added in.

"I'd just like to say that I'm going to be getting back into the swing of things." Grayson said, feeling left out.

Scarlett smiled at him. I don't think I much like him. Reign fell over laughing in the back of my mind.

"I've always been so proud of you. Since you're the only one who can keep me on a schedule." She grinned, reaching over to the table and grabbing the first book of the stack.

"What are you looking up baby?" I asked, looking down at the pages she was flipping through.

How can she read so fast? Alex sat down in the chair opposite of Grayson. Grayson was on his phone, sending a text message to someone. Probably his mate.

"I know that talisman is here. It has to be. I know what it's

from, it's gotta be why she kept showing us the talisman."
Scarlett explained. "I watched this talisman in the pack house
for... Well for as long as I can remember. It was from one of the
first members in my pack. And more important it was from the
first Alpha female ever recorded in history. It was her and then
me. Her people turned on her and let the Alphas of the world at
the time kill her. But she wanted to stick it to them and put her
power in this talisman..."

I nodded, listening to her. "And do you think that this
talisman will help you keep your energy up? Or what do you
think the importance of this is?"

I would burn the world to the ground to find it if that necklace would help her.

Scarlett stopped as the picture on the page showed the
talisman. She sucked in a breath as she skimmed through the
reading.

"The great Caitriona Winterfall refused to give them her
power... Relying on the pendant her mate gave her right before
the birth of the first of ten sons... It's said to give the owner
access to her great gift..."

"Ten kids. That hurts me and I don't even have a vagina."
Reign cringed.

I looked over her shoulder, before I growled and looked at
Grayson. "Get your mate over here now."

I need to get that necklace back.

"Why?" Grayson asked, standing up. "I don't think I want
her coming over here if you're mad about something."

Does he think I'm giving him an option in this? Reign was
ticked off.

"How dare he not listen to us." Reign growled.

I stood up, my eyes blazing red. "Are you denying a direct
command from your alpha right now?"

"You're not my Alpha. She is." Grayson said, standing up as

he looked directly in my eyes.

Scarlett stood up quickly as I leaned down to get in Graysons face. This should be fun.

"You're testing my limits, Grayson. Text your mate and tell her to come over here. Or I will have the guards go to your house and drag her here." I said, my voice was deeper than usual, showing my irritation.

Scarlett put her hand on my lower back just in case she had to get in the middle of it. She wasn't going to get in the middle of it. Even if a fight started.

"What did you read?" Alex asked, already holding his phone if he had to call someone.

"They really think we couldn't take Grayson." Reign growled.

I don't think that's the point. I could freaking kill him.

"Oh. Yeah. Might not wanna do that." Reign shrugged.

Grayson growled. "I'm not having her come here if you're just going to yell at her."

"Why don't you read the sentence I'm referring to my love?" I asked, not once breaking my eye contact with Grayson.

Grayson will submit to me. I don't care what I have to do to get it. Scarlett looked at Alex.

"It's said that the Talisman of Caitriona will protect pregnant Alpha Females who are destined to birth the better generation of Winterfall heirs..." Scarlett said, causing Alex to immediately get on the phone.

I want to know what Grayson is going to do. Am I going to have to force him to submit?

"So this is your final command, Grayson." I said, my eyes turning darker. "Get your mate over here now. Or I will have no choice but to step in to protect my mate." I commanded, my power rolling off of me in massive waves.

Grayson tried his best to stand up to me, but he couldn't maintain eye contact with me any longer. He brought his phone out of his pocket and called his mate.

I took a deep breath in. I don't have to fight my mates twin.

TWENTY-TWO

"She's coming." Grayson said, crossing his arms.

I bared my fangs at him, not liking his attitude. I might punch him if he keeps this up.

"Just force him to submit." Reign offered. *"It might be a little better than punching him. But I'm here for whatever you decide."*

"Everything is going to be okay... I'm still feeling okay." Scarlett assured, wanting to help try and calm me down.

I rolled my shoulders before looking down at her with a soft smile. I'm not going to fight her twin.

"Not in front of her at least." Reign snickered.

That's the truth.

"I know... But I want to get that Talisman back for you just in case you need it... What if it could do more than just protect you while you're pregnant? What if someone else we love needs it like one of our children?" I asked, wrapping my arms around her waist and pulling her in front of me.

Scarlett smiled before nodding. I would kill someone if one of my children needed this talisman and we didn't have it.

"We'll get it back... I promise." Scarlett promised him, before Grayson growled unhappily.

"If we're going to stay in Scotland you're going to have to learn not to threaten my mate, you need to learn to trust her. I thought you said you were going to give her a chance? Because she's not her brother." Grayson asked, turning his focus on Scarlett.

Who threatened who's mate? What is he even going on about? Scarlett reluctantly turned around in my hold.

"I don't know. He's lost his darn mind." Reign shrugged.

"What are you even talking about Gray? What's gotten into you?" She asked, looking him up and down. "You've never given me an attitude like this before."

I don't like that he has an attitude with my mate. As soon as Scarlett let's me know. I'll take him to the ground.

"I'm talking about you letting Seth threaten my mate just now." Gray said, with an annoyed look on his face.

"First off. I don't let him do anything. He's my equal in every single way. I'm not his Alpha. He's my mate." Scarlett snapped.

I didn't let her move from in front of me. I will fight him. She's not fighting anyone. At all. It's my turn to fight to protect her and her reputation.

"But you're still the Alpha." Grayson interjected.

"Secondly, don't interrupt me. Seth didn't threaten her. He could've but he didn't. You tried to defy a direct order from your Alpha and you failed at it. So he simply let you know that if you weren't going to let your mate know she is wanted by her now Alphas. Then he was going to have her dragged here. That's not a threat.

That's simply letting you know there's more than one way to get what we want done. Is this going to be a problem? You being with her? Because this isn't going to be just something we can get over Grayson. My pregnancy is going to be difficult. It's already been difficult because I'm growing twins who are half Ember wolf.

It's not the same as everyone else. So of course my mate is going to be angry and demanding. But you can't just disrespect him like that. I'm your Alpha. But as soon as I marked him. He became your Alpha as well. Your mate will have to submit to the both of us. And she will have to know that disrespect like what her brother has done to me will result in either banishment from my territories or death.

So are we going to have an issue Grayson or am I going to have to force you to resubmit to me. Because I don't want to force you to do that but I will if I have to." Scarlett snapped, her eyes slowly turning purple as she made direct eye contact with her brother.

"Look at her GO! I'm so proud!" Reign howled with happiness.

I'm so proud of her ability to put someone in their place.

Grayson stayed quiet as he listened to everything she had to say. It took him a minute before he nodded, casting his gaze down to his feet. "I'll explain to her that you'll want her to submit to you both as Alphas. But she's my mate Scarlett... I won't let someone threaten her. He might be your equal, but you'll always be my direct Alpha." He explained.

I watched him like a hawk. Why does he hate me? Just because I have Scarlett's attention instead of him?

"Did I do something to upset you? Or are you just not wanting to submit to me as your Alpha as well?" I asked, causing Grayson to look up at me finally.

"Nothing you've done. I just know who my Alpha is. You make her happy, that's all that matters to me. But I know how difficult she has it Seth. The world will see you as higher than her, that's just the world we live in. So I don't want you to be her equal. I'm sorry if that upsets you. Or if you think that's disrespectful. But we've spent over a decade making the world fear and respect her. Yes most Alphas do... But there's still some who only respect other males as Alphas." Grayson explained.

Scarlett couldn't contain the slight gasp in her voice. He... I guess has a point. There will be men who respect other men instead of the obvious Alpha in the relationship. But I won't let anything like that happen to my mate. She is the Alpha. I will admit that until I'm blue in the face.

"Grayson!" She snapped again.

I let go of her to walk over to Grayson again. I gripped his shoulder tightly, my body nearly vibrating with my anger.

"I won't let the world see me as higher than her. We'll show the world that we are equals. She's the stronger Alpha and I frankly have no problems admitting that to the world. But one thing I won't stand is your hatred towards me. I get that you haven't had positive relationships with male Alphas. But realize this. I am not going anywhere. I am here to stand behind Scarlett. I am here to show the world that no one will mess with her. Everyone will respect her no matter if they want to or not. And when I get to deal with the males who think that women can't rule. I'll deal with them accordingly." I growled, letting my nails dig into Graysons shoulder.

Just slightly. Not to cause him actual pain. Just enough to prove a point.

"So. Let's get that clear right here. She has made it this far. Now it's my turn to help her rule the world. She is the Alpha. We have plans to do a ceremony that makes us both the Alphas of our packs. You can either submit to us here. Or wait until then." I said, the room was slowly starting to shake with how much power was seeping off of me.

Alex immediately fell to his knees, Grayson fell a second

later as he showed his neck in submission. No one is going to disrespect me nor my mate.

"*You. Tell. Him!*" Reign cheered.

"I'm sorry Alpha... Forgive me for I have disrespected you." Grayson whimpered. "I submit to you both as my alphas. I won't come against you again."

I walked over to Scarlett and stood beside her again. "You may rise." I ordered, causing them both to slowly rise to their feet.

Alex shivered.

"I didn't realize how powerful you really were... I don't know how to feel about you trying to order Grayson but you got me to. How were you not affected by it?" Alex asked, looking at Scarlett.

She shrugged, sitting back down on the couch. Because she has more power than I do.

"It would take a lot to force me to submit to him. He's commanded me to do something before, but he had his hand on my skin. So it was a direct contact. I directly felt all of his power flowing into the command instead of it just going out into the air around us." Scarlett tried to explain as I sat down beside her. "I don't mean this in any negative way. But I don't think he could actually make me submit, not in a public way anyway. When it's just us. Oh you know I submit all the time." Scarlett teased.

Alex and Grayson gagged, causing me to laugh. She is the definition of perfection.

"That's just disgusting. I don't wanna know that!" Alex said. "Ewwww!"

Max walked into the room next.

"So I heard Grayson was getting snippy with Seth! Come on, I miss all of the good stuff! Why wasn't I called to get the history book!?" Max pouted as he sat down beside me.

Of course Alex would tell Max. Scarlett laughed.

"I didn't want to burden you. And I also wanted to know if Alex would actually find it." She said, smirking at Alex.

"And yes... He did try to get snippy with me. But I took care of it. We're good, right Gray?" I asked, causing Grayson to nod.

"A simple misunderstanding..." Grayson offered with a slight shrug.

Max looked at Alex. "I'll tell you everything after this." Alex nodded.

I love my brothers.

CHAPTER
TWENTY-THREE

It didn't take long for there to be a soft knock on the front door. "Wow. At least she knocks." Alex said, surprise lacing his voice.

Reign snorted in the back of my mind. It would be super weird if she just walked in like she owned the place. Grayson immediately went to the door, wanting to be the first one to greet her.

Scarlett grabbed the book. "There's a possibility that she's going to try and lie to cover her brother's tail." She told me, causing me to nod in agreement.

Like sister like brother. Or however that saying goes.

"We'll be able to tell, and if that happens I'll support you in whatever you decide." I said, placing my hand on her thigh again as she placed her legs over mine.

She needs to stay right by me.

"It's tricky. I want my brother here. But if she goes back to her brother's territory, then Gray will go with her. I don't want him spending more time with Silver than he has to." Scarlett sighed, rubbing her right temple.

I frowned as I started to rub her thighs. When it rains it pours. It'll never ever stop.

"You know... If that happens. You'll have two other brothers still..." I explained, before motioning to them whispering to each other in the kitchen.

"Can I get something to eat?" Max asked, causing Alex to laugh quietly.

"Of course, help yourselves." Scarlett smiled, before leaning her head against mine. "It wouldn't be the same... Grayson is my twin... It's different."

Was that really all he wanted to ask?

"I know... I know..." I sighed, hating that I couldn't help Scarlett more.

I would take everything off her plate if I could.

Grayson walked in, holding Violet's hand tightly. She was shorter than him, with a soft heart shaped face with a scar going over her left eye. She looked down, trying to hide the left side of her face from view.

What's wrong with her face?

"I would do anything you wanted if that meant you'd ask her." Reign laughed.

"Scarlett and Seth... This is my mate, Violet." Grayson introduced.

Scarlett and I got up, extending our hands to her. Violet didn't say anything as she shook our hands. Hmm... That's a little strange.

"I don't understand why I had to get over here so quickly for... I mean of course I did it because you're my Alphas. But did I do something wrong?" Violet asked, shifting closer to Grayson as she put her hand back down by her side.

"No. You didn't. I'm wondering if while you were living with your brother, if you saw this talisman before?" Scarlett asked as I picked up the history book and showed her the picture.

Violet looked down at the picture.

"She sooo totally knows." Reign told me.

"It's the Talisman of Caitriona right?" Violet asked, looking up at Grayson before shifting her focus back to Scarlett.

"Yes. It belongs to me and my pack. Your brother stole it from me. I want it back." Scarlett said, not leaving any room for discussion.

"We would have to have your brother come here and bring it back to us. He would also need to apologize for taking it in the first place." I added in, causing Scarlett to try her best to not laugh at his request.

It's probably a foolish demand. But it was worth a shot anyway.

Grayson rolled his eyes, before smiling as he looked down at Violet. "I told them that you would probably be okay with calling him or something to see if he'd give it back. But if you don't want to, I don't blame you." Gray assured, rubbing her back gently.

I placed the book back on the coffee table. No use in me holding it if she knows what it is.

"I mean I can always call him about it... He wears it around his neck most days. He never told me why. Just that you gave it to him as a gift so he wanted to keep it close to him." Violet explained. "I guess he didn't want to get me in trouble too."

"I don't know what his motives were. I promised my brother I wouldn't talk about it with you since it was your brother making the decision and not you." Scarlett smiled. "It's a pleasure to meet you by the way. Have you gotten to meet Stormy yet?"

Reign laughed. *"She wouldn't have wanted to meet Scarlett if she has already met Kingston."*

I snorted, earning a concerned look from Grayson. "That was rude of me. It wasn't a laugh about Stormy, more so her mate."

"I have not... I heard her mate and her are kind of... Antisocial. Graysons words, not mine." Violet smiled nervously.

Grayson rubbed the back of his neck. He's not wrong.

Scarlett glared slightly at Grayson. "You told her Stormy was antisocial?"

"You can't look me in the face and tell me I'm wrong. It was the only nice way I thought of explaining Stormy. Besides, she hates Silver almost as much as you do." Grayson shrugged. "I'll see her soon, besides with her being pregnant. I didn't think new visitors would be a good idea."

"Fair point. You might want to wait until everything has calmed down. Stormy is a lot like me. So it should be fun." Scarlett said to Violet, causing her to give her a genuine smile.

"I'm sure she's amazing..." Violet shifted uncomfortably. "I am supposed to call my brother later... I can always ask him about it then."

"How about you call him right now?" I asked.

Better to do it right now so I know she won't lie to us.

TWENTY-FOUR

"Ooh I wasn't..." Violet obviously didn't want to do that. Grayson growled lowly at me. But before he could have a chance to get a response out, Scarlett's growl was a fraction louder.

That's my mate.

"Don't start something you can't finish Grayson." Scarlett clipped out, before forcing a friendly smile at Violet. "We just want our talisman back. If your brother brings it back to us, nothing bad will happen to him here. I promise."

Violet looked to Grayson for confirmation, causing him to nod softly. "If you want to do it now... You can. If not, that's perfectly fine as well."

That's super weird...

Scarlett frowned. "Her brother?" She asked, turning to her brother.

Grayson nodded, not making direct eye contact with her. Their talking to each other without saying anything is weird.

I rubbed Scarlett's back gently. "I'll call him, I don't know if he'll answer... But I'll call him." Violet offered with a soft smile, wanting to make Scarlett proud.

Hopefully she catches that... Scarlett smiled at her.

"I really appreciate this... And I promise I won't forget it." Scarlett praised causing Violet to blush.

She took her phone out of her pocket and started to call her brother.

Grayson kissed the top of her head. Violet held her phone out, putting it on speaker. Her phone rang only a few times before someone picked up the phone.

"Violet!" A male voice said happily. "How are you doing?!"

"His voice makes me want to gag." Reign gagged.

Same here Reign. Same here.

"Hi Sil... I'm doing okay. It's still a lot being away from you. But I'm adjusting well I think. I met with the Alphas, they seem really nice." Violet's cheeks turned a darker shade of red. "Um... They actually wanted me to ask you something."

"Oh? I'm not sure I like how you're acting." Silver grumbled. "You're never so upfront about things. Is Grayson with you? He better not have left you with them alone."

Scarlett had to bite back a growl. I really don't like this guy.

"Oh my apologies Silver... I'll work on it. But yes Gray is with me. He knows I don't like being around new people alone. Don't worry, I'm okay. They were talking to me about the Talisman of Caitriona... They know you have it. They want it back."

Silver's unhappy growl came through the phone. "No. It's mine. I'm not giving it back. I don't appreciate you thinking you have the right to ask me to give it back. Why don't you come home and we'll talk this through and I'll give you my side of the story?"

"Can we kill him? The world would be a better place." Reign

160

rolled his eyes. I felt my body shaking. I can't believe these types of guys exist. I can't stand him.

Grayson rolled his eyes. Violet frowned, looking down at the phone in her hand. "I'm sorry brother... I don't want to disappoint you."

That's it.

"You ha..." Silver started, but I snatched the phone out of Violet's hand.

He'll learn one way or another that that's not how you talk to a woman.

"Ah... You see Huntington. I don't think you should finish that sentence." I snapped, my hand gripping the phone tightly.

"Who is this?" Silver asked. "Where's my sister?"

Your worst nightmare.

"I'm an Alpha that's much stronger than you. Your sister is right here. But here's the thing. I don't take it well when insecure males think they can bully females just for the heck of it. So before I have to threaten you in front of your sister. Why don't you just agree to get us our Talisman back? Be a good little boy and do it." I told him condescendingly.

I looked over at him, wanting him to shut his mouth. Grayson snorted, before smothering it with a cough. Violet sunk back into Grayson wanting his comfort.

"I don't appreciate the way you're speaking to me." Silver said. "The talisman is mine."

"*Teleport to him. Kill him. Then give Scarlett another pack! That will make her happy!*" Reign offered, getting excited at the thought.

"No. The talisman belongs to The Winters family which is now my family. You're not a part of my family. I don't care what you think belongs to you. It's ours. If you don't give it back, we're going to have problems." I growled, the phone screen starting to crack underneath my strength.

I'll buy her a new phone. I don't care.

Scarlett put her hand on my arm to help keep me in control. "The Talisman belongs to my ancestor. We want it back. We won't cause you any trouble if you just give it back to us. You can come into my territory to give it back to us. I won't ask why you took it. I just want what belongs to me and my family." Scarlett said, obviously pulling out her more professional side.

"Give the phone back to my sister. I don't want to continue this conversation. She has to come home or Grayson needs to get a better handle on her." Silver said, trying to get what he wants.

"Well there's where you're wrong. She doesn't have to do anything you say. She doesn't have to do anything Grayson says either. She's her own person. The only person she has to listen to is her alpha. Who is Scarlett. So no, I won't be giving the phone back to your sister until you agree to come to Scotland to give us back what belongs to us. I have nowhere to be. I also have the ability to transport myself anywhere I want. So if you hang up on me, I will just come to you. And trust me. That'll make me angry because I'll be without my mate. You don't want to see me angry." I grinded my teeth as I tapped my foot impatiently.

Violet was looking at her feet as she felt the silence getting to her. We should maybe get this over with. Sooner rather than later. I don't want to have to deal with Grayson being in a mood again.

Grayson frowned. "Maybe we should..." He started before Scarlett shushed him.

Silver sighed dramatically.

"I'll be there in a day or so. I have to plan for a few things while I'm away. But I'll return your Talisman. Please tell me sister I love her and I'll see her soon." Silver said before hanging up.

I smirked before I cringed at the sight of Violet's phone in my hand. Oops....

"I'm sorry... We'll get you a new one. Or you and Grayson can go to the store and pick something out that you both like." I offered. "All you have to do is say that the Alpha will take care of the bill and they'll give it to you." I said, before tossing the useless phone on the coffee table.

I don't want her to cut her hand.

"It's okay... I don't really need it anyway. Grayson and I pretty much stick together, the only thing I really use it for is to call Silver." She told me, refusing to make eye contact with either one of us.

"Thank you Seth... You didn't have to stand up to him for Vi... But thank you." Grayson said, smiling at me.

"We stand up for family... You stick up for Scarlett like no one else... I appreciate that. Violet won't have anything to worry about with Silver. She's free to do whatever she wants." I assured. "I'm just happy that I could handle it for you both. Sorry you had to hear me threaten your brother."

No I really am not.

"Oh, it's okay. I know how he can get. When you get to know him he's not so bad... I just think that he's stuck in his ways a little bit." Violet explained as she looked up at Gray.

"He's not awful. But he's extremely stuck in his ways. It was weird for me being there... Having been here where women are more in charge than anyone else. Then going there. I don't like it there." Grayson shook his head. "It's part of the reason why I was so stuck on living here."

No. He sounds absolutely terrible. They don't have to lie.

"Well I'm glad you guys live here." Scarlett said, letting her eyes drop down to Violet. "I'd love to have you guys over again... Maybe next time it won't be for any official duties."

Violet blushed as she couldn't bring herself to say anything to her. Alex and Max took this as their opportunity to come back into the room.

"Did you really tell him to be a good little boy?" Alex asked, barely able to get it out of his mouth before he started laughing.

"Don't you think that's going to be bad if you guys become an alliance or something?" Max asked, as he tried to keep his face straight without laughing.

Scarlett laughed next. It was a funny line.

"Be a good little boy for me." She giggled, shaking her head.

I chuckled. "Oh it's going to be fun bullying him while he's here. He's going to wish that he never messed with one of the Alpha's family members."

I'll show him the Alpha that my father wanted.

CHAPTER
TWENTY-FIVE

When Scarlett and I were finally alone, I brought her into the kitchen to make her a snack. It took everything in me not to rub at my nose. There's too many scents in my house now. I hate it. She sat down at the island, watching me as I prepared our food.

"Why does it have to smell in here?" Reign complained.

I want to know so much about what happened to Violet.

"Are you going to ask what you want to ask?" Scarlett teased, tilting her head slightly. "I can feel your curiosity... I can also read your thoughts."

I chuckled. She knows me so much... Without even having to read my mind.

"I know you can feel my emotions and read my thoughts. That happened when I marked you. I was waiting until they left for us to talk about it. But I guess my question is what was all of that? Her looking at Grayson before doing anything? Did her brother abuse her?"

It's kind of weird to watch... Violet being so submissive.

"Obviously I don't know if her brother abused her since I

didn't live with them. But I know her brother enough to know that he probably has it in her mind that well... There's no better way of saying this. He has it in her mind that she has to ask her male's permission to do anything. That all she's good for is to birth kids and to take care of the household. He says that he values women so much that he doesn't want anything to happen to them. But obviously that's an outdated thought process since women are capable of much more than that."

I couldn't help the look of disgust on my face. "Even in my pack we respected women. So that's saying something about him teaching his sister that."

My pack knew that oh... We grew out of the thoughts of women being only useful to birth kids and make food.

Scarlett shrugged. "I'm shocked that Grayson stayed in that territory for as long as he did. It has to be drastically different from ours. I can see why I never got along with him. He's too misogynistic." She explained, taking a sip of water from the cup I placed in front of her.

I can't wait to make him uncomfortable with my presence. It'll be the most joyful thing.

"What are your thoughts about Silver coming here? Do you want him just to give us back the talisman and then leave? I'll support you in whatever you want." I told her as I moved around the kitchen like I've been there all my life.

I feel like I have... Like I know this house like the back of my hand.

"I don't know. I guess it depends on how he acts when he's here. He stole the thing, and I don't necessarily have to have him admit it. But I'm curious as to why he did it. The information on Caitronia's Talisman is in most history books... Granted they don't like talking about it since she was the first female alpha. But the information is accessible. There's no way he didn't know the power it held before he stole it. I want to know why he stole it." Scarlett huffed, obviously still annoyed with the topic.

I smiled at her, placing the freshly made sandwich in front of her. Silver just sounds like an awful person in general.

"It's a tricky situation... Only because your brother is now involved in their family by proxy. But obviously he doesn't enjoy her brother. Seems like none of your family does." I shrugged, leaning against the island to watch her eat.

I'll make my sandwich in a minute.

"Nope." She said around a mouth full of food. "Storm hates him because of why I hate him. She doesn't like it when people try to stand against me. But I also think she hates him because he picked on her about her powers."

I nodded, my eyes trained on her mouth. Reign's rumble came through my chest. Just thinking about her mouth around my cock has me hard. "It's rude that he picked on her. Is it just because she has special abilities?"

"Probably. He probably hated that we had special powers and he didn't. Why do you keep staring at me?" Scarlett asked after she swallowed her food.

I shrugged. "It's hot that you eat my food..." I told her, blushing slightly.

It's the truth. I love how she lets me take care of her. She doesn't complain and she just lets me.

"For an Alpha she likes to be taken care of." Reign growled.

"It's a turn on for you that I eat the food you cook for me?" Scarlett asked, wanting to make sure she heard me right.

"Yup." I said, unashamed. "I love it. I love that you let me take care of you. And knowing that you're letting me take care of you while you're pregnant with my children? It's so hot to me... I love being able to take care of you and make sure you eat enough during the day."

I'll never lie to her.

Scarlett smiled at me, giving me a come here motion with her hand. I pushed off the island and moved to her side. She reluctantly put down the sandwich to dip her fingers into my waistband to pull my closer. If only her hand would come down a little more.

"I love that you love to take care of me... That you worry about me eating enough... That you love that I'm pregnant." Scarlett grinned. "I love you for every single reason."

"I love you too baby girl." I said, leaning down to press a kiss to her forehead. "Now. Finish your snack, we gotta talk more about Silver coming. Before tomorrow we have to talk about the stupid ceremonies."

Scarlett snorted at my obvious hatred of the ceremonies. I want to get them done and over with.

CHAPTER
TWENTY-SIX

"The stupid ceremonies huh?" Scarlett teased before taking a sip of her water. "It's not bad... We have a few options for it actually."

I don't know if I even want to hear what she's going to come up with.

"Hear the woman out." Reign growled.

Of course I'm going to listen.

I nodded as he started to clean up. "And those are?" He continued, acknowledging that he was listening to me.

"Well, the first one would be us having three different ceremonies to acknowledge you as my mate and our Alpha. One for Spain, Scotland, and Ireland. But that would have a lot of things that we would need to plan for. Who would be keeping track of Scotland and Ireland while we were gone. And getting Link on the phone to start getting things ready for us while we're traveling." Scarlett explained, smiling as she watched me move around the kitchen.

It took everything in me not to cringe. That sounds like the worst option she would have thought of.

"That sounds like actual torture. Next option." I smirked, giving her a wink.

"I'm glad you didn't pick that option." Reign cringed. *"Sounds like actual hell."*

"Next option. We would have one ceremony to acknowledge you and everything. Probably picking either Scotland or Ireland to host it. But this option would have to be recorded and put online for everyone to see. Which might not be a bad thing considering we would need the world to know about my change in relationship." Scarlett said, causing me to give her a growl of approval.

That. I want everyone to know who she belongs to.

"I like that one. Telling the whole world that you're mine. That one. That way more people know you're mine." I told her, turning back towards her so I could pick her up.

Scarlett laughed as I grabbed at her hips and picked her up, carrying her back to the living room. I want everyone in this entire world to know that she is my mate. That I'm with the only Alpha Female in the entire world.

"Well okay, so we'll decide to do Scotland or Ireland then and then stream it online for the other packs to watch. Next thing we'd need to agree on. What are we going to do? Are we going to follow The Bloody Rose Packs traditions? Are we going to follow The Winterfall Packs traditions? Or are we going to create our own traditions? I mean it's not like my pack really has any traditions. It wasn't very much liked that I took over my pack. But they couldn't say anything because me killing my father was public. Everyone knew I did it. No one could deny it and I made sure of that."

I leaned back into the deep cushion and thought about what she said. "You do know right that my packs traditions is that you'd have to submit to me. We've never had a female alpha, so you know everyone loves seeing their mates submit to them." I sighed, obviously not wanting to continue this conversation.

I don't want her to submit to me. But if that's what she wants. I need to figure out something else for us to do.

Scarlett pouted, knowing I was starting to stress out. "What are you talking about? You love seeing me submit to you." She smirked, shifting so she was sitting on her knees to better balance herself across my lap.

I chuckled, placing my hands on her hips. In private she can submit to me all she wants. In public. I'll do the submitting.

"Yeah! You tell her!" Reign cheered.

"That's different and you know it. We're in private. You submit to me in private." I explained, leaning forward as my hands went up the back of her shirt. Her skin was warm underneath my palms.

"You are the Alpha of the pack. I don't want to change that. But I like being able to take a load off of your shoulders while it's just me and you. While I do that when we're in public, I can do it better when we're alone. So no. I don't want you to submit to me in front of everyone."

Scarlett smiled, resting her forehead against mine. "I love you so much. More than the moon and stars. But we might not have a choice... There's some people from your pack who doesn't like that I'm a woman. But... It's essentially the same ceremony from me submitting to you than it would be for you to submit to me. So it wouldn't be hard to change our minds later on if you wanted to."

Does this mean we can change the subject now?

"Okay. That sounds good to me. So the one ceremony, but it will be live streamed in Scotland or Ireland for the whole world to see. What are we going to do about Spain?" I asked, rubbing at her tense back muscles.

Spain could just join the live stream?

"Just have Lincoln and Octavia make an announcement that everyone has to listen into the live stream. Or they can travel to us and witness it in person. Link and Octavia will probably have to come, just so people see that the people I have running my pack submit to us as Alphas. But yeah, they can come or they can listen in. As long as they're seeing the ceremony I don't think it matters." Scarlett said with a relaxed sigh, she leaned forward resting against my broad chest.

I wrapped my arms around her back and leaned back against the couch. Max is going to have fun planning all of this for us.

"Okay... So we'll let Alex and Max know about this so they can start planning things. Who do you want to read off the ceremony words?" I continued, wanting to get it all out of the way.

Better now then have to talk about it later.

"Well... One of our brothers can do it. Or we don't even need someone to do it. For my coronation, no one stood up there with me and read me words. I talked to everyone and pretty much said hey I'm your alpha now and there's nothing you can do about it." Scarlett smirked at the memory. "So whatever works."

I nodded. "I guess we'll decide that when it comes closer to the ceremony day huh?"

If we can push things off we will. Her healthy matters more.

Scarlett groaned slightly as she moved so she was more comfortable. "Yes. Preferably after having to do with Silver." She growled unhappily.

"Ahh yes... Our next order of business. How do you want to handle that? I'll stand by you no matter what. Even if that means I have to be the bad guy to your brother." I told her, causing her to sit up and look at me with a tilt to her head.

I would take the fall for her. I would more than happily do whatever she needed from me. No one will hurt her while I'm around.

"You would do that for me?" Scarlett asked.

"Of course I would do that for you. I would do anything for you. I know how much you love Grayson so I don't want him to be upset with you. I can take him not liking me." I told her with a smile, I leaned forward pressing a gentle kiss to her lips.

I wanted to hold her to me... I wanted to take this stress away from her. But I couldn't. So I'll take whatever she needs me to.

"Honestly... I say we should probably have a guard group around him just in case he tries to do anything fishy. But I mean as long as he doesn't try anything and gives me back what belongs to me. We won't have any issues. If he tries anything then we'll banish him." Scarlett nodded, being confident in her answer.

"I like her confidence." Reign told me.

"Okay. After we lay down for a little bit, I'll send Max an email about everything we decided. Probably the Silver stuff first since that's in the next day or so. And the ceremony will take time to plan and set up. Probably about a month. But I also want to schedule an appointment with the doctor tomorrow to see if he would know anything about the talisman and to see if it's a good idea for you to wear." I told her, causing her to groan.

"I don't wanna gooooo." She whined, dramatically flopping onto the couch beside me.

Oh well. I'm not giving her a choice in this one either.

"I know. But it's for my peace of mind." I smirked, getting

off of the couch to pick her up in my arms. "The more information we get the better."

Beds are way more comfortable.

Scarlett nodded, leaning her head against my chest. "I know... The more information the better. I just hate having to go and hear that they have no idea what's going to happen. Since we're two different wolves. Like that shouldn't be such a big deal."

I laughed shaking my head. It shouldn't be a big deal but it is. "It's only a big deal because Shadow wolves are nearly immortal and Ember wolves are one if not the only thing that can actually kill them." I teased her as I opened the door to our bedroom and went to our bed.

"Think of how cool our kids are going to be." Scarlett joked as I laid her down on the bed.

"Our kids are going to be the coolest. No one will ever change my mind." Reign danced around.

I smirked down at her as I climbed in beside her.

"We're going to make the next generation of the strongest wolves this world has ever known." I promised.

CHAPTER
TWENTY-SEVEN

The next morning, I was on my phone as Scarlett was sitting in the bath soaking in the warm water. Grey was quick with texting me back... I asked him to take some time to meet with me about building a new house for me and Scarlett. She leaned back letting her hair hang off the back of the tub.

"Gray is setting up an appointment for us at the hospital." I told her, before setting my phone down and walking behind her.

She opened her eyes as I squatted down. Pressing a quick gentle kiss to her forehead, I grabbed her brush from the table beside the tub.

"Are you wanting your hair down for the appointment or maybe a ponytail?" I asked as I gently brushed her hair, making sure there were no knots through her strands.

I loved her hair... I loved how soft it was... The color was beautiful. I loved how curly it was. Scarlett groaned as I rubbed at her head.

"Anything you want." She told. "Anything as long as you keep messaging my head like that."

I chuckled, shaking my head. I knew how much she loved it when I gently brushed my fingers against her scalp.

"I'll pick then. Maybe just a braid to keep your hair out of your beautiful face." I smiled down at her.

I couldn't help myself, I leaned down and inhaled her powerful scent of rose and vanilla. "Gosh. You smell delicious."

I want a candle of that smell so even when she's not with me I can still smell it.

"It won't be the same." Reign groaned at the thought.

Scarlett laughed as she felt my nose against her scalp. "Well I'm glad you love it so much. It's all for you."

"Oh it better be all for me." I growled, lacing my hand through her hair and tugging gently.

"Tug harder!" Reign told me.

She smirked up at me. Oh I know where this is going.

"And what would you do if there was someone else?" She taunted.

In the blink of an eye, I was in the tub on top of her, causing the water to splash out onto the floor. Scarlett laughed as I got down in her face.

I would fight anyone that even looks at her with interest.

"Wanna test that theory baby?" I asked, my hand drifting to go around her neck. "I'm mated to the most feared woman in the entire world. I might just mess around and match her ruthlessness. I'll kill anyone who looks at you twice."

"She could totally test that." Reign smirked.

Scarlett bit her bottom lip as her cheeks turned pink. "I love how possessive you are of me." She grinned before she leaned forward and nipped my bottom lip.

"No one will take you away from me." I told. "No one."

"No one will take me away from you. I promise. You are the only one for me." She promised, moving my free hand to her stomach. "If you ever worry about that, listen to their heart-beats. Let them reassure my connection to you."

I leaned my forehead against hers, closing his eyes. "You deserve more than I can give you..." I whispered.

I want to give her everything... I want to be her everything. I need to get her everything.

Scarlett whimpered, not liking what I said.

"I deserve you. I don't deserve anymore or any less than what you give me. You are my other half. Please don't talk down on yourself baby..." She placed her hands on my cheeks. "You mean the world to me. You are the air that I breathe. You are the reason I get up in the morning. I don't want anyone else. And I'll never want anyone else. I promise you."

I gave her a soft smile. "I just... I feel this stress weighing me down... I don't want anyone else coming near you... The last time someone came near you..." I trailed off, my eyes darkening at the thought.

I can't... I can't lose her. I won't make it. If Silver tries to kill her? I'll burn him alive.

"Is this about Silver coming?" She asked, tilting her head slightly.

I couldn't make eye contact with her as I climbed out of the large tub.

"Please talk to me." Scarlett told me, but before she could even move to get out of the tub.

I was there lifting her out and wrapping a warm towel around her immediately.

"I don't trust him." I explained. "I've only heard bad things about his pack. Obviously with how brainwashed his sister is, all the rumors are true. I don't want him anywhere near you. I don't want him touching you. I don't want him knowing about you being pregnant. I want him to know that if he so much as even thinks about touching you. I'll know and I'll kill him."

I'll burn him alive. I'll burn his entire country to the ground.

Scarlett nodded, following me into our bedroom. "I'll double the guard around us while he's in town. I don't imagine him staying long. But if it helps you, I don't trust him either. You're going to be there every step of the way. Everything will be okay."

"You say that. But you said that same thing about my father. Everything will be okay. But you almost died Scarlett. You could've left me." I told her, my eyes darkening as the brown was getting lost to the deep red of my inner wolf.

Scarlett's frown deepened before she rushed over to me and wrapped her arms around me in a hug. Flashes of that scene threatened to show their ugly faces again. I don't want to see it. I don't want to see her drop. I don't want to feel that pain again.

"I know... I know... I'm sorry about that. I can't tell you how sorry I am that that happened and you had to witness it. But you saved me. You saved me and our babies' lives. I trust that you'll protect me. I know you won't let anything bad happen to me. To us. What can I do to help you know that things are going to be better now?" She asked, wanting nothing more than to help me feel better.

I wrapped my arms tightly around her. "I need people to stop coming to our house for now... I don't know how long. But I just need people to stop coming over here. Especially not unannounced. Don't do anything without me. I don't care what it is. But just don't leave me okay?"

"Okay baby. You got it. I'll send a text to Alex, Max, and Grayson about not coming over unannounced. Is it still okay for them to come over? Or just not unannounced?" She asked, wanting to make sure.

"Just not unannounced. But outside of them, no one else. The guards can patrol outside of the house. But not in." I explained, reluctantly letting her go so I could strip out of the wet clothes I was wearing.

I feel ridiculous. I feel stupid admitting this to her. They've done nothing to us... They've been nothing but helpful. And here I am being stupid.

"I'll do whatever you need to feel better. I'll have the guard detail wait outside to escort us to the hospital then." Scarlett offered, sending out a few quick text messages as I grabbed her a set of clothes to change into.

"I'm sorry I'm being so... Difficult. I just feel like I could lose it at the flip of a switch." I tried to explain as I pulled on my boxers.

Scarlett smiled, quickly getting dressed in the matching outfit I picked out for her.

Everything is going to be fine.

"I completely understand. You don't have to explain your-self at all. I understand you. We're going to take this one step at a time. We went through a lot. So it's only natural to have to heal from that." She promised. "I will do whatever I can to help you."

"Thank you." I smiled, walking up behind her and kissing the top of her head. "Let's do your hair and then head out to the doctor. How about a side braid so that everyone can see your mark?"

"That is the hottest thing I've ever seen." Reign groaned at the thought.

Scarlett laughed, smiling brightly at me. "Perfect. I wouldn't ask for anything better. Thank you for taking care of me."

"Thank you for letting me." I told her before leading her

back into the bathroom. "And don't worry... I'll clean the bath-room when we get home from the doctor."

I don't want her trying to clean up something that's completely my fault. I just couldn't help myself.

"I don't know what I did to be blessed with the best." She smiled, letting me move her in anyway I wanted.

CHAPTER
TWENTY-EIGHT

I took a deep breath in as I pulled into a parking spot at the hospital. Just because something bad happened to Scarlett. Doesn't mean something bad would happen again.

"Or it means like it's more likely to happen again and we should hide her away at our house." Reign nodded, obviously happy about the thought.

No. Reign. You aren't helping! Shut up. Scarlett frowned again, before reaching over and taking my hand.

"This is just an appointment to ask questions about the talisman. To see if they think that it will help with my energy levels. Which have been good so far today! Today has started out as a good day baby." She tried to reassure me, wanting to get my hopes up.

I love that she's feeling better... It means the world to me. But I just hate people. I can't stand them being around her. I turned to her and gave her a small smile. I leaned over, placing my forehead against hers.

Just because I'm stressed doesn't mean that she has to be stressed too.

"I know... Today has started out as a good day." I repeated. "But things could turn so quickly... Especially when people find out Silver is coming. They might want you to leave me for him. And I don't want that to happen." I told her, closing my eyes as I let my power flood into her side of the bond.

Scarlett couldn't help the small gasp that escaped as she felt my power overwhelm her senses.

"Mmm... She likes our power." Reign grinned.

"I always forget how much power you're hiding away." Scarlett shivered slightly. "But you are mine forever and then some. You are mine for the rest of time. Nothing and no one will ever change that. If our pack has any problem with that. I will deal with it."

Oh no she won't.

I growled unhappily, my eyes snapping open to glare at her. "I will let you deal with it duh." She smiled innocently. "I won't do anything PROMISE!"

I smiled at her, my eyes changing slowly back to brown. "That's my good girl." I praised. "Are you ready to go inside?"

I smirked at the blush that crept up her cheeks. She loves it when I praise her.

"Are you ready to go inside?" She asked, pulling away to look at my body slowly.

I was wearing a tight black t-shirt that showed off all of my muscles, and a pair of blue jeans that hugged my thick thighs. She nearly whimpered at the sight. I smirked, putting my finger under her chin and gently tilting her head up to meet my eyes.

My outfit had its added effect on her like I thought it would.

"My eyes are up here my mate." I teased before unbuckling myself and her. "I can't wait to get you back home and alone again."

I climbed out of the car, glaring at the guards who were waiting patiently for our alpha to get out of the car. This caused them to take a few steps back from our car. I opened the passenger side, holding out a hand to help her get out of the car.

Scarlett took my hand and stepped out of the car. She was dressed in an almost identical outfit to me. Her t-shirt showed her cleavage, a silver of her stomach, before dropping down to her ripped light blue jeans. "We should get something to eat after the doctor's appointment."

My perfect sexy beautiful mate. I was seriously blessed with the best.

"Already planned babygirl." I placed my hand on her lower back, letting my fingers dip into the waistband of her jeans.

Scarlett smiled at me, shifting closer to me as we walked into the hospital. No one better touch what's mine.

"Ehhhh, is it really that big of a deal? We could just kill them." Reign laid down.

"No one would dare touch me." She told me. "Are you sure you're comfortable with having your hand in my pants?"

I smirked, running my fingers over her bare buttcheek. "Yes. I am comfortable. I am more than comfortable with touching any part of you baby."

More than comfortable. I like being able to touch her.

Scarlett blushed, before she reached over and pressed the elevator up arrow. "You guys will get on the elevator after us." She ordered, getting a course of grunts as a reply to her.

I rolled my shoulders as I felt the guards behind us. I don't like having my back to them. Anything could happen and they would have the upper hand to me.

"Thank you." I told her, before one of the younger guards got too close to Scarlett for my liking.

I reacted quickly, pulling Scarlett to my other side so I was face to face with the guard.

"Fight fight fight fight!" Reign chanted.

Not. Helping.

"Do not even think about touching her." I growled, my body towering over his smaller form. My body was shaking with anger as I refused to back down. "Don't even come that close to her ever again. Next time I'll break your neck." I grabbed his shirt, lifting him up so I could better be in his face. "Do you understand me!?"

The guard nodded, whimpering to show his submission to me. I dropped him, letting him fall to his butt. "That goes for all of you. Don't touch my mate or you're dead." I snapped, placing my hand back on Scarlett's lower back and leading her into the now open elevator.

"Aw... No fight. I got my hopes up for nothing." Reign pouted.

Scarlett couldn't help but grin as she leaned into me.

"That was so hot." She told me, making direct eye contact with me.

I took in a deep breath, my eyes showing the worry I felt. Scarlett frowned, placing her hand on my chest.

"I'm okay... Nothing happened. He didn't even touch me. I think he might've tripped or something." She told me, I growled unhappily at her excuse. "Not that I'm making an excuse for him or anything!"

That's such a believable excuse.

"Good. Because if I see him again I might just kill him still." I growled as I picked her up, wrapping her legs around my waist.

When the elevator opened, I carried her to her private room on the top floor of the hospital. I love that she has a private room. It makes going in there far easier with no smells of other people.

"I would never make any excuse for another male." She promised, before I walked into the room and shut the door.

"That's my good girl." I told her, sitting down on the bed with her still in my lap.

I started rubbing her thighs, needing to touch as much of her as possible. Her body calmed me down.

Scarlett leaned into my touches. She couldn't help the small moan that slipped free. "Ugh, I'd do anything if you just keep touching me like this."

Her moaning is going to make me hard in the freaking hospital. I groaned at the sound, leaning my head back against the hospital bed.

"The things I'd do to you if we were alone and I could know for sure no one was going to walk in on us or hear your delicious sounds you make." I grunted, shifting slightly.

Scarlett laughed.

"You're the one who absolutely wanted to have an appointment today." She couldn't help but tease me.

I peeked my eyes open to look down and see her smirk. I swatted her butt, causing her to gasp. Of course she wants to act like a brat when I can't do anything about it.

"You're such a brat. But I love it." I told her, before kissing the top of her head. "It's better to get it out of the way.... No matter how much I want to be alone with you all the time."

"I know... Are you going to be okay with Alex probably coming in with Carter?" She asked, laying her head against my chest.

"Yes. I know he knows you're mine... And he knows that you're pregnant. Maybe we should just announce our pregnancy... Maybe that will help calm me down." I offered with a slight shrug.

Everyone knowing we're a forever thing might help. Who knows at this point.

"You'll be more calm once Reign realizes that the threat is gone and nothing is going to happen. Don't rush his healing. He deserves his own time to process what happened." She almost demanded, causing me to chuckle. "What?" She asked, obviously not understanding what I was laughing at.

I have never had someone care as much about me as her.

"She's so hot. Of course she cares about me." Reign smirked.

"It's nothing... I've just never had someone who cared about me AND Reign before. No one even cared about his emotions... They just cared to agitate him but that was about it." I explained, putting my hands up the back of her shirt and massaging my back muscles.

My chest rumbled in approval causing Scarlett's to rumble with contentment. Reign and Xena love to talk as much as possible.

"You have me now... And I promise I care about you. Reign. And every single itty bit about you both. I want to take care of you both." She promised.

CHAPTER
TWENTY-NINE

There was a soft knock at the door. "Come in," I called out.

Scarlett groaned, not wanting to move from her comfortable position. I couldn't help but smirk. I love how comfortable she is.

"Don't worry. You don't have to move." I promised, turning my head to look at the door as Alex and Carter moved in.

Hmm... I wonder how this is going to go.

"Back again my wonderful Alphas?" Carter asked, holding her tablet against her chest.

Alex smiled at us, but didn't move from beside Carter.

"Is everything okay?" Alex asked, looking down at Scarlett as she laid against me.

"Alex sounds like he wants to be a doctor." Reign laid down.

"Yeah. We just had some news... And Seth had an idea about the Talisman of my ancestor Caitriona Winterfall. It was previously stolen. But we know where it is and it will be back in my possession." Scarlett explained. "This is just too comfortable for me to move. So I'm not going to move."

No one is going to make her do anything. She's the Alpha after all.

"That's fine. If I don't need to examine you, I won't need you to move. What is the Talisman of Caitriona Winterfall?" Carter asked, turning her focus back to Alex.

"It's something that was taken from Scarlett's collection from another Alpha. It's said to hold the power of Caitriona, the first female alpha in history, in this talisman because she didn't want to let the other Alphas steal her power when they killed her." Alex explained, smiling down at Carter. "But I don't know what that has to do with anything? I didn't think that anyone could access that power?"

We really don't know what happens with the talisman. But anything to help Scarlett... It's better than nothing to help her.

"We don't know obviously. But I was thinking. What if to help with Scarlett's low energy and dizzy spells, what if the talisman could help her?" I asked, turning my attention to Carter. "I know it's a long shot. And I am always giving her my power to use. But what if it stops... I don't know. What if one day it stops being enough for her? Like when the twins grow and need more power? What if ours aren't enough for them?"

What if they need more power now anyway? Since they're so powerful... The added ability might calm them down? I really don't feel helpful at all.

Carter nodded, listening to what we were saying. "Well. I mean that's a good idea. I would have to feel the talisman in my hands. But I think it's worth a shot honestly. Are there any books about the talisman or any information other than what Alex told me?"

Nope. Because everything has to be a mystery apparently. If you ask me that's ridiculous.

"Definitely ridiculous." Reign growled.

"Nope. Not really. I can always have Max bring you the book I have. But it has very little information about it. I'm sure back then people didn't want people to know that there was a female Alpha. I mean, not just back then, people still hate now that there's an Alpha female." Scarlett rolled her eyes. "Males can be so dumb."

"She can say that again." Reign added in.

It took everything in me not to laugh at his comment. A lot of men really are stupid.

Alex chuckled. "It's not all men."

"No. Just annoying sexist men that don't realize that women are just as strong, maybe even stronger than men." I added in, causing Scarlett to smile.

"That's my mate." Scarlett grinned.

"That's understandable. But yeah, before I say one hundred percent that it's a good idea. I would like to feel it first, just to feel it's power. I know you probably hate me saying this, but it's kind of just a learn as we go type thing. We'll at least know all of this information for your future pregnancies." Carter looked down at her tablet for a second before looking up at us again.

I shrugged. We're both open to anything. The possibility of something to make our experience better.

"At this point. We have no other option." I looked down at Scarlett.

"What's going to happen if she can't lead the packs while she's pregnant?" Alex asked.

"How many brain cells does he have?" Reign groaned.

Scarlett is going to flip.

This caused Scarlett's eyes to pop open before she sat up abruptly.

"Are you hearing things? Do people think now that I have a

mate that I can't lead my packs?" Scarlett demanded the answer. "You didn't tell anyone that I was pregnant did you? No one can know until we announce it. What's happening Alex you're not talking fast enough." She was stressed, she struggled to get off of me.

Her eyes slowly turned to a deep purple.

Alex shook his head no. "No no I wouldn't tell anyone about your pregnancy." He explained.

I quickly got off of the bed and grabbed Scarlett before she could do anything else. I wrapped my arms tightly around her, my power soaking into the air causing both Carter and Alex to whimper in submission. No way am I letting this make her lose control. Xena needs to calm down.

"They'll try to overthrow me. They'll kill me just like Caitriona." Scarlett was panicking, her breathing coming in quick pants.

I looked at Carter before looking at Alex, but Alex knew what to do. Scarlett won't want for anyone to see her like that. He immediately grabbed Carter and brought her out of the hospital room.

Scarlett fought against my comforting hold, a growl ripped free from her. "Let me go!" She commanded, her power started to dance with mine.

I won't let her go till she calms down.

"No." I snapped, turning her around quickly in my arms.

"I said let me go!" She snapped, her eyes shining that same beautiful purple.

My eyes started to shine red, I bent down to be level with her. I won't step down from this. This is important.

"You are going to calm down." I ordered. "You're going to submit to me." My power soaked through our bond, pulling her in closer to me.

She'll submit. I'll make her. She growled, shaking her head no. Her claws came out, digging into my arms.

"That's out." Reign growled.

"No! You can't tell me what to do!" She growled, her bone in her arm breaking as she shook in my arms.

My growl overpowered hers, my eyes shining brighter as my hand went around her neck, not in a harmful way but possessive. Xena will see this as what it is. Me putting her back in her place.

"It's not a suggestion babygirl. It's an order. Get to your knees and submit to me." My voice was deeper, causing her to sink closer to me. "You won't like it if I have to ask you again."

Scarlett started to growl, before she heard my chest rumble. Her knees began to give out on her and she fell to her knees in front of me. Her head was hanging, her dark hair hiding her face from me. Finally. I sighed out a breath of relief.

"I'm sorry." She whimpered, her eyes were closed as she was breathing heavily.

I smiled softly, sitting down in front of her. I gently lifted her chin so I could see her face, with my free hand I brushed the hair out of her face. It's okay. She didn't shift. That's what's important.

"You have nothing to apologize for babygirl." I promised, leaning forward to kiss her forehead. "It happens to the best of us. I'm just glad I could stop you from shifting."

Scarlett nodded, she looked into my eyes. "I don't know what came over me." She shivered.

I frowned as I grabbed her and stood up. Things happen. We make mistakes.

"Stress. Anxiety." I offered with a shrug. "I'm going to take you home, and everything will be better. I promise."

"I'm just tired." Scarlett promised. "I'm okay. I'll feel better after a nap." She laid her head against my warm chest. "I love how warm you are. It's so comforting."

I chuckled, tightening my hold on her as I went to the elevator. "Go ahead and take a nap. We'll be home before you know it."

That probably took a lot out of her... Or my power made her super tired.

CHAPTER
THIRTY

The next day, Scarlett was up before me. I hated when she got up before me... Waking up with her in my arms. She helped me have good dreams all night and it just feels weird having to wake up without her. She was sprawled out at the kitchen table, her laptop open, a notebook, her phone, and a bag of chips were placed around her.

Alex and Max were on the screen in front of her.

"When is he coming today? And what do you think about me being late to meet Silver?" She said, grabbing her phone and typing out a response to Grayson.

"Do you really think that's a good idea?" Max asked. "Won't that annoy Grayson and his mate?"

Hmmm... I should've known that that was what this was about.

"I didn't ask what he thought. I know how my twin will react to me being late. But if I show up late, it will show Silver he's not important to me. I won't let him dictate my day." Scarlett huffed, her eyes slowly moved up to where I was leaning against the wall listening to their conversation.

It's super easy to sneak up on her I think it's cute.

"I think showing up late would be funny. Show him who's the boss." I smiled at her. "And I'm sure Grayson and Violet will be showing him around anyway."

At least I assume. I don't know for sure.

"I'll make sure that I text you when he gets here so either you can be late. Or show up before him and kinda threaten him. Scare him. Wouldn't that be great?" Alex offered.

Scarlett laughed, rolling her eyes.

"That actually sounds like fun. Did you ever find out what time Silver was coming?" Scarlett asked again, needing to know the answer.

I walked behind where she was sitting, moving over her chair so that I could sit beside her and be in view. He probably doesn't want us to know when he's coming. That would be just like him.

"Why don't we add Grayson to this videochat? He would know more than us?" I offered, pulling out my phone to send him a text.

"No. That's fine. I'm sure he's not happy about this whole thing anyway." Scarlett told us. "He can have time to spend with his mate and his new family."

Scarlett's voice dropped, causing me to look at her and tilt my head. Scarlett looked at me, shaking her head slightly. I nodded, knowing exactly what she was thinking without her having to speak it out loud.

"Did you notice that too?" Reign asked.

Of course I did. I always notice.

"I hate when they talk in their minds." Max complained.

"Why can't we talk through a mindlink like other packs?" Alex asked.

Scarlett groaned, leaning back before rubbing her forehead. Just another thing to add to the list.

"My sister's mate gave me a little information about this." She growled lowly. "I have to deal with an elder that seems to think he can control my packs."

"I can always deal with it instead of you. I don't think it's a good idea for you to do it..." I said, trailing off since I knew she didn't like to talk about her problems in front of people.

Not just that. But think about it? If she sent me to deal with it. It shows everyone that she likes to delicate the less important problems away.

Scarlett looked at me, before looking at Max and Alex on her laptop screen. "After I get the talisman back. We'll let Carter use her power to see if it'll help me. If it does, we'll set up a meeting with the elders. If it doesn't. I'll let you kill him. Is that a good enough deal?" She offered.

I smirked, giving her a quick nod. A healthy compromise, I like it.

"And that is called growth." Reign added in.

"Ewwww did she just ask him permission?" Alex asked. "Ew. I don't think I like this."

Max chuckled, scribbling into his notebook.

"Ew? I don't ask him permission to do anything." Scarlett growled, flashing her purple eyes at him. "If anything. He asks me for permission." She taunted.

We both know that that's not true. But I'll let her mess with them a bit.

"EW! I'm totally leaving this conversation! It's like talking about sex with not only my Alphas. But my brother and sister. It's disgusting! I don't want to KNOW! I don't wanna know anything!" Alex whined, getting up and heading out of frame.

Max tilted his head, obviously not focusing in on the conversation beforehand.

"Someone sent me a text from the border." Max told her. "They said they saw Silvers carav..."

Scarlett's eyes widened. "What do you mean caravan? How many cars? Who was in those cars?"

I placed my hand on hers and squeezed gently. "Um..." Max trailed off for a second, looking down at his phone. "Three cars. Actual cars, not like SUVs or anything. And... Two people in each car."

Scarlett breathed out a sigh of relief. "I thought I was going to have to go and kill him."

I nodded. "But at least we don't have to kill him. At least not yet. We're going to let you go Max. We'll get some food, and then I'll send you a text before we're on our way. I love you Max."

He is on top of everything.

Max smiled. "I love you too. I'll get things settled, and to make sure everyone is more comfortable. I have extra security stationed around the pack house."

"You're the best Maxxy. The best. I love you." Scarlett told him, before ending the videochat.

I closed the laptop before turning my full attention to Scarlett. She's so going to tell me.

"What was that back there?" I asked, causing Scarlett to smile innocently at me.

"Look at that cute smileeee." Reign smiled at her.

No! She's doing it on purpose to try and make us forget about what happened before!

"I have no idea what you're talking about." She told me, trying to change the topic.

She stood up, starting to pick up her things to clean off the table.

"You know exactly what I'm talking about." I growled, following her into the living room.

She bent down, starting to plug in her electronics. I almost groaned as she bent down in front of me. I'm done for. But I need to focus.

"It's honestly nothing. Really. No big deal. Pregnancy hormones or whatever." She offered with a shrug as she stood up again.

I stood in front of her, crossing my arms over my chest.

"You do realize right that I can feel when your emotions change right?" I asked, causing her to smirk at me.

"It's really no big deal. Honestly. Just me overthinking." Scarlett tried to shrug it off like it was nothing.

"If it's 'really no big deal'. Then you won't mind telling me." I pressed.

Scarlett groaned as she headed to the kitchen.

"Fine!" She huffed.

Yay! I won!

CHAPTER
THIRTY-ONE

"It's honestly no big deal. I honestly do think part of it could be that fact that my hormones are changing." She explained, before sitting at the kitchen island.

I leaned against the counter, never taking my eyes off of her. I feel like she's just trying to make excuses. I want her to be completely honest with me.

"So if part of it is about your hormones. What about the other part?" I asked.

"I wonder if she'll respond with the truth or not..." Reign thought out loud.

"I just... I don't think I have it in me to be nice to Silver. I think Violet is a sweet girl honestly. But I don't know if I can be nice to him for Grayson. I also don't like that he's a part of that family anyway." Scarlett tried to explain as she rubbed at her right temple. "Does that make me an awful person? Does that make me an awful twin that I can't be nice to his mates brother?"

I moved closer to her, gently tipping her head up more so I could look into her eyes. I just want to make sure she's feeling okay. When he noticed they looked fine, I placed my hand over her temple and allowed my power to flow through our bond more. I think it'll help her with her pain.

"I don't think that it's a bad thing. Silver betrayed you. He took something that belonged to you. He lied to you. I don't think it's a bad thing at all. Besides you're the alpha of this territory. You get to do what you want." I assured, smiling down at her. "How is your head feeling? Are you getting a headache?"

It could be stress related. Or hormone related. Or could be from the children.

"But don't you think I need to... I don't know. Make sure my brother is happy? I don't want him to leave me." Scarlett frowned. "My head's feeling better now that I feel more of your power through our bond."

"I don't think he's going to leave you. But you can always talk to him about it." I offered. "I'm sorry I'm not much help on this..."

I don't think Grayson could make it without being near Scarlett. Or vice versa.

"It's not your fault or anything." Scarlett smiled at me. "I just have to believe that everything is going to be just fine. I just don't know what I'm going to do if Silver tries to start something with me."

"I'll kill him if he even touches you." I said, keeping direct eye contact so that Scarlett knew I was being serious.

Scarlett grinned at me. I don't want him even within reaching distance of her.

"Perfect! Grayson will hate you and not me." She teased with a smile.

"And think of it this way, you'll be the first Alpha to ever have four packs under her control." I chuckled, starting to pull food out of the fridge to cook us breakfast.

No way I'm taking control of that dreadful pack.

Scarlett laughed, crossing her legs on the chair. "Oh that would be perfect." She smirked. "More people will hate us cause they ain't us."

That's the way to live life. After all, everyone has haters.

"We do have a way of making people mad huh?" I asked, placing a bowl of strawberries in front of her.

"Yeah, but I mean. You could do absolutely nothing and people will still be mad because you're with me. I make people hate me by just breathing." Scarlett giggled, grabbing a strawberry and placing it in her mouth.

My eyes dropped to her open mouth as I watched her tongue peek out. I couldn't help but groan at the visual. She's going to be the end of me.

"Is something wrong baby?" She asked, feigning innocence.

I playfully growled at her. I want to suck that strawberry right out of her mouth.

"Don't make me bite you." I snapped his teeth at her.

Scarlett blew me a kiss.

"Don't tempt me with a good time." She winked. "I like it when you bite me if you haven't noticed."

I licked my fangs at the thought. "I've noticed." I answered, before turning back to finishing her sandwich.

I love being able to nibble on her. Scarlett fidgetted before climbing onto the countertop and moving to sit beside where I was working. She feels energetic today which is a good thing.

"I feel like my body is vibrating." She explained. "I need to run. I need to do something. I can't sit still. There's too much power in my body right now."

I looked up at her. "No running. No letting Xena out. You know this. Not until you give birth. Then we can ask when you can run again." I told her. "Maybe the talisman will help your body calm down."

"Jogging might be okay? But no shifting of course." Reign offered. *"We'd have to ask to be one hundred percent sure."*

Scarlett groaned. "It's not fair that I can't let my wolf out. I used to run for hours every single day. Every. Single. Day. And now I can't! I CAN'T TAKE THIS!" She complained, leaning back against the counter and letting her head hang off of the side.

"Look at that view..." Reign groaned.

That's... Almost the perfect height. But she needs to eat first.

"I feel like a caged animal, which is probably insensitive considering what you've gone through. But I feel trapped inside of myself and I don't like it." She fidgeted. "Like there's three people inside of my body now. Two of them like to apparently stress Xena out."

I couldn't help but laugh at her. She's the sweetest person I've ever met.

"It's not insensitive. I was technically a cage animal. But I wasn't conscious for a lot of it. So I knew I was trapped but I didn't feel trapped? I don't know how to explain it." I rubbed at the back of my neck. "But even if I did. I don't think it's insensitive. I know you're going through a lot. You can vent as much as you want."

I wouldn't make her not vent to me just because of what I went through.

"I just don't like this feeling of not being able to do anything." She shrugged, looking up at me as I came to stand in front of her.

I tilted my head as I looked down at her. I can't help myself.

"This is almost perfect height." Scarlett teased me.

I groaned, my shorts not hiding my arousal. I bent down and pressed a kiss to her lips. She gets me going so easily.

"I could make it work. But I'd rather you eat first, and then we go meet with moron so we can get it done and over with." I rolled my eyes. "I'm also just about to tell Max he can plan the Alpha ceremony for us in Scotland. So he can take care of everything."

It would make him so happy to be able to help us with everything.

"Perfect! Let's do that!" She said as she tried to sit up, but couldn't due to the angle she was at. "I'm stuck."

I chuckled, placing the food down beside her and pulling her off of the counter. "Not comfortable huh?"

"Not at all. But I would do it for you." She smirked up at me as I pulled her back into my front.

There's plenty of other ways to make that more comfortable for her. I smiled, one of my hands came up to wrap around her neck.

"That's what we have a bed for babygirl." I smirked, kissing the top of her head. "Be a good girl and eat your sandwich for me."

Scarlett whimpered, her thighs pressed together as she nodded and went to sit back in her seat again.

Her praise kink is the hottest thing to me.

CHAPTER
THIRTY-TWO

Scarlett rolled her shoulders before she closed her eyes. "It feels weird having him around again. Back then, we were supposed to be such good friends..." She sighed, before rubbing her temples.

I frowned before I parked in the front spot labeled for the Alpha. I turned towards her and placed my lips against her right temple to help ease her pain. I don't think her headache will go away until Silver goes home.

Scarlett relaxed into me, her body calming as she felt my power run through her body. "I'm going to be right here every step of the way. If you want to kick him out immediately after he gives you back the talisman. Then we can go home, and schedule an appointment where Carter can use her ability to see what kind of power it holds."

Scarlett snorted before shaking her head. "You're really not going to let me forget that huh?" She asked with a teasing smile.

I smirked, gently nipping her bottom lip. If it helps her? I'll never forget. She's my top priority.

"Of course not. If this is going to make your pregnancy easier. Then I'm going to make sure you have as easy of a pregnancy as possible." I explained before getting out of the car, and quickly heading to the passenger side to open the door.

I was dressed in a deep red hoodie, with black ripped jeans. Scarlett grabbed my hand and got out of the car.

Scarlett was dressed similarly, with a matching hoodie and black jeans and combat boots. "I'm going to laugh at him if he over-dressed for this." She smirked at me as we headed to the pack house.

I chuckled. We get to do whatever the heck we want to do. If he's over dressed that sounds like it's his fault. Not ours.

"I didn't think to ask Max how he was dressed. But I'm sure it won't matter." I shrugged, wrapping my arm around her shoulder and pulling her into me.

Scarlett smiled, bumping her hip against mine. It definitely won't matter. She's my mate. I'll fight anyone who says otherwise.

The guards followed behind us, keeping their eyes peeled for any danger. "Is he here yet?" She asked, looking to Max who was waiting for us by the front door.

"Yes. Has been waiting for you for an hour." Max nodded, casting his eyes down in respect and submission.

It took everything in me not to laugh. I'm glad he's been stuck waiting. I frowned slightly, gently placing my hand on my brothers shoulder. I feel his nerves... I want him to know that I won't let anything happen to Scarlett/

"Everything will be fine. Promise." I assured, giving me a quick squeeze.

Max perked up, a bright smile crossing his face. Scarlett squared her shoulders, before leading us the rest of the way into the meeting room.

I opened the large wooden doors in front of us so she could walk right in. Her eyes immediately met with Graysons. She smiled kindly. "Brother..." She spoke softly as she walked into the room. "I'm going to have to ask you and your mate to wait outside while we discuss the situation."

"If they want to stay. I'll speak freely in front of them." Silver said, slowly standing up but keeping his head bowed in submission to Scarlett.

I growled unhappily before standing directly behind Scarlett. My eyes never left Silver's form. If he even makes one wrong move. He's done before.

"We can leave... It's okay." Violet tried to say, looking up at Grayson.

"Whatever you want Vi... It's your choice." Grayson said, before looking at Scarlett.

"It's actually not. It's mine. Leave the meeting room, I will have a guard come and get you when we're done." Scarlett said, her eyes flashing purple at him.

I don't think that it would be a good idea for them to be in on this conversation.

"I will escort you to where the others are waiting." One of the younger guards, Boyde, told them.

Grayson nodded, taking Violets hand and leading her after where Boyde was heading.

This is going to be good.

"Oh this is going to be soooo hot. I'm excited." Reign howled.

"Now we can speak freely without your sister getting upset with what might be said." Scarlett said, I immediately pulled out the chair at the head of the table for her.

She smiled, gently pressing a kiss to my cheek before sitting in the open chair. I might fight Silver if he tries to sit by her.

"You may sit." She ordered.

Silver nodded, sitting in a seat a few seats away from her since he didn't like how I was staring at him. I stood right beside Scarlett, not wanting to sit down in case I had to intervene. I'm going to be prepared. No matter what I have to do to protect my mate.

"Aren't you worried about your brother getting upset?" Silver asked, trying to make awkward small talk.

Scarlett's eyes settled on a black velvet box with an amethyst stone in the shape of the crescent moon with a wolf howling up at her. Is that where the talisman is?

"No. That's his phone." Reign snorted.

That was a good one.

"My brother is used to this life. I didn't shelter him. He needed to know how I handled things so that he trusted me as his Alpha." Scarlett explained. "Is that my talisman?" She asked.

Silver nodded, reaching to grab it for her. But I beat him to it. I growled, my eyes a dark red. "Do not make a move to come any closer to Alpha Knight." I snapped causing Silver to whimper and nod.

I grabbed the box and handed it to Scarlett. I'm not afraid to break every single bone in his body.

"If you would let me..." Silver swallowed thickly, "I would love to explain... Well not love to. But I want to explain why I took it... Why I didn't tell you I took it."

Scarlett sighed, placing her hand on top of the box. Her eyes immediately looked brighter, a wave of power rushed through her body quickly. It almost made me stumble from the brunt of it. That was more than I was expecting. But I was able to stay standing.

"I guess you can tell me why you destroyed our friendship

for a talisman that wouldn't even work for someone outside of the Winterfall bloodline." She glared, moving the box closer to her since she didn't trust that he wouldn't try to take it again.

I don't blame her at all...

CHAPTER
THIRTY-THREE

"I ... Honestly there's no excuse for what I did. In the moment, I felt like I had no other choice... Vi... Before I took the talisman. Violet got attacked by a shadow wolf. She was so small... Smaller than she should've been because our mother died during childbirth so she didn't get the proper things she needed from our mother. But I was reading every single book in our library. And I came across the talisman..." Silver started before Scarlett raised her hand to tell him to stop.

Is Scarlett and Stormy the only known shadow wolves?

"*Pretty sure yeah.*" Reign offered with a shrug.

"Wait. What? Are you sure it was a shadow wolf?" Scarlett asked, giving Silver a skeptical look.

"Yes. It had every symptom known from a shadow wolf bite." He nodded.

Silver is already annoying me. I continued to let my power roll through her body to keep her in a calmer state. As long as she's still in control. We can stay in the meeting.

"That can't be true." Scarlett said, shaking her head. "The only known shadow wolf at the time was me and Stormy."

"Maybe..." Silver stopped himself.

Scarlett bared her teeth at him. Silver's going to get himself killed.

"Stormy was in Scotland. So don't blame her for something you did. You took my talisman. Continue on with your story." She commanded, her power radiating throughout the room.

Silver's head immediately bowed to the stronger Alpha in the room. No one is stronger than her.

"My apologies Alpha." He whimpered in submission. "I came across the talisman in our book. There was next to no information about it, but I knew it was powerful. I prayed to the Moon Goddess... And her answer to me was clear. That the talisman would save my sisters life."

"And why didn't you just ask?" Scarlett asked, her eyes drifting back down to the small box in front of her.

It would've saved everyone time and effort if he had asked.

"I didn't think you'd say yes... I didn't know how to pull you aside and tell you my sister was dying and I needed your talisman to save your life. I thought you'd tell me that the talisman would only work on the Winterfall line." Silver tried to explain, he fidgeted again showing his unease in the whole situation.

Scarlett growled, her eyes starting to glow purple. "Do you really think I believe that? Tell me the real reason you didn't come to me. Tell me the real reason. Because if you lie to me again, I will break every bone in your hand." She threatened, baring her teeth to him.

"*You get em baby!*" Reign cheered.

The stink of lies filtered through the air. It kind of makes me want to barf.

Silver couldn't bring himself to look at Scarlett. I looked at him. "Alpha Knight asked you a question. The best thing you can do right now is answer her. We can both smell your lies." I threatened.

Silver swallowed thickly.

"I thought if I came to you. That it would make me look weak. And I didn't want to look weak in the eyes of the only female Alpha in the whole world." He explained, rubbing his forehead.

Scarlett sighed, leaning back into her seat. That is finally the truth... It's really stupid honestly.

"There's the truth. I hope you realize I would've helped you. I would've wanted my talisman ya know, back. But I would've wanted to save your sisters life." Scarlett told him, reaching back to hold my hand. "Do you have any questions for Silver?"

"Asking him about his sister?" Reign asked.

Of course. I needed to know everything I could.

I nodded. "Yes actually."

Silver gulped as he looked up at me. "Look Scarlett's young enough to be my daughter."

Ew. That wasn't going to be my question.

I growled, my eyes turning dark red immediately. "That wasn't my question." I snapped. "Next time don't speak unless you're spoken to."

Silver nodded. "My apologies."

"My question is why does Violet act the way she does? Why does she look to Grayson for permission to do anything? Why does she just look at the ground and not say anything?" I asked. "What did you do to her to make her afraid to be a wolf?"

That has to be some intense torture for her to act the way she does.

Silver rubbed the back of his neck. "I allowed my fear to get to me... I allowed my thoughts to spiral. I was scared. I thought if she did anything alone... I thought someone would attack her again." He swallowed thickly. "The one time I let someone else watch her... She nearly died. I had to raise her since she was born."

"You couldn't imagine living a life without her." I finished for him, causing Silver to nod in confirmation.

I could maybe understand that to an extent. But not how far Silver took it.

"How are you dealing with Violet living here?" Scarlett asked. "Do you have any plans on trying to make her move back to your territory?"

"No... Violet is so happy here. Grayson takes such good care of her. I don't want to uproot her life." Silver smiled sadly. "I miss her. Don't get me wrong. I miss her everyday. But I... Grayson helped me realize that just because I let her live her life. It doesn't mean that she'll be hurt. You raised him right."

Scarlett smiled as Seth pulled up a chair to sit beside her. "I did. Both of my siblings. Listen. I'm willing to move past this. As long as when I check the talisman out, nothing is wrong with it." She offered. "I'm not going to say you're not allowed in my territory. Because I know how it feels worrying about your siblings. I wouldn't want someone trying to keep me from my siblings. So I won't keep you from yours."

Silver smiled brightly at her. "I didn't do anything to it... After Violet wore it for about an hour or so. And a mark appeared on her arm. I took it off of her and put it back in the box and hid it away in my closet." He explained.

Did Violet say that he wore it around his neck?

"I'm pretty sure she said that he wore it around his neck. We'd have to ask to make sure. But I think so." Reign told me.

I think that might be a good idea. Scarlett scrunched her nose before looking back down at the box.

"No offense. I'm going to be looking it over to make sure that it's okay." Scarlett told him, moving to stand up.

I immediately stood up, pulling out her chair for her. Silver waited for us to stand up before he made a move. He stretched out his hand to Scarlett. But before Scarlett could react, I did.

No one his stank is going to be on my mate.

I put my hand in Silver's and shook it. "Not a chance Silver." I growled. "You don't get to touch my mate. Make sure not to leave our territory until we give you permission."

Scarlett smirked, grabbing the box with the talisman in it. Grabbing my hand before leading me outside of the meeting room. She looked at her guard, smiling at him.

"Silver is not to leave until I give the go ahead. Please let Grayson and Violet know it's okay to show him around. But there will be a team following them to make sure that Silver doesn't try anything." Scarlett told him, causing the guard to nod once before walking off to do as she said.

"She's so beyond hot. I'm in love with her." Reign smiled.

I wrapped my arm around her waist and walked with her out of the pack house. "How are you feeling about the meeting?" I asked when we got outside of the building.

Scarlett inhaled the fresh air, her eyes were shining brightly at me. I smiled excitely at the power I saw in her eyes. I like how strong she looks right now... It makes me happy.

"You seem like you're already feeling better." I complimented, opening up the passenger door for her.

She immediately got in, before I rushed to get in on the driver's side.

"Honestly... As soon as I felt this get into my hands. I felt a wave of power roll into me. It felt refreshing." Scarlett smiled, running her finger over the crystal.

"Are you immediately wanting to head to see Carter about it?" I asked, backing out of the spot.

Scarlett shook her head no.

"No. Let's go home. I want to look at it first." Scarlett told me, I nodded once to confirm that I heard her.

I quickly sped off to head back to our home. Going home sounds like heaven to me.

CHAPTER
THIRTY-FOUR

Scarlett fidgeted, her hand constantly went back to the black velvet box on her lap. "It feels weird... Weird having this back in my possession. I never realized how much my body missed this until I got pregnant." She explained, she was mesmerized by the crystal on the top of the box.

I think she's feeling fine... She should be feeling okay? Like through the bond she feels completely fine? I looked over at her for a split second.

"Are you sure that you don't want to head to Carter?" I asked, worry evident in my voice.

I thought it would be best to ask just in case I'm not feeling her feeling off.

"Yeah, no I'm good. I feel honestly better than I have in the last few days since having this in my hands." She told me. "Do you want us to go to Carter?"

"I... I don't know. I just don't want anything bad to happen. I can feel how good you're feeling right now through our bond. So I of course trust you. But we can do whatever you want." I told her with a soft smile.

My hands tightened on the steering wheel. I sped up, I just want to go home. I want to be alone with her. That way I can really make sure she's feeling okay.

"What if something bad happens? What if she needs to see her?" Reign questioned.

I really need you to stop talking Reign... I don't need to think about this right now.

"I do feel good... I want you to feel good about this too." She said, pouting. "Would it make you feel better to go to Carter?"

I shook my head, bringing myself out of my thoughts. "No. No. No. I'm fine. I'm fine. We don't have to go see Carter. I just need to get out of my head. Everything will be fine." I forced a smile, his eyes kept changing between red and brown.

My breathing started to quicken. I feel Reign itching to take control and I can't let him. I want to be present. I don't want to shift.

"Baby..." Scarlett spoke softly, placing her hand gently on my thigh. "Pull over... Everything will be okay."

I nodded, pulling over to the side of the road and putting the car in park. I couldn't bring myself to look at her, my eyes stared straight ahead at the clear road in front of us. My mind is spiraling... This talisman could do more harm than good...

Silver being here could do more harm than good. I feel like I won't be able to protect her. And she's going to die just like before.

"Tell me what you're thinking... What's going through your mind? Everything is okay." She kept her voice even, not wanting to trigger me.

I looked down at my lap. "There's too much going on..." I whimpered.

Scarlett frowned, reaching over to place her hands on my

cheeks to make me look at her. Just feeling her skin against mine makes me feel calm.

"Pick one thing and we'll start there... We can stop when you want to." She promised with a caring smile.

I nodded.

"I... I'm just worried... Worried that everything my father told me will eventually come true.... I know that he was just trying to hurt me. But he told me I'd lose everything I hold close to me because I don't deserve the happiness..." I swallowed thickly, tears welling as I tried my best to fight them from falling.

I don't deserve her... I'm scared she's going to figure that out. Scarlett gently ran her thumbs over my cheeks.

"We are all okay I promise." She said, moving one of her hands so she could move my hand to rest on her still flat belly.

My large hand rubbing her stomach, almost as if the babies could tell I was stressed. A wave of warmth spread through my entire body causing me to smile.

"Woah... Did you feel that!?" Reign asked.

Of course I did!

"Did you feel that?" I asked, dragging my eyes from her stomach up to her eyes.

Scarlett grinned, her dimples showing. It's like they knew I needed to feel them.

"I did... I think they might be worried about you." She smiled.

My smile was genuine as I looked down at her stomach again. I unbuckled myself and leaned over to kiss her stomach again. I want to feel their power again.

"I worry that I'm not going to be good at this... That I'm going to not only fail you as a mate. But fail them as a father... As a leader. As a wolf in general." I said, leaning my forehead against her stomach.

Scarlett leaned back so I could have more room, she gently ran her hand through my soft brown hair. *I want to be perfect for them... I want to be their everything.*

"We both have a lot to learn about being mates... And parents. You're already doing such an amazing job at not only being a leader but being a mate. We have each other to lean on. I promise I won't let you fail as long as you won't let me fail." Scarlett told me, constantly keeping her hand against my skin.

I reluctantly moved back to be more comfortable in my seat. *I wish we were home.*

"We can do this together." I promised, taking her hand gently to bring it up to my lips. "Thank you for calming me down..." I told her, before I put a hand on her stomach again. "And thank you both for making me feel that you're okay..."

They're going to be one of the greatest blessings for me.

Scarlett smiled at me, licking her lips slightly. "I'm sure they'll start doing it more often now." She said, placing her hand overtop of mine on her stomach. "I think they're going to grow up knowing how amazing you are."

I blushed at her compliment. *I really do love when she compliments me... It makes my insides all warm.*

"It's because she's amazing." Reign smiled.

"I still don't know what to do with myself when you compliment me." I chuckled, before putting the car back into drive and heading back to our home.

"Well, I mean same." Scarlett looked outside of the window. "But we both deserve it. Cause we're top tier, or whatever the kids say nowadays."

I laughed, shaking my head. "Don't ask me, Max tries to use that lingo on me and I don't understand half of what he's trying to say. Cause like? What does this "slaps" mean?"

Children's slang is hard to understand.

Scarlett snorted. "I don't know but that sounds terrible."

"Exactly. But I'm just happy that he's happy here... He's finally acting like a person again. I'm so proud of him for putting himself out there." I smiled at the thought of my brother.

Max deserves this...

I slowed down as I pulled down the long driveway to our secluded home. Scarlett perked up when she saw Alex pacing back and forth from one side of the driveway to the other.

This isn't going to be good.

"What's happening?" She asked, looking at me.

I shrugged, pulling slowly up to the garage. When Alex saw us, he quickly moved out of the way. I didn't want to accidentally hit him.

After I parked, we both quickly got out of the car and headed to where Alex and Carter were outside.

"Everything is fine. Look, they're here now. You can talk to them now!" Carter said, causing Alex to look at Scarlett.

"What's going on Alex?" Both me and Scarlett said at the same time.

"I had a vision from the Moon Goddess about your kid." Alex said, forcing himself to stop pacing long enough to talk to us.

When it rains. It pours. What does she have in store for our children now?

THIRTY-FIVE

"About our kid?" Scarlett asked, looking at me before looking at Alex again.

About our children. Isn't that what he said?

"Yeah. I think so." Reign shrugged. "I wasn't paying any attention."

"No. Yours and Carters." Alex rolled his eyes. "Obviously you and Seth's. Yes. I don't know how much I should really tell you about it. But I can't just not tell you ya know? I feel like that would just be wrong. I don't even know why the Moon Goddess thought it was a good idea to give this to me because I tell you everything!" He babbled, the smell of his stress drifted into the air around us.

Oh she's not going to like that smell. Scarlett gagged, before I immediately looked her over. I knew it. I hope she doesn't throw up though. She'll get upset.

"Shut up for a minute Alex." I told my brother. "Are you okay? What's wrong?"

Scarlett nodded, covering her nose and mouth with her shirt.

"Definitely the smell getting to her." Reign nodded.

"I'm okay... His stress just makes me want to throw up." She mumbled from behind her shirt.

Alex frowned, looking down at his feet. I nodded. If she thinks he feels bad. She's going to feel bad. So let's get this thing rolling.

"Okay, before you start up again. Let's go in the house. She'll put on my hoodie and my scent will overpower yours." I explained, turning Scarlett so that I could lead her into the house.

Before we went into the house, I opened the passenger door and grabbed the velvet box that held the talisman. No need to forget that. She won't like that.

"It's not my fault my emotions just have a strong scent to her!" Alex complained. "Alphas have heightened senses than the rest of us." He huffed, grabbing Carter's hand so they could walk into the house together.

Her senses are more heightened than most. But it's not his fault anyway. She's just hypersensitive to certain stuff.

"Yes, it's not your fault. She has a heightened sense of smell in general, but now that she's pregnant it's even more heightened. I wasn't trying to make you feel bad." I told him, sitting Scarlett on the couch before grabbing a hoodie off the back of the couch to give to her.

Alex and Carter walked into the livingroom next, Carter sat down on the chair. But Alex was so restless, he couldn't bring himself to sit down.

After Scarlett put on my hoodie, she nodded to Alex. "Okay. Continue on with what you were saying. But please talk slower. We're not going to be mad at you." I sat down beside Scarlett, nodding in agreement to Alex.

I want to hear everything. If I have to fight The Moon Goddess I just might.

"I don't know what happened. It happened a little bit ago, I was just talking to Carter and then I just randomly blacked out. When I opened my eyes I was in the middle of the woods, I don't know where though. Anyways that's not the point. I was walking in the woods, trying to figure out what was happening. Well, as I was walking around. I heard this... Person scream. So of course I went to check it out on what was happening. When I found the person, they were on their knees on the ground. And a burst of power left them. Before you ask I'm not telling you the color." He said, causing Scarlett to snort and grin at him.

Dang. We were so close to finding out what we were having.

"I wasn't going to ask anything. But keep going." I told him, placing my hand on Scarlett's stomach again.

"You so totally were going to ask." Reign snorted.

I so totally was. But he doesn't have to know that.

"Well anyway... This other person came running up to them... I'm going to skip over this part because I don't want to accidentally say something that I wasn't supposed to say. I... I just think you should call Lincoln and Octavia." Alex said, biting nervously on his bottom lip.

Lincoln and Octavia? What do they have to do with this?

"Well first off, how do you know this is our child?" Scarlett asked, wanting to make sure she understood everything.

Alex crossed his arms and glared slightly. I growled. He might be stressed. But I'm not afraid to fight him.

"Watch how you look at my mate." I snapped causing Alex to whimper.

"Let me just say. The kid looks exactly like you both." Alex said, rubbing his forehead as he was overwhelmed. "No doubt your child. The power I felt... Felt just like your guys power. I just... Can you just trust me please? I don't know how to tell you that it's your kid without giving away too much information. And I'm not looking to get in trouble with the Moon Goddess okay!"

I don't think I like this at all.

Scarlett nodded. "Yes... We'll trust you. Why should we call Lincoln and Octavia? If this has to do with our baby?" She asked.

I nodded. That's exactly my question? I don't understand what's happening.

"I don't really like him." I rolled my eyes.

Scarlett smiled, placing her legs over mine. This was what she does when she wants me to calm down.

"He's just my friend. That's all." She teased, nuzzling her nose against my mark. I groaned, moving my head to the side so she could have more room. "You're the only person I've ever wanted."

I love it when she nuzzles my mark.

I gripped my thigh tightly. "Good. I'll kill another man if they want you."

Alex gagged. "Nope nope nope. I don't want to see any more of this! Okay stay on topic! You need to call Lincoln and Octavia and trust that theres a reason! Or bring it up to the Moon Goddess! And if you do that, tell her to leave me alone. I don't want to have to deal with this again. This is freaking stressful." He complained, Carter got up quickly and rubbed at his back to try and calm him down.

I wonder what he saw that has him so worked up.

Scarlett nodded, leaning her head against my chest. "I will call him. You don't have to worry anymore. Everything is going to be okay. I promise." She smiled sweetly at him.

"Besides, I can worry enough for the both of us." I joked, wanting to calm my brother down.

I might've joked. But I'm deadly serious. I need to calm down actually.

Alex nodded, looking down at Carter now. "Will you call right now if we leave?"

Scarlett looked confused, before looking at me. "Um... Sure. Just hand me my phone it's on the table and I'll call him right now." She told him.

Alex quickly got the phone off of the table and rushed it back to her. Okay... This isn't good at all.

"Are you okay?" Scarlett asked, holding Alex's hand so he had to look into her eyes.

Her eyes turned purple, glowing enough to keep Alex mesmerized by her power. Alex took in a relaxing breath as he nodded.

"Just worried... I'm feeling much better." Alex told her with a sleepy smile.

Scarlett smiled at him before looking at Carter. She's really good at calming him down.

"He's probably going to be asleep by the time you guys get home. It's completely normal." Scarlett assured.

Carter nodded, holding Alex's hand to lead him out of the house and to where they parked the car. I smirked at her.

"You do that a lot don't ya?" I asked as she got into her phone and pulled up her contacts.

I wonder if she's ever done it to me before.

"Not like a lot. But I can do it with people I have a bond with. Like Gray or Stormy. And then obviously you. They just calm down because they feel my power. So it's not hard for me to do." Scarlett smiled at me, pushing the call button when she brought up Lincoln's contact.

"Thank you for taking such good care of him." I told her, rubbing her legs as we listened to the ringing tone.

CHAPTER
THIRTY-SIX

It only took Lincoln a minute to answer the phone. "Ugh you couldn't have called me at a better time." Lincoln groaned, plopping down onto the couch.

Scarlett smirked at me. I wonder why... Maybe Alex was right about whatever is going on.

"Why is that? Mated life that hard? Octavia ruling your house?" She teased, causing me to laugh quietly.

"No. It's not hard. She's just having a tough time being pregnant, and I'm constantly worried about her. And yes, I'm not afraid to say my woman runs my household. She's amazing at it, and she deserves it. So I don't want to hear anything about it." Lincoln almost whined.

Scarlett bit her bottom lip, trying to refrain from laughing at him. A man after my own heart. I get it.

"Well, I can't really say anything. My mates the Alpha and she rules the house. So I feel you there brother." I said, getting into the conversation since Scarlett put the phone on speaker.

I wanted him to know I was there so he didn't think that I was listening in.

"Perfect. We're two peas in a pod. Although it's only a slightly different situation because mines not the Alpha. But she's still struggling all the same, I don't know what I'm doing wrong. I leave our bond open all the time. But she's progressively getting weaker and weaker as the pregnancy progresses. They're talking about having to deliver the baby early. They're talking about how she could die. And I can't do it. I can't live without her. I've already lived without her and I was miserable. I can't do it again Scarlett. I can't think about it. I can't. I can't. I won't be able to make it without her." Lincoln rambled, his voice was thick with emotion.

"Wow... He really understands what we're feeling." Reign laid down in my mind.

I've hated that guy for as long as I can remember... And here we are going through the same exact thing... Feeling the same exact thing.

Scarlett frowned, hating that her friend was struggling so much. "What's been happening? Do you want to give me any details?"

"It started out great ya know. We got to know each other pretty good before she was starting to randomly get weak. We immediately went to the doctor. And they suggested that it's because her wolf has been neglected from love and attention for so long. That her wolf needs her mate bond to be complete. So we ya know, marked. Mated. Everything. And everything was fine, at least for a while. But then she started getting exhausted so I pushed more of my power at her, and that helped for a while. But it just kept getting worse and worse.

And now... Now she doesn't even want to leave our bed. I take care of her of course. But I'm worried. The doctors don't think she's going to make it." He swallowed, before taking a deep breath.

I squeezed Scarlett's thigh tightly, my eyes starting to blaze red at the thought of something even happening to Scarlett. Reign whimpered in the back of my mind, he didn't like the feelings rolling through us.

"I'm okay..." Scarlett said, shifting so she could put more of her body on top of mine. "Nothing is wrong with me." She promised, needing to calm me down before she continued on with their conversation.

I swallowed, unable to say anything so I just nodded my head in confirmation. Nothing is wrong with her... She's okay. She's safe. No one is going to take her away from me.

"What's going on?" Lincoln asked. "What's happening? What's wrong with you? You aren't dying are you? I can't take having to lose anyone else. Or frankly having to worry about someone else dying." Lincoln started, causing me to growl.

Showing my unease with this conversation. No one else is dying.

"Okay! No one is dying. We're not going to talk about anyone dying okay. Nothing is happening. Let's talk about you first and then we can get into me if you want." Scarlett promised. "How about you guys take a trip here? I'll have the doctor waiting to check Octavia out. We actually have a new doctor, she's pretty good at her job."

I scoffed, rolling my eyes. "Yeah, pretty good at her job for not being on the job for long." I needed to add in.

"And for her favorite line to be, I don't know." Reign rolled his eyes.

"Okay when, should we leave tonight? Can we come in tomorrow at sometime?" Lincoln asked immediately. "I'll text Antonio and have him look after things while we're gone. I mean he's already been doing that since I've been staying home to take care of Octavia, but it's fine. I'll get things ready and we'll leave so I'll see you in the morning!"

Lincoln didn't even give Scarlett a chance to say anything before he hung up. I bet she didn't like that he hung up on her.

I looked at her. "What's going through that beautiful mind of yours?"

"I have many plans... And I think it all ties into that talisman..." She explained, looking directly at the box that sat on the coffee table in front of us. "And it might just fix all of our problems."

I'm hoping that whatever she has planned will help. I don't know what I'll do if something bad happens to Scarlett.

THIRTY-SEVEN

The next morning, I was able to sneak away from Scarlett. Not real. I said that I was going to go say hi to Max and Alex. It's not a lie. It's also just... Not the full truth.

"We don't have to tell her everything. It's a surprise. She'll love the surprise!" Reign offered, trying to give me a positive thought.

I appreciated it. But it still stresses me out hiding this from her. Yes I know it's a surprise. It's supposed to be a good thing. That it technically isn't hiding anything from her. But I still feel like I'm hiding something. I don't want to make her upset that I didn't tell her immediately.

I forced myself to shake those thoughts off. It's going to be fine. If she feels me being stressed out. She's going to think something is wrong and then try to come and find me. And I definitely don't want that.

"You letting this get to you huh?" Grayson asked, crossing his arms with a smirk.

"Maybe... Just slightly. I don't want Scarlett to think I'm

lying to her." I shrugged, rubbing the back of my neck. "I feel like it could go both ways. Whether she hates it or she loves it."

"She's not going to hate it." Alex rolled his eyes playfully.

"I just feel like this could go badly. Especially with everything else we're going through right now." I growled, turning my focus back to Grayson. "You got my sketches right?"

Grayson snorted. "If you could call what you sent to me sketches. You and Scarlett rush through things so fast sometimes." He teased.

"We're going to just let this one slide because he is keeping this secret for us." Reign growled. *"He's getting a thin line though. Super thin."*

"I had to do it quickly so Scarlett wouldn't find out. But you got the dimensions. How many rooms I want. Bathrooms. All the specific details that I had scribbled down?" I asked, following him as he walked down the hallway.

"Yup. I had someone come up with an official blueprint, I have people heading out to the field to start prepping the land and start a foundation. We're going to add in a basement for added space too. Even though the house is already obnoxious." He continued to teased and I was getting annoyed with it.

"Grayson." I growled in warning.

"Ohhhh someone's getting in troubleeee." Alex teased, trying to calm the tension.

"I'm sorry. I was just trying to joke around with you. Everything is getting started for the building of the house. Including the blacktop. We should be able to get it all done on the timeline that you requested." Grayson offered with a smile, before looking down at his phone. "I have to take this." He explained before walking away.

"I feel like me and Grayson will never get along." I sighed, running a hand through my hair.

"You might just have to give him more time... He's so used to being Scarlett's go to... Her everything. For the longest time it was just them. Now... It's them... Me... You... Max... You get my point. He has a lot to handle right now. Adding in his new mate and her brother too. He's going through a lot. Just give him a bit of time. I'm sure he doesn't hate you." Alex tried to assure me.

But I don't think that it was working... I just need to get my mind to focus on one thing at a time.

"I don't know. It just seems like everytime we talk... I mess everything up. I don't know how to talk to anyone besides Scarlett, you, and Max. Everyone else stresses me out." I rubbed at my temple. "I don't know how Scarlett does it."

"She does it because that's what she's been doing for the longest time. This is all she knows. She's the best at it." Alex smirked. "You are mated to the only Alpha female in the entire world. This is where it gets you. Is Grayson the only one stressing you out?"

I almost rolled my eyes. No. He's stressing me out. The pack is stressing me out. The ceremonies are stressing me out. The fact I feel like my mate's going to die on me and I can't do anything to stop it is stressing me out. I could keep this going for as long as he wants.

"*Seth...*" Reign warned.

What?

"*You're spinning.*" Reign continued.

So? I can spin. I'm allowed to spin. My mind is allowed to do whatever it wants.

"*Stop spinning. We don't spin. We are in control. Everything will be fine. Scarlett and our children will be fine.*" Reign growled at me.

I know... I breathed in deeply... Everything will be fine.

251

"No... He's not the only one stressing me out. But everything is fine. I'm handling it. Scarlett takes care of most of the talking, and let's me talk whenever I feel comfortable. She's letting me take the lead on my healing or whatever and she's helping me feel more comfortable being in an Alpha position. I just don't want to fail her... I don't want her to hate me." I vented out.

I really shouldn't be telling him this. I should just keep it to myself or wait until I can vent to Scarlett about everything. I can't let the pack know that I'm struggling. It would look badly on her. I closed my eyes, taking another deep breath.

Everything is going to be fine. Everything has to be fine.

"You're right. Everything is going to be fine... We will make sure that everything is completely fine." Reign assured me.

I felt this power roll through me and I felt better... I felt calmer. I felt more in control.

"A run might help?" Reign offered.

Nope. Can't do that. Scarlett can't shift so I'm not doing it either. I don't want to throw it in her face that I can do what she wants to do. I stand with my girl.

Alex waved his hand in front of my face causing me to snap my attention back to him.

"Were you saying something?" I ask, scrunching my nose.

"Yes. Did you not hear a single word that I just said?" Alex asked with a chuckle.

"No. I wasn't listening. What were you saying?" I asked, we were heading back towards Scarlett's office.

I didn't want to leave her for so long... I hated even leaving her for the short time that I did.

"I said... That I could talk to Carter about maybe figuring out something to put in the air to help calm Scarlett down. I'm not sure though, but I'll talk to her and see what we can come up with with the new house." Alex smiled brightly at me. I smiled at him.

"Thank you... I would really appreciate that. Maybe throw me into that mix too." I chuckled, giving him a wink before I opened the door to her office and walked in.

CHAPTER
THIRTY-EIGHT

The next morning, Scarlett was sitting at the pack house. Her eyes locked on the talisman in front of her. I was standing beside her, my arms crossed as I didn't know what she was doing.

I feel like she's been staring at this thing for a while.

"Please tell her I'm bored." Reign groaned.

I am not doing that. She'll get upset.

"But I'm bored!" Reign whined.

"You know it might do something better if you pick it up?" I offered, leaning down and pressing a kiss to the top of her head. "It might make you feel better to get your hands on it."

She felt better the other day when she touched it? So maybe it'll help now? I don't know anything about this thing honestly.

"I don't think any of us do?" Reign snorted.

"I don't know... Just looking at it makes me feel better if you want me to be honest. A part of me wants to touch it, but the other part of me just... I don't know the other part of me feels better knowing that it's there." She shrugged, turning her office chair to be able to face me better. "After Carter gets her hands on it... We'll make the choice to wear it or not."

I like that she says we will make the decision. It makes my heart happy.

I smiled, squatting down in front of her. "We will make the decision that's best for you." I promised, reaching up to brush a piece of her long brown hair behind her ear. "You look beautiful today."

She smells like mine. Looks like mine. Everyone knows she's mine. What more could I ask for?

Scarlett blushed. "Well thank you, you look amazing too." She said, before her eyes trailed down to her stomach. "When do you think I'll start showing?"

I placed my hand against her stomach, smiling brighter when I felt their power warm my hand. It's like they know when I need a bit of their calmness. "I don't know... But obviously they're progressing quickly since they can do that." I smirked. "Of course our kids would be the ones to progress quicker."

I can't wait for them to be here... I'm so excited to be a dad.

Scarlett laughed. "Pretty sure that that's because we're both Alphas but sure let's go with that one." She teased, pressing a kiss to my lips. "I think we're due to meet Link at home now... Or maybe we were supposed to meet him at the hospital?"

"I think it was the hospital. But we could always call him to make sure before we head out?" I offered. "That way we're not making him wait or anything?"

Doesn't hurt to ask.

"Look at you baby. Thinking about saving time for someone I thought you hated. Someone I was supposed to marry." She couldn't help but taunt me.

I growled playfully at her. I might bite her. That would be a lot of fun for me.

"Don't make me bite you. *Again*." I taunted with a slight glare.

Scarlett grinned, getting up and kissing me on the lips. Now I might just do it for the heck of it.

"You know I just love to get a raise out of you." She grinned innocently. "Are we going to walk to the hospital since it's so close by?"

I rolled my eyes. I can't tell her no.

"You can. You just won't do it. You simp." Reign teased.

I will happily be a simp for my woman.

"I guess so. That is if you're feeling up to it." I said, grabbing the box that held the talisman in it. "I don't like that you're overdoing it so much."

"How am I overdoing it when I feel fine?" Scarlett asked, heading to her office door.

I was about to say something when my eyes landed on Alex with the door open.

No way he found him that fast?

"Alphas." Alex said, bowing his head in respect. "I have what you requested. And a little information as well." He smiled, before he shoved in an older man that was shorter than all of us.

Scarlett's mouth fell open as she stared at him. I motioned for Alex to shut the door behind him. Alex stepped further into the office.

"You're the reason why our packmind link isn't working? I thought you got the message when I delivered your mates head to your doorstep." Scarlett growled, her eyes blazing purple as she refused to take her eyes off of the man in front of her.

"That's so hot." Reign groaned.

So hot.

I looked between Scarlett and Alex. "Who is he?"

The elder smirked as he looked up at me. "I'm her Uncle."

"Oh snap." Reign gasped.

Oh snap... That's messed up.

Scarlett was shaking, her claws growing as she slapped her hand across his face. Making sure to leave a swipe of her claws.

"Do. Not. Speak." She ordered.

Her power flowing through the room, Alex stumbled before catching himself. The room started to shake as it darkened, I kept my eyes on her.

I'll step in if I have to.

"Scarlett." I said, worry laced in my voice.

Scarlett snapped her eyes over to me for a split second. I know she's in control. I can sense it. But Xena needs to chill out.

"I'm in control." She clipped, before reaching for the talisman in the open box.

As soon as her hand wrapped around it, a wave of calm shot through her body. Her eyes held a new dangerous look to it. Her uncle stared up at her, fear crossed his face almost immediately.

"This is so hot." Reign repeated.

I don't think she's ever been this attractive.

"You decided to test me dear uncle. I won't make this mistake again." She growled, she pressed the talisman into his forehead.

Immediately he started to scream in pain, his skin turned pale, his eyes dulled as he tried to move away from her. But it was no use, Alex grabbed one arm and I was quick to grab his other. Effectively holding him in place so Scarlett could do whatever she wanted.

"I won't kill you. That would be your escape. No." Scarlett

grinned, her canines were sticking out. "No. I'm going to make you live out the rest of your sorry excuse of life living as the thing you- hate most in this world."

"No. No!" Her uncle tried to shout, but her power was making her office completely soundproof. "Don't do this to me! Don't do this to me! I'm sorry!"

"It's too late for apologizes." She growled. "You'll learn the hard way." She snapped, removing the talisman from his forehead when the symbol was burned into his head.

Alex and I immediately let his weak form drop to the ground.

She really just did that? She just took away his wolf?

"I didn't know she could do that." Reign added in.

Scarlett was shaking with her anger. "Make sure he leaves Scotland and Ireland. I don't care what you have to do, make sure he goes to the rogue territory. They can have their fun with him." She ordered, her shadows slowly melted away like nothing happened.

I followed after her as she left her office.

As she was walking she looked to Max, making him follow after her. "I don't care what you have to do. I want the coronation ceremony done by the end of this week. I won't stand for disrespect by the elders in this pack. Get it done." She snapped, before her eyes softened as she looked to see who she was talking to.

"I'm so sorry... Please. Do what you can to get it done." Scarlett offered with a soft smile.

I wrapped my arm around her shoulder.

"Max gets it." I assured, giving Max a nod.

I don't want her to feel bad for snapping at him... We all make mistakes.

"I completely understand Alpha. You're under a lot of

stress, I'll make sure the ceremony can take place no later than the end of the week." He promised before rushing off.

I held the open box to Scarlett, letting her gently place the talisman back in the box. When she let go of it, it immediately stopped glowing. "Do you wanna talk about what happened back there?"

Scarlett shrugged, letting me lead her down the path to the hospital. "I... I don't know. I just felt so angry. There was so many emotions. But then Xena told me the talisman... That I needed to grab it and it would do the rest of the work." She tried to explain what she was thinking.

"Not many Alphas can take someone's wolf away." I offered, wanting to cheer her up. "So that makes you even more special."

She's truly one of a kind.

Scarlett smirked up at me. "We are made to make the world around us angry apparently. Their anger and jealousy is just going to keep getting worse... And worse... And worse. Especially if they find out about this."

The world will rue the day that they ever doubted Scarlett Knight.

CHAPTER
THIRTY-NINE

When we arrived at the Hospital, they went straight up to the top floor to meet with Lincoln and Octavia. I rubbed my hand across Scarlett's back. She seems tense... Stressed. Worried. Does she really think something is wrong with Octavia?

"Wouldn't he have called sooner if it was really that bad?" Reign asked.

I don't know. If they were that close. Probably?

"He's probably scared of you." Reign teased.

Good. He should be. I'm not afraid to kill him.

"Why are you worried?" I asked, sensing her stress through our bond.

She shrugged, rubbing the back of her neck. She better not try and lie to me. I'll know and I am not afraid to spank her for it.

"Oh. Yeah! Do that do that! You know she likes it!" Reign told me eagerly.

"I never expected for Lincoln to have this kind of issue with his mate... He has been one of the only nice people in this world to me." She tried to explain. "He's been the sweetest person for his pack." She shifted closer to me, rubbing her head against my chest to scent me.

My chest rumbled with approval, knowing that by her scenting me, my scent would linger on her in return. I want everyone to know that she's mine. Also... I feel a little bad for Lincoln. I also want to tell her that it's not his pack. It's hers. She killed the Alpha so that means it's her pack.

"That's my girl." I praised, a slight growl to my voice.

Scarlett smirked up at me, loving when I praised her. I wouldn't have thought an Alpha would like it... Especially one who pretty much has always been an Alpha. But it's okay. I'm good with it.

"How about let's get this going... I have a feeling things are going to start moving fast when Max gets things moving." Scarlett held my hand tightly. "I've been feeling my phone buzz for the past five minutes."

"Why didn't you check it?" I asked, leading her out onto the floor when the elevator stopped.

To be honest, I don't really blame her. I had a phone, but I don't know where it is. I can talk to Scarlett through our minds if we're not together, even though we are always together.

"I didn't think about it... I figured that I would be able to deal with everything later. Especially if it's about the coronation, I won't be able to give him the proper time he needs anyway." Scarlett shrugged. "I'm sure he won't care. He's one of the better helpers I've had. Literally my beta and deltas are my brothers. It works out well for me."

I think it works out well for the both of us. I don't have to worry about them trying to take my mate away from me. And she also doesn't have to worry about me killing her Delta or Beta for looking at her.

"Alex and Max and Grayson make killing people less likely. Which I guess is a good thing." Reign rolled his eyes.

I'm not allowed to kill anyone. It's kind of boring.

I smiled at her, before opening up the door to the VIP room. Scarlett smiled brightly as she saw Lincoln fussing over Octavia.

"Really... Really Link I'm feeling fine. Much better than before honestly." Octavia smiled, trying to reassure her mate.

"I know.... I'm just worried." Lincoln pouted.

"You're probably feeling much better because of Scarlett's power... But it feels a bit different than last time. I... I don't know. Somehow it feels much more powerful than the last time we were here." Lincoln explained, obviously not seeing that me and Scarlett were in the room with them.

But he does have a point. Her being home is probably the best for her wolf... Feeling Scarlett's power again probably helps a lot with her symptoms.

"Well. I do have to agree with Link... Your wolf probably feels more comfortable knowing that she's home... Even though she should feel that same way while in Spain because that's technically my territory as well." Scarlett looked towards me, holding her hand out for the box.

Lincoln rushed over, not caring about me standing right beside her. He wrapped his arms around Scarlett in a tight hug.

I kind of hate him again.

"I thought you felt bad for him." Reign teased.

Nope. I hate him again.

"I missed you." He said, Scarlett wrapped her arms around him.

"I missed you too," Scarlett told him.

Removing her arms as I growled uneasily at someone else touching her. Lincoln blushed, quickly moving to where Octavia was laying. That was too long of a hug. I don't like it.

"It's okay... I'm assuming you're pregnant too?" Octavia asked, looking Scarlett up and down. "Is that why he's being over the top for you?"

I growled. "I'm always over the top for her." I huffed.

Why not be over the top? She's the most powerful Alpha in the entire world. I should be over the top.

Scarlett laughed. "Yes. I'm pregnant. But there's been some other things that happened that we get to be over the top." She tried to explain without saying too much. "But we're not telling anyone until the ceremony anyway."

"The ceremony is happening this soon?" Lincoln asked, looking between us.

Extremely soon.

"Yes. By the end of next week." I nodded, crossing my arms as I stood behind Scarlett.

"Wow... That's... Wow." Lincoln said, not sure what he needed to reply to that.

Good thing to keep his mouth shut. I moved to sit down in a chair since Scarlett was going to be the main one talking to Octavia. I'm still close enough to her that if something happens I can stop it. But I'm also just far enough away to give them a little privacy.

I haven't known them long... I don't want to intrude. But I also don't want my mate to be alone in a room with them. Who am I kidding? I don't want to be away from her for even a second.

"We can talk about this later. We're talking about you right now." Scarlett said, moving closer to where Octavia was laying. "Has anyone come in here to check on you yet? What has been going on? Links told me a little bit about everything. But I want to know from your side of things."

"Yes. Everyone has been so nice, wanting to make sure I'm settled and everything." Octavia smiled softly. "They were heading to get Carter I believe was her name. But I've been feeling really tired. Like I don't feel like I can get out of bed. I've been less hungry... Just feeling less of myself. I know my wolf is tired. But no one in Spain can figure out why she's exhausted."

Scarlett nodded as she listened. "Do you think you might want to try something? To help give you more energy and power? I think I might have an idea of what's happening..." She said, looking directly at Octavia.

Lincoln snapped his gaze back to Scarlett. I snapped my gaze to Lincoln. I don't like how he's acting right now.

"Absolutely not. We're not trying anything new that might make things worse." Lincoln snapped.

I moved to stand beside Scarlett as I got up out of my chair. No way that this is going to happen.

"Watch the way you speak to my mate." I commanded, my power soaking into the air around us.

"Yeah! You tell him! Make him submit to you!" Reign cheered.

CHAPTER
FORTY

"It isn't new. It's been around for a long time." Scarlett told him, glaring slightly at Lincoln.

Link bared his fangs at her. Reign growled, showing his anger to this situation. I could totally just break his nose.

"It's been around for a long time. But no one has been able to use it, and for the last who knows how long. It hasn't been in your possession. So don't try me Scarlett." He snapped, taking a step towards Octavia as the monitor started to beat faster with how she was stressing out.

This isn't good for Scarlett. This isn't good for Octavia. How does he not see that?

"This is the only warning you're getting Lincoln. Watch your tone." I growled my warning.

I don't want to have to fight him in front of his mate. But if he gives me no choice. I'll do it.

"It hasn't been used because it hasn't needed a reason to be used." Scarlett tried to explain. "It came back for a reason. Obviously it's needed in some way."

It helped Grayson's mate, who obviously was connected to

the Winterfall line. It helped Scarlett. Obviously this Talisman likes to help the women in the family bloodline or connected to the bloodline.

"Not on my mate." Lincoln shook his head.

Scarlett looked down at Octavia, wanting to know her answer.

"If Link isn't comfortable with it, then I'm not either. He's the only one who has ever cared about me... We're equals in this choice." Octavia said, lifting her chin slightly.

Lincoln smiled at her, proud of her. I mean it's good that they stick together. They at least have a good relationship together.

"I think it's worth a shot. If it could make you more comfortable for the rest of your pregnancy. Wouldn't that be a good thing?" Scarlett asked, turning her focus back to Lincoln.

Lincoln looked at me. Why is he looking at me? I don't want to be dragged into this.

"Tell him to leave you alone then. Duh." Reign laughed.

"Answer me this. If you were me. And Scarlett was in this situation. Would you want her to try this talisman? Would you risk this unknown object hurting your mate and your unborn children? Would you risk the only person in the entire world that was made for you?" Lincoln asked, his eyes showed his fear and worry.

I looked at Scarlett, before wrapping my arms around her and pulling her into my side. I don't like that question... I don't want to imagine her in this situation... Not after her dying because of me. I would be worried. I would be stressed out. Heck. I already am because I don't know what this will do to her.

"No. I wouldn't. But at the same time... We know some information about things. Things we can't exactly talk about fully with you. And I trust Scarlett. She wouldn't hurt Octavia nor you." I said, looking at Lincoln now. "I'll ask you a question in return. You have this option. This talisman that has the possibility to take away your mates pain. Wouldn't you take that? Wouldn't you want your mate to live a life without being in pain?"

At the end of the day. I want Scarlett to be happy and healthy. That's what matters. If she trusts the necklace. So do I.

"Can we stop talking about me like I'm not here?" Octavia asked. "I'm literally sitting right here in between you three."

Scarlett smiled, looking down at her. "Yes. Yes we can. What are your thoughts about this? I can have Carter check out the talisman before you even touch it if that makes you both feel better."

"I'm assuming that this talisman only works with people that are linked to your family?" Octavia asked, Lincoln sat on the bed beside her.

"We aren't fully sure, but from what we know. Yes. It's claimed that only the Winterfell line can use the talisman." I answered, refusing to move from Scarlett's side.

So far that's been the truth... Women in the line or connected to the line are able to use the talisman.

"So our son... Our son is linked to your child?" Octavia asked, turning her focus to Scarlett.

"I think so." Scarlett smiled, placing a hand on her stomach. "I think that's why this can work on you. Because he's linked to one of them in me..."

Lincoln shook his head. "I don't think I like this. I don't think I like this at all."

Scarlett looked down at the box in her hands, she gently opened it before taking the talisman out. "I used this earlier. I didn't get hurt or anything. It actually helped me." She explained, the crystal starting to glow in the presence of Octavia.

It's like the Talisman speaks to her. I don't really like it but it's fine.

Octavia looked intently at it, before looking at Lincoln. "What are you thinking?"

"I'm thinking that this could end badly... Or this could help you with your energy problem." Lincoln shrugged, placing his hand on Octavia's stomach. "I want you to feel amazing... To feel perfect. So if you think this will help you... Then I guess I'm okay with it."

Octavia looked at Scarlett. "You're going to be holding it the whole time?"

Scarlett nodded. "I promise I won't let it go." I placed my hand on her lower back.

I'm going to be standing right here with her in case I have to step in too.

Octavia nodded, her hand was shaking slightly as she gently placed it on top of the talisman in Scarlett's hand. Immediately, Octavia gasped. Her eyes were shining much brighter than a minute ago. Lincoln tensed, his heart hammered as he waited impatiently to see how this would turn out.

Scarlett's eyes were glowing purple as she held eye contact with Octavia. "Wow..." Octavia breathed, withdrawing her hand as a small purple and red flame danced up her arm towards her bicep.

It stopped before disappearing into her arm and returning as a mark of a purple and red paw mark. That's weird...

"Well. I didn't think that was going to happen." Scarlett said, placing the talisman back into the box.

I tilted my head as I looked at the mark. I guess our families are really connected now.

"I guess we really are going to have kids that are connected." I said, shrugging slightly.

Lincoln looked at Scarlett.

"You need to get that ceremony done. Before my son is born. I want him to be protected." Lincoln told her, causing her to nod.

"It will happen as fast as we can make it happen. Nothing will happen to your family. Because if they come for you. They will come for us." Scarlett told him with a confident nod.

FORTY-ONE

A couple days have passed... I feel like things are moving way too fast for my liking but I just have to deal with it. I had plans to meet with Grayson today... They've apparently made a lot of progress on our new house. But I want to go and see what it looks like... See if we need to change anything. I want to see it with my own two eyes.

"It's going to be crazy to see... See our house being built... The place where our children will grow up..." Reign told me.

I know... I swallowed thickly as I looked back at the house Scarlett built... Scarlett grew up here... Raised Stormy and Grayson. What if she doesn't want to leave the house? What if she's mad at me for even suggesting us to move? I just don't want to have to raise our children in a house that I was so weak in...

Yes... Yes she saved me. Yes the torture wasn't my fault. Yes I didn't have a choice. But this... I have a choice in this. I have a choice in giving Scarlett the option. I want to have everything done for her. Surprise her with this. I hate leaving her. But I know she'll be safe.

I have a feeling she'll love that she gets a day where she doesn't have to worry about anything. I tried to think of everything she could want to do or maybe eat while I'm gone. I don't plan on being gone all day... I don't even plan on being gone long. Maybe a couple of hours. But I have enough planned to give me all day if it's needed.

I walk down the path, shoving my hands in my pockets. I don't know how they did it... But we can't hear any of the construction from our house. Maybe it's just The Moon Goddess giving me some help. Maybe I'm delusional. I'm not going to question it. I'm just going to be thankful that I've kept this from her for so long.

Surprises are good. Surprises are fine. I'm just stressing out for no reason.

"You have a reason. We've never done this before. It's okay to be stressed out. We just need to keep going. And then remember not to think about it. Also don't get too stressed out Scarlett will sense it and she'll come and find us. And then surprise ruined." Reign reminded me.

Like I needed that reminder. She's not that far away from me. It would be easy for her to smell my scent and track me here. It would be more than easy since I didn't think about driving. Not that she would care if I took her car. I just don't feel right driving it without her being with me. That's her baby. I don't want to do anything to it.

I shook out my nerves. Okay. This is going to be just fine. I took a deep breath in... I couldn't help but gasp as I walked up to the field... The fencing was being put up, it was almost done. Or well... The framing was almost done. They need to do interior work... Insulation and electricity.

"So. Not almost done." Reign teased me.

Don't start with me Reign. I was just shocked it had come

through this much already. I thought there would be work done. But not this much work done.

"Hey!" Grayson waved with a bright smile on his face.

I swallowed thickly as I walked over to him. "Hey. This is... Incredible. Like I didn't think it would have this much progress... I told you like not that long ago."

"Yeah. But when it's something the Alpha wants. It gets done. We make sure it gets done." Grayson beamed.

He was obviously extremely proud of himself. I was proud too... I didn't think he'd get this moving so fast for me.

"Does everyone know that this is a surprise for Scarlett? That the request came from me?" I asked.

I couldn't help but ask. I wanted to know if they knew and were still moving this fast for me.

"I don't think that this is a good idea..." Reign winced slightly.

I don't know if it's a good idea, but it's too late. I've already asked and I'm not going to ask that he doesn't tell me now.

"Of course! I told everyone working that it's for a home for our Alphas. Something that you want to surprise Scarlett with. They want to please you as well. You guys might have not come out officially as Alphas. But everyone still respects you as an Alpha... They love how happy you make Scarlett. So of course they want the praise of the Alpha... And their Alphas mate." Grayson smiled, walking up the steps. "Of course everything isn't done... We have a lot of things ordered. I spoke with Alex... He's working with Carter at getting something crafted to have a scent that will bring peace to the house when you both walk in." He talked to me, before bringing out his tablet to pull up the blue prints to the house.

I looked over his shoulder as we started to walk through the house. We'll have a lot of rooms on the main floor of the house... Not including the basement. Although I don't know if a basement is necessary...

I think basements are stupid.

"I am not going down there. You can't make me. And if you try I'll take control because that's not happening." Reign shook his head.

I hadn't been in a basement since Scarlett found me... And I am not going to try to go into one without Scarlett. Absolutely not. That's a no for me. Heck no.

Grayson walked towards the basement entrance. He walked down a few steps and I didn't follow him. I swallowed, looking down into the darkness below... My vision started to blur. My heart started to race. I felt a weight on my chest. I took a few steps away from the basement.

I can't do it. I won't do it. Grayson looked up at me.

"Seth?" Grayson asked.

I swallowed thickly. "I... I trust that the basement is... Fine. I trust your judgment... I can't do that... I can't go down there. Scarlett can when she sees the finished project. But no. No. I... No..."

Grayson nodded. "Of course... My apologises Alpha... I didn't think about showing you..." He tried to explain.

I didn't blame him. I couldn't. Scarlett and I decided that we weren't going to tell many people about me still working through some stuff. I'm not going to talk about this with Grayson either. Absolutely not.

"It's okay. Not your fault... Let's just keep going... Keep moving... Away from the basement." I said, taking a few steps away.

Grayson followed after me. "Of course. We've started with getting the walls up... So we can move to wiring and insulation... We're wanting to get everything in the guts of the house done so we can move into decorating and everything. Are you wanting me to order stuff or how do you want to go about that?" Grayson asked.

I rolled my shoulders. "I figured that I'd send some links... Maybe draw up a general theme to what I want for the house... But for the nursery... I want to do it. I want to plan everything... I already know everything that I want for the room." I smiled.

I've been dreaming about this... Thinking about the perfect cribs... I've been so excited. I have always wanted to be a dad. I've always wanted to be extremely... Involved with my family.

"That sounds like a perfect plan... The master bedroom is over here... Has a door that leads outside so that you guys can just walk out onto the back deck... Kind of like the setup she has now... Good to shift and run out of." Grayson explained. "I thought that would be a good thing to have here."

I nodded, listening as he kept talking. The house is coming together perfectly... I think it's amazing... I'm hoping they kind of hurry up so that everything is done and I'm able to make final decisions on things.

That might be a little rude but that's why I didn't say it out loud.

"The master bedroom has a walk in closet that you requested... Same with the ginormous bathroom. But it's your house." Grayson teased slightly.

I think he's uncomfortable with me... Or maybe I look stressed from the basement. I freaking hate that thing. I don't want one in my house. I'm not going to be able to not think about it being under me. I took a deep breath.

"Is there a way we could fill in the basement?" I asked, swallowing. "I can't have a basement in my house."

Grayson paused for a second. He looked down at his tablet before looking up at me. "Yes. Of course. I'll get people on that today. We'll get it done and taken care of by the time you come out to check on progress again... You won't have to think about it again." He promised me.

I'm glad that he didn't ask me questions about why I'm

being so weird about this. I wouldn't have answered. He probably would've complained to Scarlett about me and it would've been a whole thing.

"Thank you... Thank you for also not asking me any questions about why..." I trailed off.

I really don't want to have to get into this. Not with anyone besides Scarlett.

"When are we going back to her anyway?" Reign asked me.

Soon. So freaking soon. I miss her and I want to make sure she's okay. I'm surprised she hasn't tried to come and find me... Or question me through our bond. But I'm glad she's relaxing.

"It's probably because she likes that you're putting in an effort with Grayson." Reign explained.

It took everything in me not to laugh at his remark. Of course she knew that I felt like he didn't like me. I almost flinched when I felt Grayson's hand on my shoulder

"Are you okay Seth?" Grayson asked.

He sounded genuinely worried about me. I'm not going to lie I'm a bit shocked. I shook my head.

"Of course... Sorry... I got a little lost in thought there..." I told him as I looked away

This is going to be a good new start for me... For us... For our family.

"Do you need to go back to Scarlett?" He asked softly.

It's like he was walking on eggshells. Probably a good thing because I feel like I'm one wrong step away from Reign stealing control. He doesn't like the basement. I think he probably hates it as much as I do...

I nodded, shaking my head yes. "I... Yes... Please just... Please take care of the basement thing. I thought I could handle it. But it turns out I can't. Thank you for all of your hard work today." I gave him a soft smile.

Before I walked away, I looked at him. "Before I leave. I

want it known that Scarlett isn't going to submit to me. The day of the ceremony. I know she thinks she's going to. But she's not. I'm going to submit, and she's going to take control of my pack. I won't let her lesson herself for me. She's the Alpha Female of this entire world. I'm not going to let any stupid male think that he can disrespect her all because she submitted to me publicly." I told him, he grinned at me.

"You are perfect for her... I'll make sure everything is ready for it. I won't tell her." He told me, before I turned away and walked away.

I am excited for this... I'm excited for this new start for me. I just need my mate. I need her comfort. Everything will be okay when I get back to her... I started to run home... She's close. But she'll never be close enough.

FORTY-TWO

The next week, Scarlett was in the dressing room at the dress shop. Which I feel like she wants to stay in there forever. Like she just hasn't come out. I should've just gone in there because I don't like having to wait for her to come out and show me her gown.

"Are you going to come out?" I whined, pouting slightly.

"Should just go in there." Reign rolled his eyes.

"I don't know. I think I look fat." She complained.

Fat? What does she mean fat? Nothing about her is fat. I don't know what she's even talking about. I popped the door open easily.

"What do you mean fat?" I asked. "You can't be fat." Scarlett turned around and looked at me.

She had a long purple and black strapless dress, the talisman rested against her breasts. My mouth fell open as I took her outfit in slowly. Holy Goddess... She looks...

"Wow..." Reign breathed out.

Definitely wow.

"Wow..." I said, licking my lips slightly as my eyes stopped at her stomach.

She's actually showing... This dress is actually making her show... Scarlett blushed, looking down at her stomach.

"I didn't think I was going to be showing so quickly. What are we going to do? We have to announce it after the ceremony so it will be shown all around the world." Scarlett told me, the talisman on her chest started to glow before she shivered slightly.

"What was that?" Reign asked me.

I don't know but I don't think I like it. I gave her a look.

"What was that?" I asked, my eyes dropped to the talisman as it stopped glowing slowly.

It makes me anxious... I don't want that thing messing up my children.

"I don't know, when I start getting overwhelmed. It just sends a wave of power into me and I don't know I feel so much better." She shrugged. "I don't think it's a bad thing."

"Why are you stressing out? You showing is a good thing." I frowned. "You showing means they're growing."

Means they're growing... She's able to actually function... Maybe thanks to the talisman. Like I thought all of these things would make her happy. Not stressed out. Why hasn't she told me?

"Probably because she knows you're stressing out already." Reign offered.

I will be less stressed after I show her the house.

"I know..." She trailed off, turning to look into the full length mirror. "What do you think of it?"

I wrapped my arms around her and pulled her against my front. "I think you're breathtakingly gorgeous babygirl. I've never seen anyone more beautiful." I smiled, kissing the top of her head. "I think mine will match yours. But I'm not worried about trying it on or anything. I want you to be the star of the show."

She's going to be the star of the show anyway... Everyone is going to want to see her... And I'm the one who gets to take her home at the end of the day. My chest rumbled at the thought. Everyone wants her but she's mine.

Scarlett blushed. "I think either way, both of us are going to be the star of the show. Everyone used to talk about how I wouldn't be able to get a mate. Because I'm defying the laws of nature and everything. Said it was my punishment or whatever. So everyone is going to be looking at you because they want to see if you can keep me in line." She teased with a smirk.

I chuckled, leaning against the wall as I watched her. "Oh, if someone looks at you the wrong way. It'll be the other way around." I winked.

I make no promises to be able to keep control of myself.

Scarlett rolled her eyes playfully. "Help me out of this dress please." She asked, causing me to nod and move to help her.

"We're going to need to be on the same page... We're not going to announce the kids names. We can tell them we're expecting twins, but I want to keep their names private until much closer to their birth." She explained, moving slightly so she could step out of the dress. "We claim Spain, Ireland, and Scotland as ours. So coming for Octavia and Lincoln will be like coming for us."

"What's so important about claiming them as our family?" I asked, sitting down on the chair to watch her get dressed.

They are like working for us. So claiming them as our family shouldn't be any different. They're helping us completely with everything. But then again people really are stupid.

"Because... I know Link's worries. It's extremely possible

that people are gonna figure out that our kids are going to be together. So by going after them, it'll be like someone coming after us." She shimmied into her jeans. "Does that make any sense?"

"Not really. How are they going to figure out that they're mates?" I asked, scrunching my eyebrows.

We didn't know that they were mates until Alex told us about it. And he didn't know until the Moon Goddess gave him a vision. Which let me just say is unfair. I should've been the one to have a vision about our future children.

I still have too many questions then I'm comfortable with... But I trust Scarlett. I know she wouldn't lead us in the wrong direction.

"I don't think they'll figure out that they're actually mates. But I think they'll assume that because he's my close friend, and he's been public about how he accepts me as his Alpha. I think they'll assume we're going to match them up in hopes of them being actual mates." She explained further before pulling on her t-shirt.

"It's starting to make more sense. So there's that. I'm just going to follow her lead." Reign shrugged.

I nodded. "I guess that makes more sense. I'm completely on board. I just wanted to understand it more. Thanks for telling me." I smiled, standing up and putting my arms around her.

Who am I kidding? I would've been completely on board even if she told me to shut up and follow along. She has my life. She owns me. That will never change.

"I will always explain everything to you." Scarlett smiled, kissing me on the lips.

The next moment, someone walked back into our VIP room. "Is everything going okay in here? Do you want anything changed on your dress? I'd be more than happy to help you however you need." The woman bowed her head, not wanting Scarlett to be mad at her.

"No. It's perfect, thank you for getting it done so quickly." Scarlett praised, causing the woman's cheeks to turn pink.

"And I won't need to check my suit. I trust that it'll be just perfect." I told her, before tugging Scarlett along with me.

Scarlett was confused at first, but followed me anyway. I like how she'll follow me without question even when I don't say anything at first.

"She's equally as obsessed with us." Reign growled with approval.

"It's time to get some food, and then we're going to go see Carter. Since I want to make sure that thing you refuse to take off is actually working." I told her.

She might be the Alpha. But I'll always make sure to take care of her first.

CHAPTER
FORTY-THREE

Scarlett was happy, shimming in her seat as she was eating her cheeseburger. I couldn't help but smirk at how happy she was. I can always tell how hungry she is... Even if she doesn't want to admit it.

"Someone has to get her to eat something. Eat more often than she did before. That's for sure. You know... Looking back? I don't understand how she survived. She definitely didn't eat enough to survive." Reign told me.

I mean... He had a point. She definitely needed to eat more. I'm glad she's actually doing that now. I don't know what I would do if she didn't eat enough now.

"Be more stressed out." Reign teased.

Stopppp, I get it. I need to relax. But I can't. Not right now... I'll relax later. Later when Scarlett is relaxing. Not a second beforehand.

"I didn't know you were that hungry. I would've gotten you something sooner if you would've told me." I explained, placing my free hand on her upper thigh.

Like I knew she was hungry... But she's really chowing

down on it. I feel like I should've gotten her more. Maybe I can see if Max or someone will go back and get more food for her. Scarlett reached over to grab her drink, after taking a gulp she set it back down.

"I wasn't. But then I smelt the food and it hit me. It's so so good." She smiled happily as I parked at the hospital.

I smirked. She'll never tell me no.

"She's as much of a simp for you as you are to her." Reign teased.

Wouldn't that be a good thing that we simp for each other? I'm more than okay with just being the simp of the relationship. She deserves someone to put her first.

"I know you very well baby." I winked, before getting out of the car so I could get her door.

Scarlett took one last bite of her food before she got out with me. Should I take her food in with us?

"Maybe? Maybe not. Maybe we could just have the cafeteria bring something up for her if she's that hungry?" Reign offered, tilting his head slightly.

That's a really good idea.

"It's not really hard to tell when I'm hungry. Even before I was pregnant, I was pretty much constantly hungry. So now it's like amplified." She shrugged, holding my hand as we walked into the hospital together.

"I wonder why you were hungry all the time Scarlett... Because you weren't eating enough pretty girl." Reign sighed.

It's okay. Things are different now. Better. Everything will be better here on out. I'll make sure of it. No matter what I have to do to get it done.

"I figured. From everything I've been reading lately it's completely normal. And those are studies geared towards lower ranking women. So it'll be even worse for you." I told her, proud of myself for studying up.

I've been reading a lot lately... I want to be the best dad there can be. So I'm reading and writing things down. Scarlett smiled brightly at me, we quickly got to the elevator and got on.

"I love how you're so into learning about all of this." She squeezed my hand. "I didn't think it was a bad thing, but it's still a little annoying. Are you really uncomfortable with me wearing the talisman?"

I feel like that's a double ended question. I need to be honest with her. But at the same time. It could just make her mad and I really don't want that to happen.

"Not necessarily uncomfortable. I just don't know if I trust it. It could've been cursed a while ago, things could've happened before you had it. Caitriona could've cursed it as a joke. I don't know. We don't know much about it. I just would rather be safe than sorry." I told her, wrapping my arm around her shoulder to hold her closer to me.

I'm being overly cautious... I know. But I can't lose her... I just can't. Scarlett nodded in understanding.

"I don't think Caitriona did anything to it... I think she knew the world she was leaving behind, and wanted to give the next Alpha Female a little bit of an upper hand. But that's also why the Moon Goddess gifted certain people with certain abilities." She tried to calm me down.

I rolled my eyes playfully. She really wants to look at everything in the most positive way possible huh.

"If she was as amazing as you. She would have." I led her to the VIP room where Carter was already waiting for us.

I'm not going to lie. I'm a bit shocked. I thought we were going to have to wait for her.

"Don't say it out loud." Reign snorted. *"She doesn't need to hear it."*

CHAPTER
FORTY-FOUR

"Well there's my two favorite people!" Carter smiled.

I gave her a nod, before looking around the room for Alex. She's such a suck up.

"Pretty sure that's everyone in the pack. They want to suck up to the Alphas to make them like them more." Reign shrugged.

You my sir, have a good point there. Doesn't mean that I have to like it.

"Where's Alex?" Scarlett asked, since they were typically always together.

Carter couldn't help but roll her eyes. Oh... I think I know what that means. He's doing something for the house and she doesn't want to say?

"Oh I'm sure he's off somewhere helping Max. I know they wanted to get somethings done before your ceremony tomorrow. I think he's worried something bad is going to happen. He wants it to be perfect for the both of you." Carter explained, moving so Scarlett could sit on the bed. "Is something going on that made you want to come in today?"

"No." I answered for Scarlett. "She's just obsessed with that talisman and I just want to make sure that she's okay."

Oh... I should probably stop doing that. Considering we're in public... And I don't want anyone thinking I'm trying to control the Alpha.

"That wouldn't be good... So close to the ceremony and everything." Reign agreed.

Scarlett smirked at me. "This sounds like you're jealous of the talisman baby. Is that true?" She teased.

I growled, bending down to kiss her lips. I really wish I could spank her for that one.

"There's always later." Reign growled.

"I'm jealous of no one." I looked directly in her eyes. "You are mine. And that's that. I'm not worried that the thing is going to do anything to our relationship. I just want to make sure it's not doing anything to the kids."

I know where I stand with my woman. I am hers. She is mine. No one is going to take her away from me. I won't let them. Not even death will keep her from me.

Scarlett's cheeks turned pink as she stared at me. "Oh Goddess." She said, covering her face with her hands.

I smirked, crossing my arms as I stood beside where Scarlett was sitting. I love it when I fluster her... I can't help myself. I'll keep at it though. It's just Carter. She's not going to tell anyone but Alex.

"And that's how you fluster an Alpha." I chuckled. "Do you want to hold the talisman again? Or?"

"Oh. Yeah." Carter said, laughing uncomfortably. "I'll hold the talisman if you don't mind Alpha Scarlett?" Scarlett nodded, taking the necklace off that held the talisman.

I wonder why she's addicted to it. Well... Maybe not addicted. But obsessed with it.

"I don't wear it all the time." She said, before I growled at her in warning. "Okay I guess I wear it all the time." She explained, before handing the talisman to Carter.

Carter turned to look at me. She knows I'll tell her the truth. All of the truth since Scarlett won't.

"All the time. Even when she showers." I corrected. "I tried to take it off of her so she doesn't choke in her sleep. But she woke up and put it right back on."

That totally freaked me out. She sometimes moves a lot in her sleep and I don't want her to ya know die.

"That's right, because the only thing I am allowed to choke on is you right?" Scarlett asked with a wink.

My grin widened. She's got that one right.

"I'm so proud of her for not being afraid to say that in front of Carter." Reign growled softly.

"You got that right babygirl." I couldn't help but chuckle at Carter's uncomfortable expression. "You're just going to have to get used to this."

We could be making both her and Alex uncomfortable with our comments. Too bad he's not here.

"He's just out there helping get the house completed." Reign said.

Exactly.

"I know... I just feel a little weird being around you guys without Alex." She told, before closing her eyes as she put her other hand on top of the talisman.

Her hands started to glow softly. That still is weird to me.

Scarlett looked at me. "I don't think that it's necessarily a bad thing that I like having it near me." She huffed.

I sat down beside her on the bed, placing my hand on her thigh. I never said it was a bad thing. I just want for her to make sure she's safe.

"No. It's not a bad thing. But if you don't need it, then you don't need it." I explained with a shrug.

I have a feeling that she doesn't need it. But I'm not going to tell her that. That's for sure. I don't need her to be mad at me for anything. I don't think I would survive if she was mad at me.

"I'm not going to be wearing it at the ceremony... I don't want anyone thinking that my power comes from that instead of myself." Scarlett was sure about her decision. "I would kill someone."

"And that's my job, while people are here. While you're pregnant. I get to take care of all of the difficult things. You don't need to be stressing out." I explained, turning my focus to Carter when she opened her eyes.

I finally get to show the world how I'm not afraid to kill someone for the Ruthless Queen.

"So?" Scarlett asked, impatient for her answer.

Carter smiled, handing the talisman to me to hold on to. "Everything feels fine with the talisman. Or... Well I should say everything feels like the first time I felt it. But I'd like to feel you now too... Just to make sure everything is going good with the twins." She explained, holding out her hand to Scarlett.

Scarlett was hesitant but placed her palm in Carters. I held my breath as I waited impatiently for Carter to be done with her exam. I feel like these take so long...

And each and every single time I feel like my heart is going to beat right out of my chest. I just need to keep telling myself that I can't kill her if she tries to say something is wrong with my mate. She's technically my sister... She's my brothers mate.

I can't kill her.

I shouldn't even yell at her. But here I am... Contemplating yelling at her if she doesn't hurry up and tell me that my mate is going to be fine. That my children are growing and they're healthy.

After a few minutes, Carter opened her eyes. But I was the

first one to speak. "Now it's my turn! What's happening? Is everything okay?"

Carter nodded. "Excellent actually. Everything seems to be progressing quicker than what we're used to. But that was to be expected since you both are Alphas and will give the kids more power than a typical couple." She grabbed her tablet to start writing down notes. "I do think you'll start to be showing more within the next week or so. I'm honestly surprised that you're not showing more."

It could just be that because of her Shadow wolf abilities... Xena is using her power to hide the pregnancy to keep her safe longer.

"I've been eating, a lot actually. Before Seth starts to say that I haven't been." Scarlett teased, bumping my shoulder gently to try and pull me out of my anxious thoughts.

I forced an uneasy smile. She's been eating better. I can admit that.

"Oh I believe it, it's a good thing to eat a lot during your pregnancy. But I'll have to look it up to be sure. But certain shadow wolf do tend to hide their pregnancies. I'm happy to send you some articles, or maybe my father has some books you can borrow." She offered without looking up from her tablet.

See. That's what I said. I'm learning... I'm actually learning a lot about Shadow wolves. It's interesting.

Scarlett scrunched her nose. "Sure. That's sounds great." Carter's head popped up.

"If you need anything else please don't hesitate to ask!" She said before rushing off.

Scarlett gave me a look, but I just shrugged. She doesn't have to tell me that this was a waste of time. I know. But it makes me feel better wasting Carters time to make sure she's okay.

"I know it's a waste of time okay? But it makes me feel better knowing that someone confirmed that you're doing okay." I explained, my cheeks turning pink. "But, I love how you're not afraid to make some dirty comments in front of anyone."

"I will happily do it, in front of anyone and everyone. Everyone will know that you're mine." She promised, leaning her head against my shoulder.

I won't rest until everyone knows that she's mine.

"Everyone will know that you are mine as well." I repeated. "You are everything to me." I kissed the top of her head. "Are you wanting to head home? Since we have to get up early for the ceremony tomorrow?"

Scarlett nodded, moving so she was straddling my waist. "I think that sounds like a perfect idea. Because I'm sure I smell pregnant, and I'd rather tell everyone tomorrow after the ceremony."

I gave her one nod before getting up and heading back to our house.

CHAPTER
FORTY-FIVE

The next day, Scarlett looked at the dress sitting in our bedroom. I was in the bathroom, I thought a shower would help lessen my nerves... Today is the day that she finds out that I'm going to submit to her in front of everyone.

"All of this is for you two... You hear me in there?" Scarlett asked, no doubt looking down at her stomach. "We're building this for you... So you're safer. No one will come for you knowing you're my children."

I wonder what she's doing in there. I opened the bathroom door, leaning against the doorframe. My arms were crossed over my bare chest. She is considering wearing the talisman?

"I thought that she wanted to leave it here so no one tried to steal it?" Reign asked me.

I... Don't really know. I thought so.

"You know you can wear it if you think you need it?" I offered, just watching her for a moment before heading to where she was standing in front of the mirror.

Holy Goddess I love her belly. I love how she's showing... Everyone is going to see it and I can't wait.

"I don't think I need it, but I don't know. I feel just fine, like everything is going to where it's supposed to be finally. But it feels like one of them is calling for it. I don't understand it." She tried to tell me what she was thinking. "It feels better having it on. But I don't think I need it."

It's because she doesn't need it.

"Don't you dare tell her that." Reign growled at me.

I'm not stupid. That would just be giving her unnecessary stress.

I wrapped my arms gently around her stomach, placing my palm straight on her stomach. "Carter says everything is going good with them. Do you have a feeling that says otherwise?"

"No... Nothing like that. I think they find comfort in the extra power..." Scarlett shrugged. "They feel healthy to me. They feel safe. Like everything is going to be just fine. But maybe after today they'll feel better since we'll be officially adding another pack to our power?"

It'll give them more power... It'll secure their position in this world. I think that'll help, but I don't know if I'm being honest.

I rubbed my thumb over her belly, before turning her in my arms. "I don't know. But I trust you... I trust you completely. If you think you don't need it, then you don't need it. You're the most powerful person in the entire world. Are you sure you're okay with this happening so fast?"

I don't want her to be doing this just for me... I'm okay with waiting. I'm more than okay with postponing this. I don't need their acceptance. All I need is her.

"I want everyone to know you're mine... We're equals. Things might change a little... But you are what matters to me. Not what other people think of me. I'm happy to get this done and over with honestly. I don't need the acceptance of the world, but I know by doing this. It'll help the world know they have to respect you, or I might just kill them." She teased, winking playfully at me.

I frowned slightly. That just makes me feel like she's doing it just for me and that's exactly what I don't want.

"Are you doing this just for me?" I asked. "Because we can cancel this. You don't have to do this for me. I'm happy with us. I don't need their acceptance either. I just need you."

She is all I need in this world. She and our children. This family is all I need.

Scarlett shook her head slightly. "No. I'm not just doing this for you. I'm doing this for Lincoln and Octavia. I'm doing this for our packs to recognize us as their Alpha. I'm doing this for our children. I'm... I'm doing this to show the world that everything they said about me was wrong. That I am here with my mate. That I am getting the happy ending that I deserve." She sniffled, wiping at her cheeks. "I want to show them that every single thing they said about me was wrong. That I'm getting everything I've always wanted and so much more."

That breaks my heart... But I'm so incredibly thankful for this woman. I don't know what I did to deserve her. But I will thank the Moon Goddess that she gave me this blessing. I won't let her regret for even a minute that she is my mate.

I smiled, bringing my hands to her cheeks and wiping her tears. "You my love... My mate. My Female. The mother of my children. You are the sun to my day. You are the Moon to my stars. You are everything to me. This is what we deserve. This is what we need. The world will see that The Knights and our friends are not to be messed with. Our children will come into this world and show them what true power is like." I kissed the top of her head, before leaning my head against hers.

My eyes locked with hers. I want her to know that I'm telling her the complete truth. I'm not lying to her. I would never lie to her.

"We will show them that we're better than them. I promise you I won't let any of them hurt you. I won't let any of them disrespect you. I'm here to protect you, mind, body, and soul. I'm yours for the rest of time. In this life and whatever comes after."

Scarlett's bottom lip trembled as her eyes watered again. "Seth." She sniffled. "I'm trying not to cry." She complained, wrapping her arms tightly around me and shoving her face in my chest.

I chuckled, wrapping my arms around her again and holding her tightly. Happy tears are good tears. I don't want her to ever cry sad tears.

"I love you more than the air inside of my lungs. I need you to know how much I love you. How much I appreciate everything you're giving me and have already gifted me." I told her, needing her to know how much I loved her. "I need you to realize what you mean to me. That yes to the world you are the Ruthless Queen. But to me you are my world."

She is the only thing that matters to me. The only thing. That world is only going to grow when our children come into the picture.

Scarlett cried into my chest, listening to me love on her. I gently rubbed her back, letting her cry as I held her. I picked her up, wrapping her legs around my waist before sitting on our bed. I didn't speak, I was just sitting in her space.

I knew that sometimes this was all she needed... She just needed me to sit with her and let her feel her feelings outwardly so she didn't have to hold in it like everything else. I'm more than happy to sit with her, let her know that she's safe with me.

Once Scarlett was done crying, she leaned away from me and looked at my face. "Seth... You. I don't even know how to explain to you how much you mean to me. Everything you've done for me. Everything you've given to me... I don't know how I got so lucky." She sniffled, wiping at her cheeks again.

I smiled, leaning forward to lick away a straw tear.

"Her tears taste delicious." Reign groaned.

I don't need to think about this right now.

"You are my other half. The better part of my soul." We said to each other at the same time.

"You are what I dreamed of for years. I know sometimes you doubt that... That I would want someone with less power so that I could be the stronger one. But no babygirl. I want you. I've always wanted you. I like that you're the Alpha. Because yes you act like the Alpha, but at the same time you still treat me like one." I smiled, running my hand through her hair gently.

"Because for... For years. I've had to be the strongest one. For years, everyone needed something from me. They needed me to do something for them. They didn't care about me as a person, but me as their alpha. Or to me it just felt like that. Then I found you... And you let me show you the weaker parts of myself and you didn't judge me. You've held me while I cried. You've saved my life. You've done more for me than anyone else in my life. You are my life." She told me, getting out of my hold and standing in front of where I was sitting.

What is she doing?

I tilted my head, confused at what she was doing. "What are you doing baby?" I asked, watching as she dropped to her knees.

"I don't want you thinking that I'm submitting to you in front of everyone because I want to please anyone else. You are the one I want to please." She promised, bowing her head and tilting her head to the side so I could see her mark.

I couldn't help myself, my chest rumbled in approval at the submissive position.

"This is the hottest thing I've ever seen." Reign groaned.

"In front of no one... I submit myself to you Alpha Seth Knight, Heir to The Bloody Rose Pack. I give you my power. I give you my love. I give you my soul. I am yours. My body is yours. I am yours to use, to need, to want. I submit myself to you, showing you I respect your power." She told me, her eyes glowing purple as she looked up at me.

I watched her intently, I couldn't tear my eyes away even if someone tried to get me to move. I don't deserve this women... I don't deserve her submitting to me without a reason.

"Scarlett..." I swallowed thickly, I got to my knees in front of where she was. "Babygirl..." I couldn't form a sentence, the air around us showed how much I loved her, my respect, my need.

I want her to know how much I need her... How much I love her. But I don't know how to put it into words. Our bond showed her every emotion I was feeling. Scarlett brought her hands up to my cheeks and smiled at me. Her eyes still glowing, causing mine to glow in return.

"You are my mate. My Alpha. The better half of me." She promised. "I would submit to you in front of everyone. In front of no one. I would do it everyday if that's what you needed. I just needed you to know that I was doing this for you. No one else."

I whimpered softly, before placing my forehead against hers again. "You are the reason I wake up in the morning." I promised. "You are the reason I'm still alive today. You are the only reason I made it through everything to get to his point. With you."

She is my life. There's no other way of putting it.

Scarlett closed her eyes as our power mingled through our bond. "You are the only reason why I didn't give up years ago..." Her voice cracked. "I hated myself... I hated being alone.

I hated not knowing if I was ever going to find my mate. I hated waking up in the morning..."

I couldn't stop myself, I wrapped my arms around her tightly and laid her down on the floor. I looked at her before smiling. "I promise you, you'll never be alone again. I will make sure you love waking up every morning. I will show you every single day that you deserve this. That *we* deserve this. You are the best parts of me."

We've both been through a lot... A heck of a lot. We both deserve this. More than deserve it. We've listened. We've obeyed. We've done our share of things. It's time for us to get our happily ever after.

Scarlett smiled brightly up at me, the normally brown eyes had purple and red flames dancing around in the irises. "And I promise to do the same for you. Every single day."

That's new... That's really pretty though. I like that.

"That's never happened before has it?" Reign asked.

Not that I can remember. But it's still super pretty.

I was transfixed by her eyes, I kept staring at them. "Your eyes are really pretty." Scarlett snorted.

"Thanks?" She said, unsure of what I meant. "Your eyes are really pretty too." She told me.

FORTY-SIX

I reluctantly got up, pulling her to her feet as well. "Aren't my eyes always pretty?" I asked, before we moved to our connected bathroom to look in the mirror.

I want to see what she's talking about. I also want her to see what I'm talking about. So it's a win win situation. I just don't know if this eye thing is a good or bad thing.

"I mean yes... But today your eyes have purple and red in them. Like flames are dancing around in them." She tried to explain as she hopped up onto the counter to better look in the mirror.

I smirked, my eyes were on the curve of her butt. I love that butt... One of my top favorite things about her. I kind of want to bite it.

"DO IT! That sounds amazing!" Reign howled.

I couldn't stop myself, I smacked her butt causing her to gasp. She looked back at me, her hair moving back of her shoulder. "It's just so perfectly smackable." My voice was a rumble as I squeezed it causing her to moan.

Smackable. Biteable. Rubbable. I literally could keep going

on for hours about this. I'll never be able to not be obsessed with this woman. Scarlett's eyes rolled into the back of her head.

"I love you but focus!" She said, moving back to look in the mirror. "My eyes are doing what your eyes are doing."

I nodded, moving to look in the mirror right beside her. I like how they're matching... They're really beautiful. The colors are so bright. It's almost like Reign and Xena are dancing together.

"It looks like our eyes are still doing that." I said, before shrugging.

I placed my hands in her pants, wanting to feel her butt in my hands. Scarlett giggled, leaning back into me. Her skin was warm... Smooth... Soft against my palm.

"I never knew you were so obsessed with my butt." She teased me, her eyes sparkling. "What do you think is going on with our eyes?"

I massaged her butt, causing her to groan in relaxation. It could be our wolves are happy? Could be because we're getting a new pack that we're feeling stronger? Who knows? I most certain don't.

I didn't stop my hands. "I don't know. Probably our wolves are happy that we are finally officially announcing us being mates. You know how old fashioned they can be." I seemed unfazed.

We could just leave it be... She's feeling great. The twins heart beats are strong. Her heartbeat is strong as well. I don't think we need to go see Carter unless she starts feeling bad?

"But wouldn't that make our eyes just... Our colors? I've never seen them be both of our colors before." She tried to figure it out.

I smiled, kissing the top of her head. I feel great too... Better than I have in a very long time.

"If we're both feeling fine... Should we really worry about it? What if we're having one girl and one boy? Each one could have our colors?" I offered, wanting to help calm her down.

I helped her off of the counter, letting her stand on her feet now. We should probably start getting ready so we aren't late to the ceremony.

"That would be kind of funny." Reign snorted.

"Each one could have their own colors." She countered.

"I think you're thinking too much into this." I laughed slightly, before running a hand through my hair. "Did you want me to shave before heading to the ceremony?"

She never said anything about me shaving before... So I thought I would ask before the ceremony so I could do it quickly while she's getting ready. Scarlett reached up, rubbing a hand gently down the scruff I had growing.

"No. I like this look on you." She smiled, leaning up to kiss my lips. "I also think you're not thinking enough into this."

I laughed harder now. "I just know we have other things to worry about. The one thing we have to worry about today is this whole ceremony thing. The whole world is going to be watching. The whole world is going to find out that you're finally taken. Goddess that's going to be so hot." I told her, gripping her hips again and pulling her against me.

I don't want to stress out today if I don't have to. I want this day to be about us... To be about our relationship. Not the drama. Not the bad days. I want this to be a good day.

"I don't know if I like how positive you're being. It's kind of weird.' Reign gave me a weird look.

"I love that everyone will be able to see that you're mine." She purred, her chest rumbling with a gentle growl.

She couldn't help herself, she rubbed her face against my chest. I'll be able to smell extra like her.

I chuckled, wrapping my arms around her. "I will tell

everyone that you are my mate without hesitation. I'm not going to leave your side the entire time. I don't know everyone coming, and I don't want you to be unprotected."

I'm not going to be away from her at all. I don't trust anyone. I don't want something bad to happen to her. To her or the twins.

"I'm pretty sure Max will have double the guards on us. But I don't think anyone is going to try anything with us today... We're combining three packs into one. Into one pack with one pair of Alphas. This is going to be big for our future." She smiled up at me, before reluctantly turning away so that she could go get dressed.

I smiled, following after her immediately. It takes me less time to get ready so I can just sit and watch the perfect how.

"I'm still not going to leave you. Better safe than sorry! I won't let anything happen to my mate or my heirs." I explained, walking into our closet with her and sitting on the floor by where she was getting dressed.

Scarlett smirked at me.

"I like how literal you're being." She teased softly. "I'll need your help with this stupid bra anyway."

"I know. My hands are way better to hold your boobs." I grinned, laying back on the floor.

This is the perfect view for everything I want to watch. Scarlett laughed, shaking her head slightly.

"Gotta stay focused baby. We can't be late. It's coronation day."

CHAPTER
FORTY-SEVEN

Scarlett couldn't help but fidget as she looked out of the passenger window. She feels on edge... I don't like it. I rolled my shoulders, instead of riding in Scarlett's Bugatti. We decided to opt for our large SUV instead. I reached over, placing my hand gently on her thigh.

It feels a little strange being in something this big. But I'm going to get used to it just fine. Because soon... We're going to have two little ones back there. It won't feel so big.

"You're gorgeous... You look absolutely beautiful in that dress." I complimented. "I love the little way you're showing already. Are you nervous about the coronation?"

I can't wait for her to show more.

"No... Yes. Kind of I guess. I'm also slightly uncomfortable in this, we probably need to start driving it more often." She shrugged. "I just can't wait for this to be done... To finally be accepted by the world."

"I agree with you baby." I agreed, turning into the pack-house parking lot.

Holy crap.

"Holy crap... That's a lot of people." Reign cringed. *"It would've been worse if it was planned months in advance..."*

He was right... This turnout is insane. It was filled, cars parked in every spot, and cars were beginning to fill the grass surrounding the lot.

Scarlett breathed out. "I haven't seen this place packed this much... In so long. The last time Silver was here was when it filled up like this." She said her foot was bouncing against the floor quickly.

She's anxious... I need to get her to calm down.

"Everyone wants to see you and we want the world to know that we are one... No one has ever ruled over two packs... And now we're going to be the first ones doing it. It's going to be great babygirl. Alpha Scarlett Knight will go down in the history books." I praised my emotions flowing through our bond.

Scarlett giggled at my excitement, before she covered her mouth. Her cheeks burned red at the sound that came out of her mouth. I love it when I get to make her giggle. It's like music to my ears.

"Okay we need to calm down." She laughed as I pulled up in front of the packhouse and put the car in park.

I smirked, turning the car off. I can't promise anything... My emotions feel so heightened right now.

"I will try my best. But I make no promises." I teased, before getting out of the SUV.

I was dressed in a three piece suit, the color matching to Scarlett's dress perfectly. I walked around to her side and opened the door for her. I feel like I do look pretty great.

"I can't giggle in front of everyone. They'll think less of me." She told me, taking my hand and getting out of the car.

Immediately lights started flashing, cameras taking a thousand pictures as people crowded around to see the Alphas arrive on our special day. A day that will go down in the history books...

Mr. and Mrs. Alpha Scarlett Knight.

My back straightened as I felt all of the eyes turn to us. "No one will think less of you on my watch. I exist to stand behind you, and show the world who the true Alpha is." I promised, placing a hand on her lower back.

I want the world to know who deserves this. She's fought everyday for this. Scarlett smiled as we posed for a few pictures.

"Are you excited Mr. and Mrs. Winters! It's your crowning ceremony!" A girl called out, I smiled down at Scarlett.

I wasn't going to say anything. She's just a kid. It doesn't really matter anyway.

"Yes. We're absolutely excited to officially show the world that we are Alpha Scarlett Knight and Alpha Seth Knight. The first alpha and alpha couple." Scarlett corrected, knowing that I wasn't going to say anything about it.

My chest swelled with pride as Scarlett started to lead our way to the Pack house, knowing our ceremony would take place behind the building in the woods. I do not deserve this woman. I know I keep saying that. But I really don't deserve her at all.

Alphas bowed their heads in respect to us as we passed by. Scarlett smiled, her cheeks warming.

'Is everything okay?' I asked through our mind link.

'I'm okay... I'm great honestly. I... I just didn't think that this would ever happen for me... For us. It's heartwarming.' Scarlett explained, we walked slowly through the hallways.

I love hearing her voice in my head... That way we can still talk without everyone knowing what we're talking about. Alphas and their Lunas were mingling with each other.

"Alpha Scarlett and the mysterious Alpha Knight. It's great

to finally meet you!" A male said, smiling kindly. "Willow! My Queen, come over here. I want you to meet Scarlett and her mate!"

A smaller woman with curly blonde hair came up to him quickly. He smiled, bending down to plant a kiss on her lips.

I knew this was going to happen. But I thought we would have more time than this.

"Alpha Abel King." Scarlett turned her head to look at me. I nodded once in thanks. "I'm so glad that you could make it. I wasn't sure with the short notice and everything."

"Nonsense! We would make time for you anyday. I see that you're expecting? Congratulations!" Abel grinned, excitedly. "Have you set up matches for your children yet? If not. I would love for our families to get intertwined."

I already want to murder someone and it hasn't even been five minutes. This is going to be an absolutely amazing ceremony.

I growled unhappily. "We don't believe in forcing matches upon our children. So thanks but no thanks Alpha Abel."

"Honey. I told you not everyone believes like you do." Willow said, placing a hand on her chest. "It's their special day. Don't bother them about this. Congratulations on your special day and your announcement. We're going to go mingle about so my mate doesn't try and bother you anymore!" Willow began pulling Abel away from us.

"*Good. Because I might've ripped his throat out if he didn't shut his yap.*" Reign growled.

"Sorry Alphas! I didn't mean any disrespect!" Abel chuckled at his mates antics. "Don't hate me!"

I rolled my eyes. Scarlett laughed, heading over to where the drinks were. "Don't think too much about it. I'm sure a lot of other Alphas are going to ask us about that before this whole thing is over. But like you said. Our children will get to meet their mates, we're not forcing anything on them."

Our children deserve their mates. Their mates and not some arranged marriage.

I moved to pour some water into a cup for her. "I didn't realize everyone was going to be here." I handed her the cup, letting her take a sip from it.

It was such short notice... On top of them also building and decorating a house... This is truly insane.

"Max and Alex did an amazing job at planning all of this... And getting everyone here in time to witness it." She said, leading me towards where the doors were open to the seating outside.

Scarlett nearly spit out her drink when she saw how many cameras were set up. I rubbed her back, taking her cup away from her. There's a lot of cameras but I should know by now that when we ask Alex and Max to do something... They go above and beyond.

"You told them to set up for a live stream." I recalled, causing her to groan.

"I know... But I wasn't expecting all of this. I mean I was, but I didn't prepare myself for it." She shrugged, smiling and waving to different people. "When is this whole thing supposed to start?"

"We're the Alphas here. I'm sure it's your call." I smirked, causing Scarlett to laugh.

Sooner rather than later I hope.

"I'm sure it's our call. Since you know we're the Alphas here." She taunted.

I chuckled, shaking my head. Max and Alex walked up next. She's the top Alpha though. She gets to call the shots.

"You both look amazing! The designer did such an amazing job! Do you like it? I... I drew it myself. I wasn't sure if they were going to be able to get it perfectly. But they did." Max beamed with pride, he was dressed in a simple black tux.

Scarlett laughed, hugging Max tightly. He's so insanely talented.

"I love it. It's beautiful. Thank you for thinking about my bump too." She smiled, kissing the top of my head. "You think of absolutely everything. I don't know what I would do without you."

Alex smiled, hugging me before taking his turn to hug Scarlett. "He is amazing at his job. I can't keep up with him."

I don't think anyone could keep up with him.

"You make this so much easier on us Max... Thank you." I praised causing Max's grin to widen. "We would be lost without you."

"Did Stormy and Grayson decide to come as well?" Scarlett asked, worry lacing her voice.

Does she really think that her siblings wouldn't come to support her?

"Yes of course. I made sure they were coming. Grayson should be here somewhere, and I believe Stormy is on her way. Give me just a minute and I'll have someone get in contact with her!" Max said, hurrying off to make sure everything was perfect.

Scarlett smiled, her dimples showing.

"I don't know what I would do without him." Scarlett turned to look at Alex. "You could step up your game." I started laughing at Alex's shocked expression.

He's so dramatic. I love it.

"Ouch. You've gotten mean in your pregnancy." Alex pouted, before smirking. "I've been helping Carter with researching about your special breeds."

I laughed. "We appreciate you too. What have you learned about our breeds?" I asked.

I actually don't know if this is a good idea to talk about this here. We don't want any news getting out. Alex looked around, before shaking his head.

"Nothing that I would want anyone else to hear." Alex explained, causing both Scarlett and I to shake our heads.

"Okay." I said, before squeezing Scarlett's shoulder gently.

We prefer our secrets.

"We don't need anything getting into the wrong hands." Scarlett said, causing Alex to nod.

"We'll get things started when Stormy arrives." I told, looking around at the groups around us. "Get the guard around Scarlett doubled." Alex nodded, before walking off quickly.

"Do you think something bad is going to happen?" Scarlett asked, turning around to face me better.

I don't know... I hope not. But I just would rather be safe than sorry.

"I don't know... But I just don't trust people." I explained, wrapping my arms around her waist to pull her closer to me.

FORTY-EIGHT

Alex looked to a guard who was standing behind Scarlett and I. I called it. Something bad always has to happen. Scarlett turned around, watching as wolves started to crowd around the entrance.

"Who's here?" Scarlett asked, tilting her head slightly.

"What are you doing here Elf!" A wolf growled.

"You don't belong here!"

"I can't believe Alpha Winters even lets this trash live on her territory."

"I hear that he's mated to her sister! That's gotta mess with their bloodline. Their ancestors must be mad."

"Where Kingston goes... So many issues follow right on after him." Reign sighed, laying in the back of my mind knowing I had this one under control.

A million other things were being shouted. But one voice rang above them all.

"If you even touch my mate. I'll behead you before you can even try to stop me." Kingston's deep voice came above everyone else's.

My body stiffened, I looked at the guards before looking down at Scarlett. If he's itching for a fight. My mate isn't going anywhere near him.

"We do this together. Don't you dare try and leave me behind." Scarlett warned, causing me to smirk.

She knows me so well. I wouldn't have it any other way.

"I lived ten years without you in my life. I can't imagine spending even a moment apart from you." I winked, keeping my arm around her waist as we walked to where the crowd was forming.

Everyone of course wants to see a fight. But they're going to get to see something even better. Scarlett commanding someone.

"Alpha coming through!" The guards shouted, forming a protective barrier around us.

My cheeks turned red as Scarlett poked my side. I flinched slightly, it didn't hurt. It just tickled.

"What seems to be the issue here?" Scarlett asked.

When everyone heard her voice, they all stopped talking. At least I won't have to yell at anyone... Yet.

"This elf is trying to intrude on a wolfs ceremony. An Alpha ceremony." A wolf growled. "We don't want trash like this here."

"If you call my mate trash one more time. I'll show you just how much I respect your position. Alpha." Stormy growled, her eyes shining a bright blue.

Kingston placed his hand on her lower back, is he going to pull her back if she starts a fight? I guess I underestimated how short tempered Stormy was.

"We don't want trash li-..." The wolf continued, before Scarlett's powerful growl shut him up.

"I would advise for you to think before you finish that sentence Alpha. Your small pack from Lungtington is no match for my three packs. You are disrespecting the ruling Alphas sister and her mate right now. That's grounds for me to do whatever I want to you." Scarlett growled, baring her fangs at him. "Do you want to go down in history as the fourth pack I took control over? Because it's looking tempting to me."

The male's face paled. "I-it wouldn't be an awful way to die."

"Did he really just say that?" Reign asked.

Yes. Yes he did. At least he was telling the truth. He'd die adding into Scarlett's great legacy.

I chuckled, placing a hand on the males shoulder and squeezing painfully. "Just take the que, and shut your mouth." I ordered, my eyes glowing a beautiful mix of purple and red.

He doesn't need to keep this going. It's rather boring if you ask me.

"But this isn't right!" Another one spoke up. Scarlett's eyes started to change colors, instead of the beautiful brown.

They slowly changed into a beautiful mix of purple and red to match Seth's. I love how our eyes match. I wonder if it would stay like that. I wouldn't be complaining.

"Your Alpha spoke!" I snapped. "Don't push your limits."

Because if they pushed limits. I was going to be able to take control of the conversation. I'd have to kill someone.

Scarlett saw a nearby table and went to go and climb on top of it. In her heels, it was a little more difficult but she managed to do it. She ran her palms over her dress to flatten it out. She's so independent. It's so hot.

I was standing right beside the table, my hand crept up her dress to be able to hold onto her leg. I needed to feel her skin against mine... It kept me calm and in control.

When the voices continued to rise, Scarlett growled loud. Her growl echoed through the air around us, her power soaked through the air. Immediately every person present started to drop to their knees to show their submission to the most powerful Alpha. She was shaking, her claws growing.

I hope Xena behaves herself and let's Scarlett have her moment. I don't want to have to step in in front of everyone. But I would if I needed to... I won't let her shift. I immediately sent my power into her body to calm her down.

"Let the Alpha have her moment to shine." Reign grinned.

He was excited. I'm excited.

"I'm about tired of Alphas walking onto my territory and thinking they can just do whatever they want!" Scarlett yelled. "Let's get this out of the way first. I invited you because I wanted you to witness me becoming what everyone didn't think I was able to. I wanted you all to witness Alpha Scarlett Knight becoming alpha to another pack. Something you all said would never happen.

I've shown you all mercy. Kindness. Respect. But do not test me! My sister and her mate are off limits. You come at them. That means you're coming for the Alpha's family. Same goes for Alpha Lincoln Woods, Luna Octavia Woods, and their children. If you come at them, you are coming for the strength and power of Scarlett Knight." She barked, looking around the entire group, wanting to make sure that no one was trying to disrespect her.

I squeezed her leg gently, wanting to show that I was proud of her. But I didn't want to distract her so that was going to have to do. I would've happily jumped in to fight someone if they tried to disrespect her.

"But it's disrespectful." A little girl called out.

Scarlett smiled as her eyes dropped down to the child. I can't wait to see her be a mom. She's so good with kids.

"Shh baby. She's talking!" The mother said quickly.

"No. She's okay. She needs to learn. You see. My whole life people have told me I'm disrespectful. A disgrace. They have spat on my name and cursed me for changing history. Nothing is disrespectful when you are creating a legacy. When you are creating new rules. A new place. A new way of life. Nothing is disrespectful when in this world. Just being a woman in power, you are called disrespectful." She explained, holding her hand out so that I could help her down.

I reached up, grabbing her by her waist and lifting her off of the table. "This world needs more women like you." I told her, pressing a gentle kiss to her forehead.

I wasn't lying... It would be a much better place if there were more people like her. Scarlett smiled, walking over to where the child was still standing. She squatted down in front of her with a gentle smile.

"You see... The world needs more women showing that things need to change. That things will be better with us being in charge." Scarlett brushed a piece of her hair behind her ear. "I hope you'll watch and take notes." She winked before standing up, and looking at all the people on their knees, bowing their heads to her in submission.

I wrapped my arm around Scarlett again, leaning my head down to rest on top of hers. "Are you ready to show the world who deserves to go down in the history books?"

I'm more than ready to witness this amazing moment.

Scarlett's smile widened. "You may rise everyone! Let's get this ceremony started. We have a lot to discuss." Scarlett commanded.

With her command, everyone started to stand up one by one. They moved to the seating area.

"Are you ready for this?" I asked, looking down at her face.

Scarlett nodded.

"I'm ready for our legacy to combine. For the world to know that The Knight family will not be messed with." Scarlett told me, before leaning up to kiss meon the lips.

CHAPTER
FORTY-NINE

This is going to be good. She doesn't know what's coming. Not with me submitting to her. Not with the new house. I can't believe this is coming all together.

"This is going to shock her. I'm so happy she didn't figure it out." Reign smiled, prancing around in the back of my mind.

I'm just glad I don't have to stress out about her finding out about the secrets anymore. I hated having to keep them from her. It made me feel like a bad mate.

Me and Scarlett intertwined our hands together, as we walked down the aisle towards the where Grayson was standing. I nodded my head once, before looking down at Scarlett. Grayson and I have been on the same page for a while. So I'm not worried about him forgetting.

"I have many surprises for you babygirl." I told her through our bond.

It feels so intimate talking to her like this. Scarlett blushed as we stopped in front of where Grayson was standing. Scarlett swallowed thickly as she squeezed my hands.

"I don't deserve you." She replied to me through our mindlink.

She deserves me... She deserves everything she wants in life and so much more than that.

"Alphas... Lunas... Ladies and Gentlemen! Wow. Let me start this off by saying. My sister hasn't stopped for even a day since we were young kids. From taking care of me and Stormy. To taking over this pack and Spain's pack. To not stopping her search for her mate. We knew this day would come. Where we get to celebrate what the Moon Goddess has given us.

Today is the day you all bear witness to the official tie of Scarlett Winters, second born to Alastair Winters, Heir to The Great Caitriona Winterfall, and Seth Knight, Heir to Pete Knight, Heir to the former Bloody Rose Pack. Today is the day you all bear witness to the joining of three packs. Making Scarlett Knight as the first Alpha in history to be the Alpha of three packs. She will go down in history, leading Spain, Scotland, and Ireland." Grayson started, looking around at the Alphas as they paid direct attention to what he was saying.

Scarlett's mouth fell open, before she quickly closed it. She was about to say something before my soft rumble made her stop. I shook my head, before I smiled at her.

She can say whatever her heart desires later... She can't look like she didn't know this was coming. Maybe I should have told her about this beforehand... I guess I didn't really think this through.

"Shut up. Don't doubt yourself. Keep focused on what's happening." Reign growled at me.

Yes. Stay focused!

"Alpha Knight..." Grayson said, turning to look at me.

"Yes?" I replied, nodding once.

Scarlett licked her lips slowly as she tried not to squirm in her place. I want to know everything that's going through that pretty mind of hers.

"Do you, Heir to the former Bloody Rose Pack, accept Alpha Scarlett Knight, leader to The Winterfall Packs as your Alpha? Do you trust that she will lead your pack, your legacy, and your bloodline to greatness? Showing the world that today. You bend your knee to the rightful Alpha to the pack?" Grayson asked, his voice echoing through the crowd around us.

Scarlett's eyes started to water as I looked back at her. I wanted her to know that this is what I wanted... That I wouldn't have this any other way. I want her to lead my pack.

"Also... Just think about how we can call her Alpha. That's gonna be hot." Reign groaned at the thought.

"Yes... I do." I said, lifting my head to show my certainty. "I accept Alpha Scarlett Knight as Alpha. I trust her with my pack, my legacy, my bloodline, and my children. I trust her with my life."

The crowd around us gasped, causing me to growl. My eyes turned a dark red quickly. Reign growled unhappily. Neither one of us was going to take this. This pack doesn't deserve me to be Alpha. They abandoned me. They should be happy that I'm giving them to someone who actually cares about this position.

"You gasp as if you all cared about me before. You saw how my father treated me. You knew what he was doing to me. But none of you did anything about it. None of you tried to stop him. None of you tried to save me and my brother from his torture. I've spent my time thinking deeply about my decision. I know in my heart that this is what's right.

Ever since Scarlett found me and saved me. She woke up and chose me every single day. She didn't have to think about it, she just did it. Even before she found me, she didn't stop searching for me. She didn't stop at all until I was safe. You all wouldn't even stand up for me. So yes. I want my mate and my Alpha to rule my former pack. I want her to change our old ways and make us better.

And I know with her, she will lead us until a new time. I trust her. I trust her with my life. And I trust her with the lives of our children." I called out, smiling before turning back to look at Scarlett.

Tears were silently falling down her face as she watched me. I gently wiped her tears away. She makes my heart happy...

"You are my Queen... My Alpha... My everything." I promised, before dropping to my knee and bowing my head. "In front of the Alphas of the world. I submit to Scarlett Knight, Heir to The Great Caitriona Winterfall. I submit my pack. My legacy. My bloodline and my future."

In front of everyone... I show the world that she is my Alpha.

"Command him Alpha." Grayson urged her.

Scarlett had to wipe her tears. I wanted to lick them away for her.

"You may stand." She commanded me, causing me to eagerly stand back to my feet.

I kind of liked feeling her power roll through me to make me listen to her. It's kind of sexy.

"Alpha Scarlett Knight, heir to the Great Caitriona Winterfal, do you accept the new territory Ireland as yours? Do you accept the responsibility to protect them? Do you accept the position as Alpha?" Grayson asked, turning his focus to Scarlett.

"I accept my responsibility as their Alpha. I accept the position." She said, her eyes starting to glow more.

Her power started to linger in the air, I grinned with excitement. Her power feels so much stronger now... It feels bolder. I like it.

"I am excited to be able to be the one person who introduces the world to Alpha Scarlett Knight, Alpha to Scotland, Spain, and Irelands packs." Grayson called out, causing all of the wolves to howl at once.

I leaned down, pressing my forehead against hers.

"You are my everything." I promised, kissing her lips gently.

"You are my world." She told me.

After our declaration to each other, a burst of our power came from our bodies. A wave of purple and red rushed through the territory. Wolves started to howl louder at the strength that coursed through them at our official union.

"Wow... I don't think I've ever felt power like this before..." Reign was in ae.

"And that's why I told you not to worry... Do you want to tell everyone the good news?" I asked, causing her to nod eagerly.

I want the world to know that we're having kids. It's going to be amazing.

"Everyone!! Give me your attention!" She shouted, causing everyone to quiet down immediately. "Thank you. Today isn't just a celebration of the naming of an Alpha... But also the celebration of the Knight bloodline continuing... The official naming ceremony will be after they're born. But we're expecting twins."

"Our family will rule over our packs." I added in. "Our Heirs will bring the world into a new power."

"We have food inside everyone! Go ahead and go eat!" Scarlett shouted, causing everyone to start moving inside.

Scarlett went to go and follow everyone, but I grabbed her hand before she could move away from me. It's time for me to show her her surprise! We don't need to go and mingle. They're all annoying anyway.

"Is everything okay?" Scarlett asked, tilting her head slightly.

I wrapped my arms around her, pulling her into me.

"More than okay... I just have a surprise for you. I want us to go see it now." I said, before leading her away from the party.

I can't wait any longer.

FIFTY

S carlett followed after me, quietly at first as we walked deep into the forest that surrounded the pack house. I made sure to read over a map so I knew where I was going beforehand.

"Well... It's not like we wouldn't have been able to find the field anyway. We always find that field." Reign smirked at me.

He does have a valid point.

"Where are we going babe?" Scarlett asked, unable to keep quiet anymore.

"I have something to show you... Something I think that you'll love honestly." I beamed with excitement, his happiness seeped into our bond.

I couldn't contain how excited I am. I want her to love this. Scarlett laughed, loving how happy that I was.

"Is it going to be much longer? I would've changed shoes if I knew we were going to be walk a while." Scarlett asked, holding tightly to my hand.

Since she was in heels, she was walking a little slower than me because of the ground. I immediately stopped, letting her walk right into me. I can't believe I didn't think to grab her different shoes. I'm so horrible.

"I'm sorry babygirl." I frowned. "I got so excited and I didn't even think about your shoes." I apologized, before leaning down and picking her up bridal style. "I should've thought more about it, I'll do better next time."

I knew I was forgetting something. Gosh dang it.

"Eh. Gives us an excuse to hold her!" Reign added positively.

Scarlett gently laid her hand against my cheek, her power danced across my skin. It took everything in me not to shiver. I loved the feeling. But it tickles.

"You don't have to apologize my love. There's no issue. You were excited, and I liked seeing you so excited about something. How come our bond feels so much... Stronger... Deeper... More intimate almost?" She questioned, watching as two little wolves danced across my bare skin.

A red wolf chased a purple one, before two little wolves appeared following after the bigger ones. So that's us and our twins. I love this.

"Probably because all of our packs accept us fully now... Honestly probably the world." I teased, causing Scarlett to laugh and shake her head.

We can kill anyone who tries to stop us from being amazing.

"I have tits. Men hate it." She teased back.

I chuckled, easily carrying her as I walked along the path. She doesn't weigh that much. Like honestly, her weight is nothing to me.

"I like that other men hate it. If they stared too long, I might have needed to kill someone." I growled, causing Scarlett to shiver as it danced across her skin.

Two can play at that game.

"That's the hottest thing you've said all day." She almost whimpered.

I smirked, looking ahead of us. Everything she's said today has been the hottest thing I've heard all day.

"I feel like our future is secure now... I feel calmer. I feel stronger. I feel like I could take on the world." I grinned, tightening my hold on her so she wouldn't fall. "I tried so hard to surprise you with this."

"I don't know what you're trying to surprise me with? So I guess that works out? Although how did you hide it from me when I can read your mind?" Scarlett asked, narrowing her eyes at me.

I smirked, looking down at her. Her naked lives rent free in my head.

"I didn't think about it. Every time I felt you creeping into my mindspace. I thought about you naked to keep my mind occupied on something else. Especially you naked and your belly swollen with my children." I groaned at the thought, my lust evident in the air.

Scarlett smirked, loving the effect she had on me. She will never not be the hottest woman to me. I don't know how else to tell that to her.

"I just thought you were horny." She shrugged.

"I mean..." I chuckled. "I was trying to keep this a secret. You've done so much for me, I just wanted to do something for you. To show that I've listened to you talking. To show that I listen to what you want and what you plan. I want you to know that me being your mate isn't a bad thing. I want you to know that I can do and be everything you could ever need." I promised. "I accepted you as my Alpha and mate in front of everyone. But I wanted to do it privately between us."

I will show her everyday if I have to that she is who I want.

"My love... You don't have to do that... I know how you feel about me already." Scarlett shook her head. "I already know that you love me."

I smirked down at her. "I want to show you every single day that I love you." I told her, before walking up to our field where a beautiful large black house stood, with a three car garage attached.

There were tons of large windows to let in a lot of natural light. Scarlett was about to reply when I gently placed her down on the blacktop that led up to our house.

I don't know if the silence is a good thing... But I'm just going to have to wait and see how she reacts.

"Maybe she's just shocked?" Reign offered.

"Seth..." She said, looking between me and the new house.

"Scarlett." I teased with a playful grin.

She cringed. I knew she hated it when I called her by her real name.

"I still don't like it when you call me that." She shuttered. "It's like you're mad at me or something." She told me before heading up to the house, unable to stop herself.

I chuckled as I followed after her. She's obviously excited. I breathed out a sigh of relief. I can't believe I was worried that she was going to hate this.

"Go ahead... Explore... I want you to see everything..." I told her, even though she wasn't listening as she started to wander around the house.

FIFTY-ONE

Scarlett walked around, marveling at the beautiful rooms. They were fully decorated, having a beautiful mix of a deep purple and red to match both of our colors. I took off my suit jacket, making sure to hang it up and grab Scarlett a change of clothes before heading off to follow her.

I knew she wouldn't think to change. But I didn't get her new shoes... So I'm definitely not going to miss out on getting her comfortable clothes.

She had already abandoned her shoes, leaving them in the middle of the floor as she walked around the house. I couldn't help but smirk at items on the floor.

"What's that smell?" Scarlett asked, sniffing the air.

I walked up behind her, wrapping my arms around her waist and putting my chin on her shoulder. It's our smell... But something else that can keep us both calm.

"It's our smell... Mixed with a special scent that should help you keep calm..." I smiled, kissing her cheek before licking it.

Scarlett giggled. It seems to be doing its job so I'm glad it's working.

"How long have you been working on this?" She asked, turning around in my hold and placing her arms around my neck.

"Months. Ever since we came back from your cabin... I... I know that you love your house and it holds so many good memories for you. But I thought for us... For our family. I thought that it would be a good thing to have something new. To not have to live in a house where the first memory you have of me is me making you leave me alone... Me asking you for space that I didn't want in the first place.

I wanted something to show our union... Our new start. I wanted something to show that we're one now. And this field... Yes it has some bad memories. Some memories that stressed us both out. But this field is where you started your reign.

This field is where I came in my mind when things got difficult... This field is where we both come to when we need peace and comfort. This house will be the calm in the storm. I have large fencing around the property, I have guards patrolling the area constantly. This is where we can be free to be us. To raise our children. This is where I want to spend the rest of our lives together." I told her, before leading her out of our office and leading her down the hallway. "I had everything planned... Gray helped me make this perfect. Violet said that the scent in the area is something that helps Grayson calm down so she wanted to try it for you. I wanted you to love this space as much as I do. I even have another surprise too!"

I planned this to the letter...

I was obviously excited, my energy ran through our bond and made her giggle with my excitement. "Seth... Baby. I love it. It's beautiful. It's so amazing. No one has ever spent this much time on something for me... I've never been surprised with something that's so thoughtful. No one has cared about me like this... At all actually."

I survive to show her that I care about her more than anything.

I turned to look at her, before leaning down so we were face to face. "I am here to show you that you are worthy of someone to fawn over you." I promised. "I'm here to show you that you are worthy of love. I know deep down it's hard to believe. It's hard to believe some days that I'm actually safe and secure here."

Scarlett frowned, before placing her hand on my chest. "I would do anything for you... I hope you know that. I would do everything to make sure you were happy and healthy and safe. You are my everything, and that's never going to change." She declared, before she moved my hand to her small belly.

I gently leaned my forehead against hers. This life is everything to me... Everything.

"This moment is everything to me. It will be something I cherish forever." I smiled, my eyes shining a beautiful red.

Scarlett's eye lit up, her normal brown changing to a brilliant purple. I moved so that I was standing straight again. Its time for our next surprise. The one day has stressed me out the most.

"Just as I hope that you cherish this moment forever..." I told her, before opening the door and letting her walk into the nursery.

Scarlett gasped, before covering her mouth as she looked around. The nursery was beautiful, a mural of the woods was painted on one of the walls, a wall of glass was on the other, and the other walls were painted a deep green.

In cursive writing, the saying *'The Queen and King will protect their Heirs.'* With two gorgeous crowns placed on shelves on either side of the quote. "Seth..." Scarlett's eyes were watering as she walked deeper into the room to look at the beautiful deep oak wood cribs. *'The Princess'* was carved into one, and *'The Prince'* was carved into the second.

"I made them..." I said, walking up behind her as I took off my shirt. "Them both." I smiled, taking two pendants out of my pants pocket.

One was a glowing emerald green, and the other a beautiful amethyst. They were both carved into the shape of The Talisman of Caitriona Winterfall. I placed each one on the cribs. I thought that she would like this little touch that I gave.

"How did you do this... All of this? Without me knowing?" She asked, burying her face into my warm chest.

I smiled, wrapping my arms around her tightly.

"A lot of late nights... I couldn't sleep anyway. So this took up my time... Obviously the building part a lot of people in the pack helped me. They were all so eager to help provide a present for the Alpha. They're obsessed with you... Even people from my pack. They all love you." I told her, before placing a kiss on the top of her head.

Scarlett smiled as she looked at the cribs before looking outside. A little part of me thought she would be angry that I designed the nursery without her. But she seems to be okay with it.

"I was worried that they wouldn't want to accept me... That they'd hate me because I'm the Alpha... And I'm a woman." She fidgeted as my hands moved to the zipper on her back.

"Times are changing... You are changing their minds. You're showing them that women in power is not a bad thing." I praised, unzipping her dress so that she could step out of it.

Scarlett's cheeks turned pink at the compliment, and the way I wouldn't take my eyes off of her. She's incredible...

As the dress fell to the floor, I couldn't help but let my eyes roam over her bare skin. I took my dress shirt I took off, and placed it around her skin. "I want them to grow up knowing that no matter if they're a boy or a girl... You have equal rights to lead a pack." She said, looking between each of the cribs.

I put her arms through the holes and started to button the shirt up for her. I want that too... I want them to know that they both have the ability to lead no matter who they are.

"They will know... Because they'll grow up seeing their powerful, beautiful, gorgeous, smart, brave momma in power." I grinned, flashing my fangs at her causing her to laugh.

"And they'll grow up seeing their powerful, amazing, handsome, and protecting dad standing by my side..." She winked, leading me out of the nursery and heading to where she assumed our bedroom would be.

I laughed, watching as her hips moved as she walked. We will show them how to make the world respect them.

"Someone needs to protect you from all the stupid people in this world." I shrugged. "And that doesn't have to be you anymore."

Scarlett smiled back at me as we walked into our bedroom.

"You are *The Kingdom's Protector*." She teased as I pushed her onto the fluffy mattress.

"If I'm *The Kingdom's Protector*. Doesn't that make you The *Ruthless Kingdom*?" I asked, before climbing over top of her.

Scarlett snorted at the saying.

"I love you." She laughed, pulling me down to kiss me on the lips.

"I love you." I repeated before sealing her lips in a kiss.

CHAPTER
FIFTY-TWO

Two months passed, Scarlett was walking back and forth in her office looking down at her phone. I was sitting in the big chair, watching her pace.

"Her pacing makes me want to vomit." Reign told me but I could feel him watching her pace.

I don't have a single idea on what she's doing.

"What are you doing?" I asked, tilting my head slightly.

"Cardio?" She offered, stopping to look at me.

"Cardio? I could think of better cardio." Reign snickered.

That would be so much fun.

"Why?" I pressed, looking down at her stomach. "Are they stressing you out again?"

She'd tell me if the kids were stressing her out? Right? At least I would hope so...

"No!" Scarlett rolled her eyes, walking towards me and sitting on my lap. "I need to fidget. I have something coming and it's completely testing my patience having to wait for it."

"When has she ever had patience?" Reign snickered.

I'm not telling her that. That most certainly wouldn't go over well.

"What do you have coming?" I asked, smirking slightly as I placed my hands up her shirt and on her breasts.

They've been growing more... And I just can't get enough of them. I just want to bite them... Mark them so when she wears shirts that show them off. Everyone still sees my marks on her.

Scarlett smirked at my hand placement. "I have something special coming! Something I've been planning for a while and I think you'll love it!"

Something's she's been planning for a while?

"How did she keep it from us?" Reign asked.

The same could be said about our house.

I chuckled, feeling her energy zip through our bond. Whatever she has planned... She's so beyond excited about it. I kind of love it. "I love everything you do. But what is it?"

Scarlett shook her head. "Nope. You can't know. So don't go looking through my mind. I really want for it to be a surprise. So promise me that you won't look through my mind." She huffed, leaning her forehead against mine.

I smiled, closing my eyes as I felt the twins' power rolling through my body. I would never betray her trust... If she doesn't want to tell me... She doesn't have to tell me.

My body felt stronger... Warmer... More content as the twins' power danced through my body.

"I love it when they do that." I smiled, keeping my eyes closed. "It's like my own personal relaxing medication. A way to constantly feel them being safe and healthy."

"When I start to worry... They send it to me too... I think it's their way of saying, I'm here and everything will be okay." Scarlett smiled, placing Seth's hand on her bump. "Two little wolves are in there..."

"Two powerful little wolves. Do you think what happened

with you and Grayson will happen with the kids?" I asked, tilting my head as I leaned back to look at her.

Could that be a possibility? That their power would roll through the land to give it a boost? Like what Scarlett does randomly?

"I really hope to the Goddess that that doesn't happen. I don't want either of the kids to almost die like Gray did." Scarlett cringed at the thought.

"Of course her mind would immediately go there." Reign laughed.

I couldn't help but laugh. "I meant... The burst of your power. But way to immediately go to the dark side babe."

Scarlett's cheeks flushed. "Okay... My mind always goes to the worst possible thing! Okay! I'm sorry. I don't know how to make it stop."

I placed my hands on her back. "It's okay... You don't have to apologize my love. It's a hard mindset to be able to get out of."

She does everything... Being worried... That's okay. I can reassure her. I can help her see a more positive option. We can work through it together.

"To answer your question... I don't know if the burst of power will happen. It seems to happen more often lately. So it's possible. It's also possible that it won't happen. Who knows? I don't." Scarlett grinned, flashing her fangs at me.

I feel like none of us know what's going to happen. I beyond hate it. But at least next time I get her pregnant, we'll know more information.

"Is that how we're living life now? Who knows? I don't?" I teased, giving her butt a swat.

"Yup! Instead of stressing out, that's what I'm going to try." Scarlett nodded once, before looking down at her vibrating phone. "OH YAY!" She exclaimed before getting off of me and heading to the door.

Whatever she must've bought, must be here.

I watched as she stopped at the door and turned around. "What are you waiting for? Aren't you going to follow me? Or are you sick of me already?" She taunted.

"Oh I do like a game of chase." Reign growled.

I growled, my eyes flashing red. "Oh I'll show you just how sick of you I am." I growled, running after her.

Scarlett squealed, rushing out of the office and to the main exit of the pack house is. "You'd have to catch me for that one my love!"

I ran after her, I wasn't going to stop until I had her in my hands. I kept my eyes on her as we raced through the hallways. I hope no one is around cause we might just barrel into them.

I grinned, just as Scarlett burst through the doors. I had my hands on her waist. She giggled as she felt my body press against her back.

"I'll always catch you babygirl." I promised, kissing her cheek.

I looked up from her, my eyes connecting with a beautiful deep red and black Bugatti. Holy Goddess... This is beautiful...

"Do you think this is yours?" Reign asked, tilting his head slightly.

"No way." I said, still holding onto Scarlett as we walked closer to the car.

"Yes way!" Scarlett smiled brightly.

I took a few steps away from her, staring at the car. "You got this for me?" I asked, tilting my head as I couldn't take my eyes off of the car.

There's no way this is for me. I feel like this has to be some joke.

"You think she's messing with you?" Reign asked.

I don't know. But just in case this is for her, I don't want to get my hopes up.

"Of course I did! I know you absolutely love my car! I wanted you to have one for yourself too." She smiled, loving how I watched the car as I walked around it with awe.

"This is gorgeous! This is amazing!" I was giddy, almost bouncing as I walked. "I can't believe you got this for me!"

This is the best present, besides Scarlett and the twins, that I've ever gotten.

"Why can't you believe it?" Scarlett asked. "I wanted to get you something special."

"I didn't mean it in a bad way! I just... It's so beautiful babe. I love it." I smiled, walking over to her and hugging her to me. "Thank you for this... Thank you so much."

I can't tell her enough how much I love this car.

Scarlett smiled as she rested her head against my chest. "I promise for the rest of my life. I will remind you in every possible way just how much I love and appreciate you. How much you deserve to be spoiled."

I kissed the top of her head, before resting against it. "I know baby... But just having you love and accept me is all I need... You and our children."

"Until the end of time... I just need you and our children." Scarlett repeated.

"Until the end of time babygirl... And then some. Time won't take me away from you. I won't let anything take you away from me." I growled, before giving her butt a squeeze.

Scarlett snorted. "As I would for you baby... Nothing will keep me from you."

I won't let time... Death... Life... Anything keep me away from the woman who owns my heart. She's mine. For the rest of my days, she's mine.

EPILOGUE

Six months pass, Scarlett was fidgeting as she shimmed the dress up and over her hips. I couldn't help but smirk as I watched her. The way she couldn't get the dress up was adorable. Also shows how much weight she's managed to gain. I thought I was attracted to her before?

Holy Goddess... This version of her is beyond attractive. I can't get enough of this.

"You need some help babygirl?" I asked, walking over to her, placing the monitor that showed the twins sleeping in their cribs on the bed.

I didn't like to leave them for very long... These past couple of months... It's been incredible. They've grown so much, they're so strong... I love being a dad.

"Maybe just a bit." She blushed. "My boobs are gonna be crushed in this thing." She huffed as I let my fingertips drag over the bare skin of her torso as I pulled the slim fit dress up and over her body.

I feel like her boobs are going to be uncomfortable in this.

"I don't think they'll be crushed. Even if they are, we won't have to stay there long." I promised. "I'll cry wolf, say I wanna go home because the twins are hungry and I don't want you to have to show your boobs to everyone."

Which could very easily happen. I just will happily throw myself under the bus. I don't want anyone to see any part of her naked.

Scarlett laughed, moving her hair to be over her shoulder so I could zip the dress up. "I'm not afraid to say that I want to go home. It's just weird... It's finally here for their naming ceremony and I haven't left this house much the last several months. What if I have a panic attack and start to lose it?"

"Simple. I'll be there every step of the way. If you need to shift, let me know. I'll think of something to make sure everyone is in on it too!" I smiled, leaning down to kiss her neck where my mark sat.

She moved her head to the side more to allow me more room. Kissing her mark turns her on like no tomorrow. I loved getting to play with it.

"You are the greatest blessing to me baby." She praised, I smiled against her skin.

I reluctantly pulled away. And she is the reason why I'm still alive... Why I am able to live and take care of her and the twins.

"Are you feeling the need to use the talisman today?" I asked, tilting my head slightly.

I think the talisman would help calm her down more... I wouldn't blame her if she did need it.

"No. I'm okay. I have you and the twins. I don't need anything else." She promised, watching as I shrugged on my suit coat and buttoned it up.

The deep red matched the red of Scarlett's dress. We matched anytime we could. Scarlett rolled her shoulders.

"I need to get back into running my own pack anyway." She said, rubbing her temples slightly.

Her eyes started glowing purple again, Xena had wanted out badly. I could feel her... She's on edge.

"I want to bite her. She'd submit so easily for me." Reign groaned.

Uh... I think you should rethink that. She wouldn't submit easily if at all.

"Dont underestimate me." Reign smirked.

I frowned. "Tell Xena to calm down or Reign will bite her." Scarlett snorted.

"You and I both know. We like biting." She said, rolling her eyes as she grabbed her shoes.

I immediately took them from her and sunk to my knees to put her shoes on for her. She smiled as she lifted one foot at a time so I could slide the shoes on her feet.

"I like marking you." I promised, caressing her leg before standing to my feet. "Our car is waiting outside. We can get the kids in their carseats before heading over." Scarlett nodded, following me to the kids nursery.

They get to come with us... And be our saving grace when it's time for us to leave and head home. I've never been more thankful.

Once we had each of the kids in their carseats, Scarlett picked one up and I picked up the other one and the diaper bag. I wasn't going to forget anything... I'm prepared for anything. I at least think so.

"Remember. We don't have to stay long... Just need to announce their names. Mingle a little and then we can come home." I promised, following her out to the awaiting black SUV.

Scarlett nodded, before a guard climbed out of the car and opened the door for her.

"Carvaning to the ceremony?" She asked, tilting her head slightly.

"Yes ma'am. I just was chosen as the one to drive your vehicle to your house." The guard nodded once, bowing his head in respect as she placed Sebastian into his place in the captain chair, letting me go to the other side and secure Kourtney.

I can't wait to tell the world their names. I want to see their reaction... Especially their reaction to Kourt being the oldest.

"Thank you." She smiled, heading to the passenger side door.

The guard automatically went and tried to open the door. I will actually kill him.

I growled unhappily. "If you want to keep your hand. I suggest removing it from my mate." I snapped, the guard immediately whimpered and moved away.

"My apologizes Alpha... It was instinct." He apologized before quickly getting into one of the other waiting SUVs.

Scarlett snorted as I opened the door for her. There's no way I was going to let someone else get the door for my mate.

"Gonna scare everyone away from me?" She teased, causing me to nod.

"Yes of course. I don't need them thinking you're not taken." I told her as I reached across and buckled her up for her.

She kissed my cheek, making sure to leave a lipstick mark before I moved to go and get in the drivers seat.

Scarlett looked into the back, both of the kids were resting peacefully. But she knew as soon as we got to the ceremony, that they would wake up and not be happy with all of the new people. New scents... New sounds... New lights.

I couldn't help but cringe at the thought myself.

"They're going to be okay right?" She asked, her worry danced through our open bond.

I'll make sure my family makes it out of this in one piece.

"No one is going to try anything." I assured, following behind the lead car slowly towards the city.

"I guess I'm just worried." She rubbed the back of her neck. "Are we going to announce that she's our first born?"

"We have no choice. She was born first. Kourtney wanted to show everyone who's boss. Just like her mommy." I grinned, reaching over to squeeze her thigh gently.

Kourtney is going to be just like Scarlett and I couldn't be happier. Scarlett gave him a soft smile.

"The world will see the reason why she's the first born..." Scarlett sent a small flame to dance around Kourtney to keep her entertained.

Sebastian whimpered, but nuzzled himself back to sleep.

"Everyone will bow to Kourtney Knight. I promise." I told her, frowning because she was so stressed out about this ceremony.

Everyone will bow to all of us... The Knight Bloodline will be one to be respected. No matter what I have to do.

EPILOGUE 2

As we pulled up to the house, the music immediately turned down. If they didn't turn the music down, I would've killed someone.

And I know I keep saying that, but I'm just waiting for someone to step out of line.

"The Alphas are here!" Someone shouted, causing everyone to head outside to try and get the first look at the kids.

Scarlett rolled her shoulders, a nervous habit that she couldn't shake. Even if I couldn't feel her feelings... I could tell she was nervous by that one motion.

"We're okay." I repeated, squeezing her thigh. "No one is going to try anything." Scarlett took a deep breath, before nodding slowly.

I pulled up to a stop and parked the car before I got out and went to get Kourtney. Scarlett got out next, making sure to get Sebastian. Camera lights flashed as people started to take pictures of the couple.

Let's get this done and over with.

"Breath my Queen. Breath. Everything is okay." I promised, talking through our bond.

I hope it brings her some comfort. Scarlett smiled, holding the handle to her car seat tightly to her body.

"Alpha Scarlett and Seth Knight everyone!" Grayson called out, holding Violet's hand with a bright smile on his face. "Now now... We know how children can be. We've all either had our own or have seen them first hand. So we're going to let the Alphas go to the microphone in the back to tell us the names and the first born heir to their bloodline! Then the music will be turned back on, and we can celebrate!"

If the music gets turned back on, we'll be leaving. There's already so many people here. I'm not going to be able to take it.

"After all! It's a wonderful time!" Alex called out, coming up to stand by Grayson. "The Knight bloodline is continuing... And mixing with the powerful bloodline of the Winters! It's a cause of celebration!"

Scarlett smiled up at me. "You wanna do it?" She asked, following me to the back of the house where the real crowd was.

"This is disgusting." Reign cringed.

It really is.

"You can do it my love. I love watching you be the powerful Alpha you are." I grinned down at her, placing one hand on the small of her back.

I looked back at Max, winking at him before holding out the diaper bag. "Put this where no one is going to touch it." Max nodded before grabbing the bag and quickly rushing off.

I'm not going to be able to be near the bag if it smells like someone else.

I carried Kourtney's seat with ease, holding it tightly to my body so no one would try to grab at her. "Are we going to take the kids out of the carriers?"

Not that I think someone would try to touch my daughter. But just in case.

Scarlett nodded, stepping onto the stage where the microphone was set up. We placed the carriers on the table, before carefully taking out the kids and holding them in a cradle position. I bit my bottom lip as I looked at Kourtney, her eyes were wide open. A wave of purple flashed through her eyes, causing mine to react red in return.

I felt Reign shiver at the command and I smiled... Kourtney is going to rule the world... And I can't wait to be able to watch her grow into her power and her future position. My heart is so happy.

"You are going to do wonderful things little one..." I smiled softly, gently rubbing my thumb against her cheek.

Scarlett smiled, holding Sebastian against her warm body. He nuzzled into her chest, almost whimpering in satisfaction.

"Hello everyone. Wow... It's been a long long time. Seems like just yesterday we were here for our Alpha ceremony huh? Bet it surprised you when we told you we were expecting?" Scarlett laughed, causing the crowd to laugh in response.

It really shouldn't have been a surprise.

I smiled, swaying slightly since Kourtney was starting to be squirmy. "Well it's been an interesting three months away from you all. I'm healthy... The kids are healthy... Everything is going as it should." She explained, I moved out of the way since there was a big screen behind us.

We've had this whole thing planned... I hope it goes perfectly.

"I won't leave you guys waiting. I know what you all came here for... The names to the heirs to our pack... Let's start with our son..." She said, a picture of Sebastian popped up on the screen with the words *'Sebastian Blaine Knight'* in a beautiful deep green splayed above him.

I swallowed thickly as I looked at the middle name... My son shares my middle name... I bit my bottom lip. I really don't want to cry in front of everyone,

"Sebastian Blaine Knight everyone!" She called out, raising him slightly. The crowd around them cheered at the name. "Wanna tell them about our daughter Seth?"

I grinned as I nodded yes. I stepped up to the microphone and looked out to the crowd. "I know all you fathers know how I'm feeling right now... The love I have for my mate and my children is unmatched." I explained before stepping to stand beside Scarlett.

A picture of Kourtney appeared on the screen with the words *'Kourtney Rose Knight'* splayed above her in a beautiful dark amethyst.

"Our daughter Kourtney everyone!" I shouted, causing the wolves to howl with excitement.

This moment seems so surreal... I can't believe I've made it.

"We've really made it..." Reign swallowed.

"Tell us who's the first born!" A wolf yelled in the crowd.

Scarlett smiled, her eyes shining purple. I'm going to leave that up to her... She deserves it.

"I'll let you tell them, beautiful." I nodded.

Scarlett looked across the crowd around us.

"They better react perfectly." Reign huffed.

You got that right.

"Well, I'm pleased to tell you that our first born is Kourtney. She is the first of many more heirs to come for our bloodline!" Scarlett called out.

A series of claps slowly started to expand through the crowd.

"Long live Kourtney Knight!"

"Long live Sebastian Knight!"

"Heirs to the legacy of Scarlett and Seth Knight!"

My heart has never been more full than at this moment...

The crowd chanted. Scarlett's eyes started to water at the acceptance from her pack. I smiled, leaning down to press my forehead against hers.

"I told you that they would accept her as Alpha... It's all because of you that they feel comfortable with it." I assured, pressing a gentle kiss to her lips.\

Scarlett nodded, sniffling slightly as she tried not to cry. My Queen deserves this moment... She's worked hard to get here... We both have.

"You my *Ruthless Queen*... Are the reason that we have a *Ruthless Kingdom*..." I smiled, my eyes shining red.

"I love you." Scarlett smiled. "I can't wait to see what the future holds."

"Our future will be bright... I will love you till the end of time." I promised.

THE END....

Or is it?

ACKNOWLEDGMENTS

I'm a little emotional now. Having finished my third and fourth book. My heart is full. I've met so many amazing people in this book community. I've met my family. My bestest friends. The people I never want to lose.

I had the honor of meeting so many people through the book community. Allie, Gabrielle, Blake, Jay, Nikki, Blaire & Tyler, Luna, Laura, Ariel, and Ciara. And I could keep going on and on. But let's get into it.

First things first, I gotta thank God. Because my faith is something I value and hold close to my heart. And I truly believe that this talent of writing comes from him.

Oran, my brother, my first best friend, thank you for being one of my biggest supporters. Thank you for never giving up on me, and for always being there for me. And listening to me no matter what. I love and appreciate you more than you know. You will always be my favorite person big brother

Nikki, my best friend, the first person who actually started talking to me from booktok and quickly became someone I can't live without. Thank you for always supporting, always listening, always being one of my favorite people. Always believing in me and hyping me up, and constantly listening to me talk about how excited I was about writing.

Allie, thank you for being in my life. Thank you for loving me and supporting me and being my biggest fan. Thank you for sitting down and reading my book in two days and needing more lol. But most importantly, thank you for being one of the best people in my life. I don't know where I would be without you. I love you.

Blake, my brother, you have no idea how thankful I am for you. I'm so happy that we got to meet, and were able to become fast friends, and quickly became family. You mean the world to me. Thank you for supporting me and listening to my endless babble about my stories. Thank you for being one of my biggest supporters, and for never giving up on me.

Gabrielle, my bestie, my sister, thank you. For being one of my biggest supporters, my sounding board, the person I could ask the dumbest questions to and have no judgment. But more importantly, thank you for being you. I couldn't have made it here without you. Thank you for being one of the best friends a girl could ask for.

Jay, you came into my life at the best of times. And you blew away my mind. I didn't know I needed you at that point, but I just need you to always know that I love you more than words express. And I can't imagine my life without you. Thank you for supporting me, for hyping me up, for always checking in on me. Thank you for everything.

Ciara. Ciara... Ciara. I'm obsessed with you. We met during Ruthless Queen & The Queen's Flame chaos and we rode it out with each other. You quickly became someone I need through my everyday life and I don't want to ever lose you. Thank you for being my person, my big sister, my best friend, and my co-host on The Moonlit Talks Podcast *Wink wink* Subtle plug.

Laura, girly, thank you I can't say thank you enough for everything you do. Thank you for keeping me on track. Thank you for helping me get through my days. Thank you for loving me even though I bounce off the walls and can't sit still to save my life lol. Thank you for becoming one of my closest friends. You mean the absolute world to me, never forget that.

LUNAAAAAA! I'm obsessed with you. So obsessed with you. I don't want you to forget that. Thank you for being so willing to help me and for becoming one of my closest friends.

Blaire & Tyler, I have so many words I want to say. Thank you for being my friends and family. Thank you for listening to all of my nonsense when my ideas were just ideas and not in book form. Thank you for being amazing, and supporting me from so far away. I am so lucky to have you guys in my life and I never want you to forget that. I love you both so much.

Ariel. I met you at a time where I needed you most. I needed someone to help me through the dark times and you were there. No matter how many times I dropped off the face of the Earth. You were here for me and it means more to me than you know. I love you. I'm obsessed with you. I can't wait to see where the future takes us!

Thank you to my readers, and anyone who has ever supported me on this writing journey. Even if I didn't say it above, or didn't acknowledge you directly above. I love and appreciate you all so much. I wouldn't be able to be here without any of you.

Stalk me on my socials and be my friend!

Facebook: Lauren Moon
Instagram: @Heartofanalpha or @Authorlaurenmoon or
@Heartoflaurenmoon
Tiktok: @Heartofanalpha
My Reader Group on Facebook: The Moon Pack

Or find my linktree in my bio on Instagram and everything will
be linked there!

www.ingramcontent.com/pod-product-compliance
Lightning Source LLC
Chambersburg PA
CBHW070907260626
47162CB00007B/2580